A chill breeze buffeted their faces as Bond was assisted from the car and roughly handled up the ramp to the helicopter. A figure beckoned him from the steps and the FBI men gave him a final push on his way. He thought he heard Broderick say that his luggage was already aboard, but the words were lost on the breeze and the wash from the rotors.

A crewman helped him aboard and showed him to a seat inside the dark body of the craft, shouting in his ear that he should fasten the seat belt. The door slammed and the engines came up to fine pitch the moment he was inside.

He felt, more than saw, someone sitting in the next seat. Then the familiar voice came loudly in his ear. 'Only a couple of hours in San Francisco, Bond, and already there's mayhem. You even managed to get your own minder killed,' M said. 'Sometimes I think the Grim Reaper sits on your shoulder, 007. One day he'll catch up with you.'

John Gardner served with the Fleet Air Arm and Royal Marines before embarking on a long career as a thriller writer, including international bestsellers *The Nostradamus Traitor*, *The Garden of Weapons*, *Confessor* and *Maestro*. In 1981 he was invited by Glidrose Publications Ltd – now known as Ian Fleming Publications – to revive James Bond in a brand new series of novels. To find out more visit John Gardner's website at www.john-gardner.com or the Ian Fleming website at www.ianfleming.com

BROKENCLAW

John Gardner

An Orion paperback

First published in Great Britain in 1990
by Hodder and Stoughton Ltd.
This paperback edition published in 2012
by Orion Books Ltd,
Orion House, 5 Upper St Martin's Lane,
London WC2H 9EA

An Hachette UK company

1 3 5 7 9 10 8 6 4 2

A CIP catalogue record for this book
is available from the British Library.

ISBN 978-1-4091-3570-8

Typeset at The Spartan Press Ltd,
Lymington, Hants

Printed and bound by CPI Group (UK) Ltd,
Croydon, CR0 4YY

The Orion Publishing Group's policy is to use papers
that are natural, renewable and recyclable products and
made from wood grown in sustainable forests. The logging
and manufacturing processes are expected to conform to
environmental regulations of the country of origin.

www.orionbooks.co.uk
www.ianfleming.com

For Ed & Mary Anna
With thanks

CONTENTS

I

DEATH IN THE AFTERNOON

The elderly man wore jeans and a checked shirt. Comfortable Adidas trainers protected his feet and a battered Panama hat was tipped forward to shade his eyes from the afternoon sun. He stretched out in his deck chair, lowered the newspaper he had been reading and looked out at the view which he had come to love.

This, he considered, could well be an English country garden in mid-summer. The long, broad lawn was precisely cut, giving that pleasing *trompe l'œil* effect of broad, perfect stripes in two shades of green. The borders were slashed with crimson salvias, overshadowed by deep purple lupins and nodding hollyhocks. Some sixty yards away from where the man sat, the lawn ended, merging into a rose garden built with a series of trellised arch-ways, giving the effect of a great corridor of colour. In the far distance there were trees, and through a gap you could clearly view the sea stippled with points of sunlight.

The man was only vaguely aware of the sound of a car drawing up outside the house behind him. This was the complete illusion, he thought. Anybody could be forgiven for imagining they were in a summer garden in Surrey or Kent. Only the date on his copy of the *Times Columnist* assured him it was September 25th and he was sitting only a few miles from the city of Victoria on Vancouver Island in British Columbia where, because of its mild climate warmed by the Japanese current, vegetation blooms all the year round.

The main doorbell of the house pierced his pleasant reverie. The maid was away for the day, shopping in downtown Victoria, so he rose, dropping his newspaper, and ambled slowly into the house, grumbling to himself.

'Professor Allardyce?' There were two young men, dressed casually in slacks and linen jackets, standing at the front door, their car parked on the gravel sweep in front of the house.

The professor nodded, 'What can I do for you?'

'SIS.' The taller of the duo spoke, and they both lifted their hands to show the laminated cards that identified them as members of the Canadian Security & Intelligence Service.

The professor nodded again; he had reason to know these people, though he had never set eyes on this pair of agents before. 'Well, what can I do for you?' he repeated.

'There're a couple of problems. The recent business about LORDS . . .'

Allardyce lifted his eyebrows and pursed his lips.

'Oh, it *is* okay, sir. We're both LORDS cleared,' the other agent said quickly.

'I sincerely hope so,' the professor frowned. 'So what's happened now?'

'The chief would like to see you,' said the taller of the two.

'At the local office,' the other added. 'He flew in this morning. Sends his compliments, and asks if you'd do him the honour.'

There was a pause during which Professor Allardyce continued to frown and the two agents shuffled their feet, the taller of the pair undoing the one button on his linen jacket.

'You mind if I call your local office?' Allardyce began to turn away as he said it, clearly indicating that he was going to make the call whether they liked it or not.

'Not a good idea, Prof . . .' The taller agent stepped forward, spinning the elderly man around while the other man secured his wrists. 'You'd best just come along with us, right?'

The professor was a thin, somewhat gangling man but he

lashed out with arms and legs so that it took both of the younger men considerable strength to subdue him. Allardyce tried to shout and the taller agent slammed his hand over their captive's mouth, at which the professor promptly bit him.

'Like trying to wrestle an anaconda,' one grunted.

'A sackful of anacondas,' replied the other.

But, gradually, they had their victim under control, dragging him, still kicking, to the car where the bigger agent pushed Allardyce into the rear, chopping the back of his neck viciously with the edge of his hand. The professor folded, slumping into a corner, while his captor climbed in, positioning himself in readiness should the prisoner regain consciousness. With the second man at the wheel the car turned out of the driveway and within a few minutes was on the road leading away from Victoria into wooded countryside.

Professor Robert Allardyce was no fool. At the age of seventy-one he had experienced much, both in his special field of maritime electronics, and in life itself. During World War II he had distinguished himself in the United States Navy, had two ships sunk under him and had been awarded the Navy Cross. He had ended the war in the submarine service, and for a short time during training, before getting his coveted 'Dolphins', Commander Bob Allardyce had been a member of the Navy boxing team.

The chop to his neck had plunged the professor into semi-consciousness, but, by the time the car was out on the main road, he was aware of what was happening. His neck ached from the blow and he figured that it would be stiff and sore if, and when, he tried to move. He remained lying against the nearside door, inert, but with all his senses gradually coming into play again. Far better to feign unconsciousness now and take advantage of the situation later.

They drove for fifteen minutes or so and Allardyce had time to brace himself for a move as the vehicle slowed to a stop.

'They're not here yet,' one of the agents said.

'We're ten minutes ahead of time. Don't get out. Stay where you are.'

'He okay?'

'The prof? Out like a light. He'll stay in dreamland for another half-hour or so.'

As he prepared to move, Allardyce noted that both men spoke more like native Californians than local Canadians. Then he sprang, arching his body, grabbing for the door handle, lashing out with his feet which connected with the body of the man who had hit him. Then he was out of the car and running, hardly realising that he was among trees and undergrowth.

Behind him, there was a shout which sounded like, 'No! No! No!' He did not hear the two shots; just a sudden blinding pain between his shoulder blades and a punch, like some huge fist, which seemed to go right through his body, then a great white light and oblivion.

2

THE MIND IS THE MAN

Eventually, the autopsy on Robert Allardyce would give cause of death as deep trauma resulting from the spinal chord and left lung being penetrated by two .45 bullets. At the moment those bullets hit the unfortunate professor, James Bond was sitting only some five miles away, in the opulent Palm Court lounge of the Empress Hotel on Victoria's pleasant waterfront.

People who knew Bond well would have noticed that his manner, and expression, were ones of disapproval, his eyes hard and restless, his face frozen into the look of someone who has just been served spoiled fish. In fact Bond was irritated by the way this old and famous hotel served what it called an English Tea. During his four days in Victoria, Bond had avoided taking tea at the hotel, but today he had played two rounds of golf with indifferent partners at the Victoria Golf Club and returned earlier than usual. Tea seemed to be in order and he was shown to a small table right by a massive potted plant.

The first thing that annoyed him was a card on which was printed a highly inaccurate history of what it called The English Tea Ritual. This claimed that, at some time in the late nineteenth century, tea had become a 'serious' meal called High Tea. Happily, Bond reflected that while he could still recall the delights of Nursery Tea, he had never been in a position to eat High Tea, but here he was being asked to believe that the fare set before him *was* High Tea – an indifferent brew of tea itself, strawberries and cream, finger sandwiches, tasteless *petits fours* and some abomination called a 'honey crumpet'. Crumpets, to Bond, were delicious items which should be served piping hot and dripping with butter, not jam, marmalade or this sweet confection of honey.

He left the meal barely tasted, signed the bill and strolled away past the main restaurant, heading for the foyer. He would take a walk, he thought, along the harbour front which, for some reason, reminded him of Switzerland. Certainly the mountains were far away – in Washington State – but the calm anchorage with its pleasure boats, seaplanes and the juxtaposition of ancient and modern buildings all had a feel of the order one found on the Swiss lakes.

For a moment he stood just outside the main door. It had been a glorious day and the sun was now low and beginning to colour the western sky. A sleek, dark blue Rolls-Royce stood in the turning circle, about thirty yards from the entrance, and a young man, nervous, his head and eyes in constant motion, talked with a uniformed chauffeur at the car's door.

'Excuse me, sir.' One of the grey-uniformed doormen was at Bond's elbow, gently moving him to one side as though someone of great importance was about to leave the hotel. At the same moment, Bond was aware of two men, reeking of 'security', shouldering their way past the doorman and moving to what appeared to be preassigned places near the Rolls. One wore the obligatory earpiece of a bullet-catcher, as professional body-guards are known the world over, the other sported a long open raincoat of the type favoured by US Secret Service men to hide the Uzi or H & K MP5A2 submachine-guns.

Three more men passed through the door and it was obvious which of them was being protected. Bond did a double take as the striking figure moved towards the Rolls, turning slightly as the nervous young man with the chauffeur came forward to greet him.

So arresting was this man that Bond almost missed the next series of events. The man was well over six feet tall, nearer six-three or -four, broad-shouldered, erect, and, from the way he moved, in very good physical shape. You could practically see the muscles ripple under the expensive, meticulously tailored double-breasted grey suit. His face was even more remarkable than his physique: – dark, almost olive-skinned, with a broad forehead, fine flared nose and a mouth that could have been perfectly sculpted by an artist – thick, sensual lips, but which were in flawless proportion to the rest of the face. The bone structure, Bond thought, was almost that of a pure-blooded American Indian; only the dark brown eyes gave the lie to this, for they were slightly almond-shaped and hooded, hinting at some Oriental blood. Certainly, whoever he was, this fine-looking specimen could never be forgotten.

The nervous young man had been speaking to him, rapidly and low, the tall one's tranquil face taking on an expression of concern as he listened, bending slightly from the waist so that he could hear without causing the speaker to raise his voice.

The pair were now very close to the Rolls and Bond had a full view of both faces. He began to read the young man's lips only as he completed his short speech.

'. . . and they say he's dead,' he seemed to say.

'The idiots shot him?' The tall one's lips undoubtedly formed the pattern of this rather shocked question.

The younger man nodded and mouthed, 'They said they aimed low . . . but . . .'

The imposing figure raised a hand. 'I'll see to them later.' His face seemed for a second contorted in fury. 'Tell them incalculable damage may have been done regarding Lords.'

The art of lip-reading had been added to Bond's armoury some time ago. While in a Hong Kong hospital, recovering after a particularly dangerous mission, he had been instructed in the rudiments of the art by a girl called Ebbie Heritage. It would be a long time before he would forget that young woman. She had taught him well, and now, for the first time, James Bond had actually put this art to the test. He was willing to swear in a court of law that the tall VIP had spoken of some recent death and the possibility of this act being the cause of irreparable damage to some scheme.

By the time he had digested what he had learned, the main subject of his attention was already in the Rolls, together with his bodyguards, and the vehicle was slowly moving from the front of the hotel.

He turned to one of the doormen. 'Who's the imposing gentleman in the Rolls?' he asked.

The doorman gave a thin smile. 'Mr Lee, sir. That was the famous Mr Lee. He's on his way to make a very special presentation at the Museum of British Columbia across the road there.' He pointed to the far left of the hotel.

Bond nodded his thanks and strolled out towards the waterfront, making a left turn on Government Street, walking quickly towards the point where it bisected Belleville, heading towards the Museum of British Columbia, which he had visited, with great interest, only two days previously. The huge and elegant presence of Mr Lee, as the doorman had called him, had somehow fascinated Bond to the extent that he wished to know more about the man.

The Empress Hotel occupies an entire block between Government and Douglas Streets, its furthest boundary being Belleville Road. On Belleville, the next block is almost completely taken up by the beautifully spacious, modern museum.

Bond glanced around him, not appearing to be in any kind of hurry, as he walked the last few yards towards the museum. Away to his right the statue of Queen Victoria stood, unamused, before the large domed Government building.

He paused by the pedestrian crossing, waiting for the lights to change, looking at the large angular museum building, flanked by a modern carillon and Thunderbird Park with its gaudy, tall totems. In his mind, Bond could hear his old Scottish housekeeper, May, cluck-clucking, 'The trouble with you, Mr James, is that you're always sticking your nose into things that don't concern you. Curiosity killed the cat, you know.' But he *was* curious, fascinated and intrigued by this large man he had only seen for a few moments. For the first time in months, James Bond was interested in something.

The Rolls was parked at the side of the large building, close to the museum shop and entrance, its chauffeur leaning against the front passenger door. Bond strolled past the shop, then ruffled his hair and went into the main entrance at a jog. There was a line of a dozen people or so waiting to pass the ticket booth, so he shouldered his way through them, beckoning to a uniformed attendant.

'I'm late,' he said, looking frantic. 'Should be with Mr Lee.'

The porter took the bait, 'Right, sir. They're all up in the Art Gallery. Third floor.' He held a couple of people back to allow Bond to move through.

He remembered the third floor from his previous visit – exhibits of the first inhabitants of this land. Wonderful lifesize representations of American Indian coastal chiefs and headmen; a magnificently detailed model of a Kootenai village; another of a Sedan coastal village, together with artifacts from the old Indian tribes who were the first organised humans to dwell in the area; tools, artworks, canoes, masks and woven garments, the whole presenting the lives of these ancient peoples set in harmony with the environment.

He ran up the escalators to the third floor, making his way past the glass cases and cunningly lit exhibits, turning right, slowing as he entered the large reproduction of a Kwakiutl Indian Big House, made of great beams and seasoned planks. Part of the roof was open to what appeared to be the sky; there was the smell of woodsmoke which drifted from a realistic fire in the centre, while two giant thunderbird totems towered above everything. Their wooden wings were outstretched and the carved faces with long aggressive beaks looked as though they might come alive, attacking, ripping and tearing at anyone who threatened those under their protection. From somewhere, hidden within this large room, came the sound of Indian chants and the steady thud of tom-toms made the short hairs on the back of his neck stiffen.

Quietly he moved on through the Big House which opened up into the Art Gallery containing more beautifully carved totems, bearing crests, faces, entwined snakes and the figureheads of a myriad supernatural beings which guarded and cared for homes and villages.

A semicircle of people was gathered around a weathered, intricately worked, tall totem with two stubby wings near the top.

Bond moved quietly into this little group of people, his eyes searching faces until he found Lee standing at the base of the totem, his bodyguards behind him. A small aesthetic-looking man, wearing pince-nez on a nose that appeared too big for his face, was speaking, and Bond noticed that Lee seemed to have shrunk, as though he could disguise his size and dominating presence. It was almost a theatrical trick, as if the man could disappear into the crowd in spite of his commanding bearing. But it worked. By rights everyone's eyes should have been on Lee, but the people gathered for whatever this ceremony represented, looked at and listened attentively to the speaker, who was obviously one of the senior curators, or a member of the museum's board.

'This generous act,' the official was saying, 'is typical of the great benevolence Mr Lee has shown to the various communities of Vancouver Island. It is a selfless gesture, to give – not lend – this ancient totem to the museum, a totem that has been connected with his family for the best part of a century. We are grateful, and only wish that Mr Lee could live permanently among us. Though, as you know, he maintains a property on the island, his business interests in the United States and in Europe allow him to be with us all too rarely. But he is here today, and I am going to ask him to say a few words to us before we take this valuable carving under our care. Ladies and gentlemen, Mr Lee Fu-Chu.'

So, Bond thought, that was it. Lee was some kind of half-breed, part Chinese and part . . . what? Before he could even think about it, he saw Lee go through an amazing transformation. Until that moment, this giant of a man had been almost a bystander, now he straightened and came forward, drawn up to his full height, his left arm straight with the hand balled behind his left thigh, the right hand making a gesture towards the official who had been speaking. His head was held high, almost arrogantly, the large brown eyes twinkled with charm and his wide mouth parted to show perfect teeth and a smile of genuine delight. He shook hands with the official then turned, his eyes sweeping around the gathered crowd as though taking each of them into his confidence. His voice was mellow, soft and elegant with no trace of any accent, neither American nor Canadian. Lee spoke in almost perfect English, with no blemish culled from any particular education. He had neither the overstated drawl of what used to be called an Oxford accent, nor any hint of mispronunciation which would reveal his English to be a second language.

'My good friends,' he began, and Bond felt that he meant it, that every person there was a good and known friend. 'It is always a pleasure to be here in British Columbia, if only because BC is my heritage. I return here from time to time to remind myself of that great heritage. Many of you already know the story of my birthright, part of which I have today passed on to this museum. Whether you've heard it or not, I feel obliged to tell the tale once more. For the record, as it were.' The eyes glittered with elation, his voice dropped slightly as though he were passing on a long lost treasure, a secret, to those gathered around him.

The story he had to tell was fascinating – how, in the 1840s, at the time of the Gold Rush, his great-grandfather had come to British Columbia from the Shanxi Province of China, where he had traded in gold. This man had been captured by a war party of Crow Indians who held him hostage, and during that period he had fallen in love with a beautiful Crow girl called Running Elk.

Eventually, the couple had escaped and sought refuge with a band of Piegan Blackfoot Indians. There, among this tribe, they were accepted, made of one blood with the Blackfoot people, and were married.

This marriage of a Chinese dealer in precious metals and a Crow woman began Lee's ancestry, for the strain of Chinese and Blackfoot Indian had been carried through three generations. Lee, himself, had been brought up in both traditions by his parents, Flying Eagle Lee and Winter Woman.

Bond thought that the man had an almost hypnotic power, for, though he told his tale simply, without wasting words, the very fluency seemed to bring the story to life. When he used the anglicised Indian names – Running Elk, Flying Eagle, Winter Woman and the like – the words required no further description, but almost took on flesh and became living humans. It was the kind of trick that the ancient market story-tellers must have possessed as they charmed their listeners with fables and legends. Lee was still speaking, allowing himself a broad smile as he said, 'To be truthful, there are times when I don't know whether I should be inscrutable and mysterious or play the noble savage.' This brought an appreciative laugh in which Lee himself joined before becoming solemn again.

'The totem I have given you today stood before my grandfather's and my father's teepees. I know it like an old friend. I played at its base as an infant; I looked upon it as a sacred object while I was with the other braves at rituals and ceremonies. It has power and a long memory within its wooden being. So guard it and keep it well.'

The applause was genuinely warm, but Lee held up his right hand for silence. 'I have heard it said,' an almost conspiratorial smile crossing his face, 'that I am a fraud; that I have invented these stories; that I am nothing more than the child of some itinerant Chinese tailor and a Blackfoot girl who sold her body in Fort Benton. None of this is true. Come to me and I have written proof. Ask, when you go to the Blackfoot reservations, of Brokenclaw, for that is also my inheritance.' He drew his left hand from behind his thigh and held both arms out, hands with palms upwards.

For a second Bond did not see the truth, then he realised that Lee's left hand, palm open, had his thumb on the right side. His left hand was his one physical blemish, as though, at conception, the hand had grown from the wrist the wrong way round, so that with palms outstretched the thumb was to the right; when the palms faced down, the thumb was on the left.

The group applauded again and the gathering started to break up. The last Bond saw of Brokenclaw Lee was his head and shoulders above a group heading towards the escalators.

Bond stayed for a while, viewing the ancient totem with its symbols of snake, bird and, he thought, scales for weighing, not justice, but gold. The longer he looked, the more he saw – strange, even grotesque, faces peering out from carved leaves and branches.

Finally, with a smile, Bond turned and left, walking back through the Indian Big House, the short hairs on the back of his neck once again stiffening at the sound of the chanting and rhythm of the tom-tom beat.

This had been a strange, and somehow exciting, diversion – to see someone as charismatic as Lee and hear his story which could well be a trunk full of rubbish. It was, though, he reflected, walking back to the Empress, the first time in nearly a year that he had become engrossed in something outside himself.

This hybrid man, Lee, had everything – presence, power, shrewdness, strength, charisma, charm and obvious success. He would be an ideal exercise, Bond thought. While he was here in British Columbia, he would spend some time trying to discover where Lee had found his success, and what was the true secret of his power. It should not be difficult, with somebody as accomplished as this.

But when he returned to his hotel room, Bond found things had changed rapidly. The message light was blinking on the telephone. A cable had arrived from the United States, he was told, and five minutes later he read the message—

TROUBLE OVER YOUR SHARES IN THE FAMILY BUSINESS STOP IMPERATIVE YOU COME TO SAN FRANCISCO IM-MEDIATELY STOP ROOM RESERVED FOR YOU AT FAIRMONT HOTEL STOP PLEASE WAIT THERE FOR MESSAGE STOP REGARDS MANDARIN

So, Bond thought, as he crumpled the flimsy paper, the old man had him marked down for some job in California from the start. He recalled M's words to him, less than two weeks before – 'You need to get away for a rest, James. Go off to California. They're all mad there, so you'll be in good company.'

The old fraud, he thought. Then he smiled and picked up the telephone to book himself on to the first available flight to San Francisco. In fewer than fourteen days his world had changed, but at least his mind had been sharpened back to some kind of normality. Strange how that could happen by seeing and hear-ing a man whose path he would probably never cross again. A couple of weeks before, his mind had been as blunt as a rusty old axe and his whole being had seemed to be deserted by any shape or form.

An old saying came back to him without bidding – 'The mind of every man *is* the man: the spirit of the miser, the mind of a drunkard . . . they are more precious to them than life itself.'

How true, he thought. His mind, the mind of an adventurer, had been lost to him and now was refound. More precious to him than life itself.

3

THERE'S A PORPOISE CLOSE
BEHIND ME

In M's office, high on the ninth floor of that faceless building overlooking Regent's Park, James Bond had just threatened to resign.

'Resign?' M shouted. 'What d'you mean by resign? People don't resign from this firm. People are jailed, shot, keel-hauled, fired, put on the back burner, but they do *not* resign.'

'Then I'll make history by being the first.' Bond's whole being had rebelled, and this personal rebellion was, he felt, long overdue. 'I still have some authority over my own life. I can take early retirement from the Royal Navy, then thumb my nose at this Service. Once out I'll be a free agent.'

'There's no such thing as a free agent.' M's eyes were like ice and his tone was a blizzard.

'All right, sir, I'll enumerate the problems.' Bond took a deep breath and looked the Old Man squarely in the eye. 'I've asked you a dozen times why my name has not yet been removed from the active Navy duty list and returned officially to Foreign Office attachment.'

A year before, Bond had been returned to the active duty list in the Royal Navy with his rank upgraded to captain. As soon as the mission was ended he had been told to report back for duty with his old service, but the correct procedure had not been carried out. No orders had been issued taking him from the active list.

As far as the Royal Navy was concerned, he was their man and not working for M and the Secret Intelligence Service.

'Is that all?' M snapped.

'No, sir, it isn't all. Since the last business I seem to have been placed on hold. My time's squandered here. Nothing to do, nothing to occupy my mind. It's as though you've put me out to grass.'

M made a little tilting motion with his right hand. 'When the time's right, 007, there'll be plenty of work for you.'

'Like sending me to a health farm? You did that once and look what happened.'

'No, health farms are out.' M's mouth clamped shut, his lips forming a straight grim line. 'Listen to me, 007, and listen well. Europe – the world come to that – is at a crossroads. What with the wind of change blowing among the Eastern Bloc countries, and *perestroika* running amok in the Soviet Union, we need cool heads. Never,' he began to enunciate his words, clipping them off one at a time, 'never since the early days of the cold war have we been so in need of human intelligence – HUMINT. The map of Europe is being changed. For good? Maybe. Who knows? Those countries are unstable. The Soviet Union is unstable. We're recruiting, establishing old networks so that, should the problems return, we shall be ready.

'In this situation, I cannot have men about me whose minds have lost their edge, just as your mind's lost its edge, James. I've kept you on the active Naval list just in case. And I want you sharp as a dagger, smart as a whip.' It was then that M added the lines Bond was to remember in his hotel room in Victoria, British Columbia. 'You need to get away for a rest, James. Go off to California. They're all mad there, so you'll be in good company.' He had said it without a smile or trace of levity.

It was dark by the time he got to the Fairmont Hotel, high on Nob Hill. He had just made a Horizon Air flight out of Victoria, clearing customs and immigration at Port Angelis and going on to Seattle where he connected with an Alaska Airways flight to San Francisco. It was dusk as they let down towards SFO International and the mist had already rolled in across the Bay, so that the Golden Gate bridge looked like a half-submerged gigantic liner with her twin superstructures visible above the murk.

During the limo drive to the Fairmont, Bond took in the lights and atmosphere distinctive to the colourful city of Saint Francis – by day a bustling, thriving tourist-ridden place, and by night a city full of life and activity, some of it dangerous. He had not been here for several years, though he had fond memories of staying at the Mark Hopkins just across the street from the Fairmont, and of a day out in Muir Woods among the aged huge cathedral of redwoods. There had been a girl with him then but, for the life of him, Bond could not now recall her name.

There was one message waiting for him. The short, type-written note said simply:

Rest. You will need it. Mandarin.

'Mandarin' was M's favourite crypto, for it was by way of a small in-joke among the intelligence community, Mandarins being the collective name applied to all high-ranking civil servants working in their secure government jobs in London's Whitehall. Governments rose and fell but the Mandarins went on for ever.

So M was already here, somewhere, and Bond began to sense some new and dangerous activity could well be waiting for him. He unpacked rapidly, took a shower and called room service for eggs Benedict and a half-bottle of Tattinger, then he dressed in dark slacks and one of his favourite Sea Island cotton rollnecks. Just before he left England, Bond's annual order of a dozen of these had been delivered to him from John Smedley & Co., the only firm who made decent rollnecks of this kind. On his feet he wore comfortable moccasins, made for him and regularly shipped to England by Lily Shoes of Hong Kong.

He ate the eggs and drank the champagne in silence, then

switched on the television. Carson was doing all the usual old jokes with his guests of the evening, Art Buchwald and a starlet of uncertain age. The humour and bonhomie, Bond thought, was all rather forced and vulgar; his tastes were a shade more sophisticated. He watched for five minutes and then consigned the images to oblivion with the remote control, knowing that he was in an extraordinarily restless mood. He was also very wide awake and would not be able to sleep for some hours. He paced the room for a time, then walked out on to the balcony from which he had a splendid view of the city. There was a dampness in the air, as there so often is in that city, and he shivered, briefly recognising the temptations rising within him. He of all men knew that there were parts of the city that were gaudy and downright unsafe at night, yet the lights were drawing him like a magnet.

He went inside, closed the windows and put on his short grey suede jacket. This might be his last chance of unrestricted action for some time. So, taking the elevator, Bond went down into the hotel lobby and out into the night, walking briskly down the hill and turning left on a path that would take him into Chinatown.

Within ten minutes, he knew that someone was following him.

First it was just a feeling born of immense experience of such things. Around him, the nightlife seethed. Garish neon signs beckoned the unwary and, as he moved deeper into Chinatown, more sordid aspects of the city at night were blatantly displayed – girls for sale along the pavements, scantily dressed, watched over by shadowy figures who lurked in doorways or in full view leaning against buildings. At every intersection, he also caught sight of the dealers who did not have to hassle as much as the whores, for their clientèle was ready made. The market for crack cocaine, straight heroin, and even grass was secure. Sometimes a car would pull up near the kerbside, its occupant calling low to ask if he wanted some action. For 'action' read 'crack', 'ice', or even 'speed'. The results of the dealers' work could be seen everywhere in drawn faces, empty or wild eyes. The atmosphere took on a more dangerous, almost tangible, feel the further Bond went, fending off girls and dealers who approached him with monotonous regularity.

He turned left into an alleyway, took ten paces and then turned back, going on to the street again, glancing to his right as he did so. He saw, among the many people along the sidewalk, one man falter in his stride, eyes flicking from left to right as he recovered himself and carried on walking. Caucasian, Bond noted, mid-thirties, clean-shaven, well-built, around a hundred and forty pounds, brownish hair brushed straight back, casually dressed in well-cut jeans and a denim jacket with soft grey leather Sperry Topsider shoes. The jeans were probably Levi 501s and the glance to the left and right could mean that he was working with a team. Remember the shoes, Bond told himself. If it was a well-trained team they would change positions, even clothes, but they seldom had time to alter their shoes.

Bond quietly recited a couple of lines from *Alice's Adventures in Wonderland*—

'Will you walk a little faster?' said a whiting to a snail,
'There's a porpoise close behind us, and he's treading on my tail.'

Immediately, the tail became 'Porpoise' in his mind.

He took another left turn, literally walking around the block. When he came on to the main street again, Porpoise was still behind him. In spite of the dampness in the air it was a warm night and a thousand assorted aromas filled the street – cheap scents used by the whores mingled with cooking smells from the restaurants, then mixed with the odour of rotting food from the garbage cans and old boxes outside the now closed grocery stores. Mix well with the sweat of the crowd which ebbed and flowed around you and you had a concoction, Bond considered, that could be found only in a few cities of the world.

There was also noise and light. *Son et lumière*, he thought. The endless stream of slow-moving traffic, the sing-song call of street traders, the brazen advances of the girls and music blaring, overpowering, coming from almost every clip joint, club and store, while the neon, reds, vivid blues and whites, flashed and strobed. Instant inferno.

He glanced over his right shoulder, waiting for a dozen or so cars and taxis to throb past, each laden with the thumping heavy bass from its onboard stereo, before dodging the rest of the traffic and crossing the street. Porpoise was still there, further back on the opposite side of the road now, but preparing to cross.

On the corner a store blazing with lights announced that it sold rare and beautiful Chinese artifacts. The usual gaggle of female artifacts paced up and down in front of the store, offering themselves for more basic services. Bond snarled at one, who was dressed only in some unlikely garment which looked as though it had come from Fredericks of Hollywood, and entered the store.

Inside, long counters glittered with jade, ivory and semi-precious stones. Buddhas, miniature pagodas, delicate fretted work, oceans of it, were all overseen by attractive Chinese girls in elaborately decorated cheongsams or attractive silk pyjama suits.

Several people were either actively buying or seriously looking along the aisles, and the girls tried immediately for the hard sell, offering to show you the choicest pieces or the best bargains. Bond had to be firmly rude to three of them before they left him to his own browsing devices, which placed him near to the windows so that he was able surreptitiously to survey the street outside.

Porpoise appeared to be haggling with one of the street girls, but with one eye permanently cocked towards the store doorway; there was little else he could do, unless he brazened it out and came into the store itself.

Bond continued to look at the Oriental bric-à-brac, appearing to centre his attention on a statuette, a six-inch-high delicate girl in the robes of ancient China. One of the omnipresent assistants was quickly at his side.

'You wish to buy? I make special price for you.' She had all the grace of a butterfly, but the sales pitch of a rocket launcher.

'You make *very* special price for me,' Bond muttered aggressively, slipping one hand into the outer pocket of his jacket.

'How special?' the girl asked, almost flirtatiously.

Bond's lips hardly moved. 'I want nothing from this store. I also do not want to see anyone hurt. So you'll take me to the back. To your store rooms . . .' He saw the girl's mouth begin to open as though she would scream. 'No!' he commanded sharply. 'I'm not here to harm anyone. Just take me to the back of the store and show me the rear exit.'

'Rear exit . . . ?' the girl gasped.

'Rear exit, quickly – or someone will get hurt. First it will be you. Understand?'

She had gone the colour of pewter under her make-up and, biting her lower lip, she nodded.

'Good girl. Now, just smile and show me the way out. A very bad person is outside looking for me.'

She nodded again and said with a choke that he should follow her. As they walked towards the rear of the building a pair of heavy-set men approached, speaking in rapid Chinese – Cantonese, Bond thought, or one of its multitude of dialects. The girl spat back at them, the gist of what she said being obvious to all. 'If you don't want trouble, keep away.'

They passed through a beaded curtain which led to a long and high store room, and the girl pointed to a door at the far end. 'You go through there. Out in street.'

Bond grabbed at her shoulder, pulling her close and sticking the forefinger of his right hand into her side. 'Take me out,' he grunted. 'Quickly. Chop-chop, okay?'

Her eyes were wide with fear, but she gave a little nod and led him towards the door.

'And nobody follow, okay?' he grunted again when they

reached the exit. 'No alarms. No calling police. Just go on as normal, yes?'

'Okay,' she breathed, her hand on the doorknob.

'Open up then and show me it's safe.'

She obeyed quickly, her hand trembling. Such a waste, Bond thought. She was probably a nice, generous girl socially. He would not have been averse to spending an evening with her.

The door led to the street, and he made her look out to ensure there was nobody lurking in the shadows. When it seemed safe, Bond told her again that she should keep her mouth shut. 'It would be very bad joss for me to have to return and alter that pretty face.' Considering the lascivious thoughts that were going on in his head, Bond considered that he sounded pretty mean.

'I promise. Not foolish. Do not wish for trouble, particularly as my father is owner of this store.'

'Good girl! Just keep that pair of Chinese cabbages off my back.'

In spite of the trembling hands and the flicker of fear in her eyes, the girl gave a little giggle. 'Those cabbages my brothers,' she said, and the giggle stayed with him as he closed the door behind him.

There was nobody in the alleyway which led to another dark and narrow passage at the end of which he could see, like a light at the end of a tunnel, the bustle, noise and glare of the main street.

Hugging the right-hand side of the passageway, Bond moved softly towards the street, pausing at the top, flattening his body into the shadow and giving himself a small view of the front of the store through which he had gone. The girls were still outside, but there was no sign of Porpoise. Instinctively he looked back down the passageway, fearing that the tail had gone through the store after him and was now behind him. But nothing moved or stirred in the darkness.

As he turned to look again at what he could see of the store front, Porpoise came into sight. It seemed possible that the man had entered the store and discovered his quarry gone to earth, for he stood looking about him, his face showing perplexity, eyes darting all over the place. Finally he gave a deep sigh, shrugged his shoulders, turned and joined the crowd, hurrying back in the direction from whence he had come.

Bond started after him, for he was now anxious to know two things. Why was he being followed? Who had put this surveillance on him? He spotted Porpoise quite quickly on the other side of the street though the man appeared to be in a hurry and moved through the crowd with long strides, twisting his body this way and that to avoid too much jostling and bumping.

Remaining on his side, Bond followed, well behind for a couple of blocks, then pushed on faster as he saw Porpoise take a sudden right at an intersection. Perhaps he was heading towards Nob Hill, Bond thought; possibly setting up a stakeout of the Fairmont. If so, he should be easy meat and 007 would have the answers to his questions quite quickly. It was remarkable how easily people talked when you applied enough muscle to certain key points of the anatomy.

He crossed the road and was around the intersection just in time to see Porpoise diving into another side street, once more to the right.

Bond had no idea whether Porpoise had spotted him or not, but he was now committed. One way or another there had to be a showdown. He rounded the corner to find himself in a deserted narrow street. He was less than a block away from the noise and glare of the main thoroughfare, but suddenly this was a different world, silent, still and poorly lit. He slowed, walking carefully, keeping away from the wall and its many doorways in which Porpoise could quite easily be hidden.

Garbage was piled against some of the buildings, the rear exits of fast food joints, restaurants, clubs and stores, while extra light filtered on to the street from the rear windows of these places.

Still no sign of Porpoise. No sign of anybody, except for one sudden explosion of a girl pushing her customer out of a door and immediately propositioning Bond, who fended her off with the snarl he was beginning to perfect. It was no good being polite to these people of the streets, no good giving them a pleasant 'Not tonight, dear, thank you.' They understood four-letter expletives much better – the kind Woody Allen had described as 'Go forth, be fruitful, and multiply.'

The street narrowed then turned abruptly widening into a kind of courtyard. There was Porpoise standing and looking about him as though lost. Now, Bond thought, now I can take him and find out what the hell's going on. He took a step forward out of the shadow, then shrank back against the wall for two figures had appeared ahead of Porpoise, advancing from a wide double doorway above which an old weathered wooden sign hung, scrawled with Chinese characters.

The two were dressed in dark clothes, running suits most likely. Each wore a visored baseball cap and held baseball bats swinging easily in their hands. Bond automatically reached for his gun before he realised that he was unarmed. He had come on holiday and was quite unprepared for any kind of confrontation that called for more than the use of fists. There was no way he could take on this pair steadily approaching Porpoise, bats at the ready.

Porpoise threw one quick look over his shoulder, then called out to the men to stop, reaching for his weapon as he did so.

Bond saw one hand come up with a pistol, the other held some kind of wallet in front of his body as though it was a magic charm to stop evil. But the men kept coming.

He felt impotent, pushing his back against the wall, hoping the shadows would conceal him.

Then, as the pair of thugs came nearer, so others appeared silently from a doorway to Bond's right, moving swiftly with no sound, bearing down on Porpoise's back.

Bond wanted to cry out a warning, but his throat felt dry and constricted as he watched the inevitable which seemed to take place in horrific slow motion.

He saw Porpoise adopt a firing stance with legs apart and his pistol held in a two-handed grip, arms rigid in front of his body. In his mind, Bond imagined the finger already squeezing on the trigger, but before he could get off a shot, one of the men at his rear came within striking distance, raised his bat and swung with sickening force to the side of Porpoise's head.

There was no human sound, only the horrific thud and crack as the bat connected and the target's head smashed to one side, followed by the clatter as the pistol flew from his hands.

The first blow was like a signal for all four men to move in, though the initial crack to the head could well have killed. The solid baseball bats rose and fell as Porpoise dropped first to his knees and then to the ground.

Even when he was down, the quartet of clubs went on rising and falling, a macabre series of drumbeat thuds, thumping and cracking in unison until all that was left was a body with a terrible bloody sponge where the head had once been.

There was nothing he could do. No way to give an alarm or prevent this brutal overkill. So Bond backed away, still clinging close to the wall. Then he moved fast, avoiding the boxes and garbage as he hurtled back the way he had come.

He stopped running once he had reached the main street and walked at speed, weaving in and out of the people who still, at this late hour, filled the sidewalks. He felt guilt wash over him for a second and cursed his lack of any weapon or means to save the man. Then, as he began the long, thigh-aching toil back up Nob Hill, he realised that the guilt was really only a reflection of frustration at not having had the opportunity to question Porpoise. Why had be been followed? he asked himself again. Who wanted him under surveillance? Come to that, was the death of Porpoise just one of those unhappy timings – being in the wrong place at the wrong time – or was there some more sinister, premeditated reason?

The questions were to haunt him all that night as he lay in his safe and luxurious room high in the Fairmont. Bond dropped in and out of sleep, sweating and plagued by nightmares of a severed head being kicked around a schoolyard by a laughing gang of Chinese children.

At dawn he woke suddenly from one bout of deep sleep. Sitting bolt upright, he captured the image of the girl in the store from his most recent dream. The girl had first giggled and then thrown her head back, cackling, which showed her to have the razor-sharp teeth of a shark.

He called room service and ordered breakfast – just a lot of coffee and toast – there was little chance here of getting his beloved precisely boiled egg or the De Bry coffee, Tiptree strawberry jam or Cooper's Vintage Oxford marmalade which made up his breakfast ritual back home.

Before the room-service trolley arrived, he had time to shower, shave and dress. Then he sat at the window drinking almost scalding coffee and eating quite reasonable wholewheat toast with at least a facsimile of marmalade or jam.

As he breakfasted, his head began to clear and his thoughts became more positive. Was there any point in reporting what he had seen to the local police? The answer to that was a straight no. He had been summoned to San Francisco by his chief, which certainly meant official business. A report to the police would only snarl him in red tape. It would also, undoubtedly, reveal his RN rank plus his identity as a member of the British Secret Intelligence Service. Whatever M required of him, Bond could bet every penny he owned that his Chief would not be attracted to the idea of his identity becoming public knowledge to local law enforcement agencies. The only course still open to him was a quick, unidentifiable call to the SFPD giving the barest details of the horrific murder he had witnessed.

He was still thinking of the feasibility of this action when the doorbell chimed. Probably room service wanting to clear away the breakfast debris, but he took the safe action of squinting through the security peephole in the door. The strange fish-eye view showed two well-dressed burly men standing back from the door.

'Who is it?' he called.

'FBI. Open up, Captain Bond, or we'll have to smash the door down.'

They looked and sounded as though they meant it, and through the peephole, he saw one of the men holding up a wallet with official ID. Even through the lens Bond could see that it looked genuine.

'Come on, Captain Bond. We haven't got all day.'

Slowly, Bond slipped the safety chain off the door, moved to one side and tensed his body, ready to fight back if this pair proved not to be on the side of the angels.

They were FBI, there was no doubt about that. One even had his automatic pistol unholstered. They came into the room in the confident way of police officers who know that right is on their side, not barrelling in, or attempting to put any restraining hold on Bond, but smartly, firm in both manner and speech.

'You are Captain James Bond, Royal Navy?' the leading one asked, while his partner stood back, the unholstered automatic held close in to his side with the business end steadily pointing towards Bond.

'Yes, my name's Bond.'

'What are you doing in San Francisco, Captain Bond?'

'I'm on vacation. Why would you want to know?'

'You're here as a private individual?'

'Yes.'

The FBI man nodded, his face blank but a deep disbelief embedded in his eyes. 'There are several people who wish to talk with you, Captain Bond.'

'For instance?'

'First our own local Bureau Chief . . .'

'He's *very* anxious to see you,' sharp from the other agent.

'About what?' He was letting them come to him.

'How about murder?' Again from the younger of the two, the one looking very angry, the one with the pistol.

'I've only been here since last night. I really . . .'

'And you went out?'

'Yes, but . . .'

'Tell it to the Bureau Chief, Captain Bond. He wants to talk to you about the murder of Agent Patrick Malloney who was found bludgeoned to death near the Embarcadero early this morning.'

'I've never heard of Agent Malloney, and I haven't been near the Embarcadero . . .'

'We think he was dumped there, Captain Bond; and excuse me if I tell you that the late Agent Malloney and yourself have a very close connection.'

'I've . . .' Bond began, but the two agents had started to move in on him.

'Come quietly, Captain Bond,' one of them said.

'We wouldn't like to mess up this nice room,' said the other.

4

LORDS AND LORDS DAY

The Bureau Chief, the senior FBI agent working out of San Francisco, was a stocky, battered-looking man in his mid-forties. He sat in his shirtsleeves, his tie pulled loose, the desk of his cluttered office giving the impression that he was not happy with paperwork. His name was Broderick, and he also did not seem to be happy with James Bond.

'Captain Bond RN,' he announced to Bond, as though passing on uncertain information. 'Captain James Bond. Uh?'

'How can I help?' 007 was not going to open the batting.

'Well,' Broderick ran stubby fingers through greying unruly hair. 'Well, we've been asked to hand you over to your own people. In fact they asked us to keep an eye on you yesterday.' He grunted again. 'Truth to tell, I'm a tad angry with myself. The boys are just angry. We all get that way when one of our own meets an untimely and brutal end. You ever set eyes on this man?' He tossed a five-by-four matt photograph across the desk, and Bond found himself looking into a pleasant young face staring out of the picture with eyes that seemed full of hope and determination.

'Yes. Yes, I saw this man last night.'

'Uh-hu? Tell me about it.'

Bond told him, for the photograph was undoubtedly Porpoise, the man he had seen clubbed to death in the Chinatown alley. When he had finished the story, Broderick sighed and nodded. 'You didn't think to tell anybody about this?'

'Yes. I did *think* about it. But it was necessary for me to wait. There's someone I felt I had to talk to first.'

'You didn't even go to the poor guy's assistance.' There was more than a hint of disgust in his voice.

'No. It wasn't in anybody's interest, Mr Broderick.'

'Particularly your own, eh?'

'One of the rules of military life is self-preservation. There was no point in my trying to help this man. I was unarmed. Better for me to live and fight another day.'

Broderick nodded again, his face grim, unconvinced by the answer. Then he rose and led Bond over to a detailed map of San Francisco which almost took up an entire wall of his office. 'Like to try and pinpoint the place where you say you saw the killing?'

Bond zeroed in on the Chinatown area and quickly found the junction on Stockton Street where he had thrown Porpoise by going into the store. He traced his own movements for the FBI man, his return to the street and his own surveillance on Porpoise. Everything was marked on the map, all the tiny alleys and passages which made up the network around the main arteries of Chinatown. It was easy to pick out the narrow street that led to the cul-de-sac courtyard where the murder had taken place.

'And you just watched him get killed here?' Broderick did not sound surprised.

'That's the place.'

'Well, they moved the body and dumped him a long way off.' He sucked in a breath through his teeth, turning his eyes on to Bond as though he despised him. 'You do realise that Agent Malloney was killed while looking out for *you*.'

Bond had already been well ahead of him. After all it had become obvious, just as the open hostility towards him was obvious. The pair of agents who had brought him down to their Bureau chief had treated him as though he carried the plague or smelled badly. They had frisked him very thoroughly and without gentleness, taken away his passport and other items, wallet, credit cards and the like.

'Well, why wasn't I told he was looking out for me?' Bond had now become angry.

Broderick raised his head, and Bond saw that his eyes held nothing but a cold and calculating disgust. 'Surveillance isn't surveillance if the target knows about it, *Captain* Bond.'

'Yes, but . . .'

'Yes, but we have to deal with your kind quite often.' Broderick faced him, and for a moment Bond prepared to defend himself. It was clear that the FBI man would have liked to tear him apart. 'We have orders not to lay a finger on you,' he said, finally. 'Seems there are people waiting to talk with you who can take care of all your problems, and you've gotten plenty of those, Captain Bond. That should be clear to a drunken June bug, let alone a man of your intelligence.'

'Sorry, I don't follow you,' he began, but was cut short by Broderick shouting for the two agents who had been at the hotel. Their names, it seemed, were Agents Nolan and Wood and they came into their chief's office like two men hoping there was going to be a fight.

'Lock him up and keep him happy until we move him.' Broderick turned away.

'Look . . .' Bond began.

'No, you look, buddy.' Agent Nolan was close, with a hand around Bond's wrist. 'You look and listen, *Captain* Bond. If it wasn't for our orders, I'd do something that wouldn't be nice, like reorganising that plummy English accent of yours or sticking your pearly whites in the roof of your own pink little mouth. So remember that and don't take chances.'

Bond let the fury build up inside himself, keeping it under control. He could probably do things to Agent Nolan that would come as a very big surprise to the man, but there was no point. Instead he asked if he was being arrested.

'Not as easy as that, Bond,' the other agent, Wood, drawled.

'You're to be handed back to your own. I just hope they know what to do with a scumbag like you.'

'I think I have a right, then, to speak to the British Embassy in Washington or one of their representatives here.'

Broderick turned sharply, face flushed. 'You have no rights! Nothing! Understand? We simply have to turn you over to people who *do* have rights, so you'd best behave yourself. I'd hate to report that you got yourself shot or messed up by falling down a flight of stone steps while being unco-operative. Get him out of my sight!'

The agents took him by the arms and led him through an outer office, down a small flight of stairs to a holding cell into which they pushed him, clanging the door shut.

'You're so damned sensitive that we had to remove the Marshals who usually deal with people in here,' Nolan said, as though indicating that Bond was causing them unnecessary work and disrupting normal routine.

He heard the heavy clunk of the key in the lock, but did not even try to protest. He did not understand what was going on or why. The only thing plain and simple was the fact that one of their colleagues was dead and he had stood watching while the man met his end. In their place, Bond thought he might feel the same, but he had not bargained on the hostility which came off all the FBI men like static on a dry cold day. There must be something else, but it was best to wait. Wait and find out what the whole damned business was about. After all these men were accredited law enforcement agents, and he was in their country.

He sat down on the small cot which took up almost one wall of the cell and tried to think it through. He had been officially under FBI surveillance. His tail had been killed and he had watched the killing. But, he told himself for the hundredth time, there was more to it than just treating him like a coward for not going to Agent Malloney's assistance, something deeper, something more disturbing.

Agent Wood came down about an hour later with a polystyrene box containing a dry-looking hamburger, fries, a plastic capsule of tomato sauce and a disposable receptacle containing what could well have been coffee.

He sipped at the muck, chewed on a couple of the fries, which were cold, and left the hamburger untouched. This was a country which appeared to be in the grip of a gigantic health kick – magazines telling you that your body was a machine which had to be cared for, advertisements, public broadcasts and TV commercials, all telling you to watch your cholesterol, watch your weight, look out for your blood pressure, eat wisely and fill your intestines with fibre – yet their fast food joints did a roaring trade in junk food. He could not even bear to let this stuff past his teeth. Cynically, he thought the world had gone crazy. For instance, they were happy about heading for a smoking-free society, yet doing little about the thousands of alcohol-related deaths in the home, on the roads and in hospitals. The anti-smoking lobby appeared to gratify that other guilt which knew little headway was being made against drug abuse.

The afternoon went by in intense boredom. He was not worried about any legal repercussions, but the big question mark remained over his current status. His mind made lazy circles around the enigma in which he found himself. He could not figure out the mystery surrounding Lee. No sense, or sudden revelation came to him. Only a numbness and the now unmistakable fact that someone, for some reason, had set him up.

Around dusk, Broderick and the other two agents came down. Bond was handcuffed to Nolan and they led him back out of the cell, up the steps and into the main offices, all deserted except for the more obvious signs of security – the coded key pads, electronically locked doors, and blinking alarm lights. They unlocked and relocked doors by punching in codes, finally reaching a deserted reception area with a double bank of elevators.

They locked one of the elevator cars in the 'up' position and

Broderick sent Wood down to make sure 'we haven't got any civilians around', as he put it. After five minutes Wood signalled through the emergency telephone system.

'Downstairs, you just move fast, okay?'

Bond nodded, asking where he should move to.

'We'll take you to a car out in back, and I want it real quick. No lagging behind. The last thing we need is some smart-ass reporter spotting you. You're probably next month's front page, Bond, but sure as hell nobody wants you to be splashed over the tabloids tomorrow.'

The main lobby of the building was as deserted as the offices above them, but they led Bond away from the main street doors, taking him along a corridor and out through the rear of the building where Wood sat at the wheel of an old brown Chevy. Bond was bundled into the back, squashed between Nolan and Broderick and was barely settled before Wood burned a great deal of rubber, pulling away and running through the gears like a racing driver.

He tried to follow the route, but the driver kept doubling back, taking last-minute turn-offs, so that he became disorientated. He tried to remember the map of San Francisco in his head and thought they were heading in the general direction of the Embarcadero. He glimpsed the TransAmerica Pyramid some-where over to the right, then suddenly they were down by the old Ferry Building, which always reminded him of Liverpool, and drawing up to the side of a helicopter pad where a big S-61 sat in the glare of floodlights, its rotors idling, the word NAVY clearly visible on the rear assembly.

As the car pulled up, the floods went out, leaving only little blue marker lights around the pad and up the ramp to the S-61. Nolan unlocked the handcuffs. 'Okay, Bond. Out we go. They're looking forward to seeing you inside that chopper. Rather you than me.'

A chill breeze buffeted their faces as Bond was assisted from the car and roughly handled up the ramp to the helicopter. A figure beckoned him from the steps and the FBI men gave him a final push on his way. He thought he heard Broderick say that his luggage was already aboard, but the words were lost on the breeze and the wash from the rotors.

A crewman helped him aboard and showed him to a seat inside the dark body of the craft, shouting in his ear that he should fasten the seat belt. The door slammed and the engines came up to fine pitch the moment he was inside.

He felt, more than saw, someone sitting in the next seat. Then the familiar voice came loudly in his ear. 'Only a couple of hours in San Francisco, Bond, and already there's mayhem. You even managed to get your own minder killed,' M said. 'Sometimes I think the Grim Reaper sits on your shoulder, 007. One day he'll catch up with you.'

The helicopter was airborne and tilting like a fairground ride, angling the lights of the city crazily below them.

The helicopter ride took them out over the bay towards the US Navy facility on Treasure Island and down to the helicopter pad of a Nimitz class nuclear aircraft carrier. Throughout the whole journey, which took less than ten minutes, Bond said nothing to his old chief. Inside he seethed with anger. 'Take a rest; take a holiday . . .' M had said. Now, Bond felt that he had been betrayed. Certainly he had been set up, the hostility of the FBI men had not been feigned, so somehow he had been used, and there could only be one manipulator – M himself.

As they touched down on the carrier's deck, the deck lighting went off. The door was opened and two shadowy figures helped him out of the helicopter, leading him firmly towards the island – that unique superstructure which is the hallmark of any carrier, though the island of Nimitz class aircraft carriers is distinctively smaller than normal.

Once through the hatchway and into a brightly lit interior, Bond turned as M followed him.

'I think you owe me some explanation, sir!' His anger was

barely concealed, but M simply gave a tight little smile and indicated that he should follow the uniformed yeoman who stood patiently waiting just inside the hatchway.

Bond gave an audible sigh and followed the yeoman along the maze of companionways, and up metal stairways until they reached a wooden door set into a bulkhead. The yeoman opened the door without pausing to knock, holding it back so that both M and Bond could enter, then closing it behind them.

'Alone at last, eh, 007?' M's voice had a slightly jaunty air to it. They were in a large day cabin, the kind, Bond thought, that would be occupied by a Naval Taskforce C-in-C. There was a large desk anchored to the deck and chairs set around for conferences. The US President's framed photograph hung over the desk which was completely clear except for a bank of telephones and a small, neat, pile of files.

M strode across the cabin, taking the seat behind the desk as though this was his rightful place. Bond opened his mouth, about to pour out a list of genuine grievances, but M held up his right hand as though staving off a blow. 'Just sit down, James. Sit down and listen to me before you even try and fire a broadside. Things are not what they appear to be.'

Bond swallowed his pride and sat, his head cocked to one side, chin lifted arrogantly.

'You say that I owe you an explanation, and maybe I do,' M began, 'but I think you'll find the boot might be on the other foot. First, you are under the impression that I tried to lure you to this part of the globe on the pretext of sending you on leave when I really wanted to involve you in some operation, right?'

Bond nodded. 'Absolutely right, sir. And if I . . .'

'Wait!' M barked. 'Just sit quietly and wait, 007. You're too fond of flying off the handle at the least suspicion. I am sorry that your leave has been curtailed because you are still very obviously in need of a rest and change of scene, but we're into something far more important now.'

He shifted in the black leather chair, taking out his pipe and tossing a tobacco pouch on to the desktop. 'Let me say now that I wanted you to get a good rest – a change of scene and a change of pace. Yes, on the charge of trying to lure you into this part of the world, I plead guilty, but I wanted you to get your leave before slamming you into an operation here, in the United States.' He began to load his pipe, constantly glancing up at Bond as he spoke. 'Events overtook me. I had thought to give you fair warning and a good briefing. Before you left London, I was pretty certain that you would end up working on this side of the Atlantic and I'm sure you wouldn't have relished two trips across the fish pond. My whole aim was a genuine attempt to get you relaxed and ready. Come to that, it backfired very badly – and that part is down to you.'

'You mean the FBI and the surveillance?' Bond had calmed a little for he knew, while M could be devious, he always played fair with him when it came to operations, even though he had, on a number of occasions, tried tricks of involvement without giving him all the facts at the outset.

'I left a note for you at the Fairmont. That just about amounted to an order. I was telling you to stay aboard the damned hotel and not go gadding off around the town.'

He waited, as though expecting an apology. When none was forthcoming, M continued, 'Instead of staying in, you went off out into the night and, as a result, an FBI agent was killed. Your fault, 007. Entirely your doing.'

Another pause and silence between the two men. Bond stared straight ahead, not even looking M in the eyes as he slowly began to face the fact that it *was* his fault.

'Death is not funny, especially in the way the poor, unfortunate Malloney met his end, but it has helped us rather than hindered a somewhat complex situation.'

'So, I am now a pariah as far as the FBI are concerned? Because some young agent wasn't experienced enough.'

'No.' M's look hardened into an all too familiar grimness. 'No, you're persona non grata with the FBI because that's how *we* want it. It's one of the reasons I did not countermand the Queen's Regulations and MoD instructions and take you off active duty in the Royal Navy. You see, we're co-operating wholly with the US Navy. Even brought your uniforms over here, just in case you need to wear them. Also we've spread the word that you've become highly disenchanted with life in the Navy. That you want *out*. Which is what you do want, is it not?'

Bond's anger briefly flared again, 'Oh, no, sir. No, we've been down that road before. Disenchanted Naval and Intelligence officer seeks employment with hostile power. Object, the passing of classified information.'

'It isn't quite like that, James. Not this time. But people like the FBI and your old friends in the CIA are probably quite interested in seeing us move you out and back to the UK. You're simply disenchanted and not a little slipshod. Inefficient, not taking life very seriously.'

'Why?' This time 007 locked eyes with M as though challenging him to provide an adequate reason.

For the first time, M smiled. 'Because of Lords and Lords Day.'

Bond's voice was heavily tinged with sarcasm. 'Sir, I know you like being cryptic and using cryptos, but a crypto's no good to me unless I know what it means.'

'Oh, you'll find out what it means, James,' all fatherly now. 'You'll know what it means, but I doubt if you'll ever know how it works. Let me call in one of the US people you're going to be working with.' He lifted one of the telephones which was answered immediately. 'Would you ask Commander Rushia to step in now, please.' He pronounced the name 'Roosha'.

Rushia was in civilian clothes, smart, tidy, even a shade of the dandy, sporting a blue white-spotted bow tie, an immaculate white shirt, dun coloured slacks and a lightweight thin-striped summer jacket. But it was the man himself whom Bond saw immediately, not the clothes. He was big, tall and broad-shouldered, about Bond's age but with hair which had gone prematurely grey. He had a rangy look about him, eyes which seemed to yearn for far-off horizons, either at sea or the edges of great wheat fields reaching almost to the sky. His hands were large, big, strong and used sparingly in simple gestures.

Bond's first impression was of a man who might just have been a mite happier on some Mid-Western farm. His whole manner and speech also seemed to betray this essential idea, as though he wanted people to think of him only as slow, charming and have the feeling that he was really not up to the complexities, let alone the niceties of his calling.

'Captain James Bond, I want you to meet Commander Ed Rushia, US Naval Intelligence.' M smiled quietly as he introduced the two men.

Rushia took a step forward and placed his large hand in Bond's, giving it a firm shake. 'My gosh,' he said, his voice soft, down-home as they say in American. 'Jiminy, James Bond. Heard a lot about you, Captain Bond. Mind if I call you James?'

'Be my guest.' Bond did not usually like the American habit of becoming almost bosom, first-name buddies within thirty seconds of meeting, but as he felt the warm, firm pressure of Rushia's handshake and looked into the friendly, twinkling eyes, he felt he might have known the man for years. 'I can call you Ed, yes?'

'That's mighty nice a' you, James. 'Preciate it. Going to enjoy working with you. You just call me anything you darned well please. Most people do.'

M watched the two men, as dissimilar as the proverbial chalk and cheese. From his own first meeting with Commander Rushia he had known they would make a team. 'Ed, we have to clear Captain Bond here for Lords and Lords Day.'

Rushia took in a deep breath. 'Gee whizz,' he said. 'Gee, that's going to be tough. I don't understand the darned thing myself – only that she's a honey, Lords and Lords Day both. Two sweet and deadly honeys.' He looked from M to Bond and back again, pursed his lips, blew a couple of short breaths as though testing some imaginary instrument and lowered his long frame into one of the remaining chairs. He then turned to Bond.

'Well, James, it goes something like this. These coupla doo-hickies, Lords and Lords Day, are two sides of a mighty impressive coin. Lords, if you want the truth, stands for Long Range Deep Sea, and that's a real humdinger, I can tell you. This thing is state-of-the-art, but don't tell Art, or he'll want one.' His voice dropped into a confiding, almost secretive tone. 'This thing can detect submarine signatures – even well-shuffled ones – at a phenomenal range, in all weathers and to depths you just wouldn't believe. I tell you, James, I hardly believe the thing, it does such fantastic tricks. Don't ask me how it works, 'cos I guess only around half-a-dozen bald-pated superbrains know that. I can tell you it's a cocktail of micro-tech, lasers and some good things we got out of studying stealth technology.' He swept his hand in a gesture which made you feel he was signifying an entire ocean. 'To boil it down, take the mystery out of it as you might say, it's a box. A box with wires. But if there's some miracle metal dolphin out there, couple of hundred miles off the port beam and full fathom five down, the box with wires'll leap up and dance like Bojangles himself. Follow my meaning?'

Bond nodded, smiling. Ed Rushia was a live one, a natural, he thought. That down-home, simple, almost country-boy language must have led many unwary people to their doom. Bond, who knew good cover when he saw it, had already begun to respect Commander Rushia. 'And Lords Day?' he asked.

'Oh, that one's more perverse. It's the antidote. Long Range Deep Sea Detector And Yaffler. Yea, I had to ask about the Yaffler thing and it appears that in some parts of the world, the common green woodpecker is known as a Yaffler. Simple, isn't it? The antidote confuses the Lords box with wires by using a particular pattern of sonic beams. They're not your run-of-the-mill sonic beams. These are special, they form a pattern that sounds just like a common green woodpecker.' He clapped his big hands together in an act of finality. 'Okay, James, consider yourself Lords and Lords Day cleared.'

'So, what appears to be the problem?' Bond asked.

'Oh, the admiral here hasn't told you? Well, San Francisco is, as you must surely know, the headquarters of the United States Pacific Fleet, and the United States Pacific Fleet is as leaky as an old kettle. There are things going on around here that make the Walker Brothers look like a Girl Scout convention.' He frowned. 'The Walker Brothers were spies, by the by, not some singing rock 'n' roll outfit.'

'I had heard,' Bond said, straight-faced.

'Well, I like to be sure, James. Some people tell me that there are British officers who don't even know the difference between Stonewall Jackson and General Sherman. Think they're baseball players or some such.'

'And what's it all got to do with us Brits anyway?'

M stepped in. 'Us Brits, as you call your own, 007, helped invent the thing, but in the last three months no fewer than three officers and two enlisted men, one Royal Navy and the rest US Navy, have gone missing. They are *all* fully Lords cleared; they are *all* highly trained technicians with stratospheric security clearances . . .'

'Six, not five, if you count Wanda . . .' Rushia began.

M turned towards the American. 'We do *not* count Wanda, because she didn't go missing, Commander. She's our asset and she's here for the night. But you couldn't have known that.'

'Who is Wanda?' Bond asked, his mind already centred on the word Lords. He had heard it before and the picture came back clearly – the huge, hybrid Chinese-Indian and the words that had seemed to pass between him and the nervous man outside the Empress Hotel only yesterday afternoon. The lip-read conversation concerning someone's death by shooting, and the big man with the twisted hand saying, 'Tell them incalculable damage may have been done regarding Lords.'

He opened his mouth, but Rushia was already speaking. 'I

might add that if those guys have gone over to *any* foreign power, even in this time of *glasnost* and *perestroika*, then heaven help us, because those guys know things we wouldn't even share with the Army, Navy and Pentagon combined, leave alone the old folks in East Jaboo.'

'What is more,' M continued as though he had never been interrupted, 'as of yesterday, the founding father of Lords, one Professor Robert Allardyce, went missing. Guess where, James?'

'Surprise me, sir.'

'In Victoria, British Columbia. Where you were on holiday.'

'Then I just might have a connection.'

'What kind of connection?' M snapped.

'I think I have the name of someone possibly mixed up in the business.'

'Really?' M sounded almost patronising. 'Give me the name.'

'He's a half-breed, Chinese-Blackfoot Indian by the name of Lee Fu-Chu, also known as Brokenclaw Lee.'

M's face hardened and his voice took on the sharp tone of suspicion. 'What do you know of Brokenclaw Lee, Captain Bond?'

'Very little, sir. But I saw him and listened to him giving a speech yesterday in Victoria, just before I received your orders to come on down here.'

'Gee whizz,' said Rushia softly. 'Gee whizz, is that right?'

'Tell us about it,' M said flatly, as though challenging Bond to perform some impossible feat.

5

TROJAN HORSE

As he recounted the facts of yesterday's unexpected sighting and observation of Brokenclaw Lee, Bond was almost anxiously aware that both M and Commander Rushia listened to him with an intensity which he found disturbing. The two men were very still, never moving a muscle, their faces blank, like a pair of predators waiting for their target to come within range.

When Bond finished speaking there was a long silence. Involuntarily, images came clearly into his mind – smoke from an old steam train, drifting away in a long stream; the view from a powerful telescope, looking into space. Then M spoke.

'Why did you become so interested in Lee?' His tone was unusually hostile.

'I read his lips; death seemed to enter into the conversation, but, above all, he appeared to be an immensely powerful man. There was an aura about him, something different, fascinating, even charismatic.'

'And that's the truth, Bond? The whole truth? You saw this man and he struck you as being, shall we say "different", not quite as other men? His power and presence fascinated you?'

As he spoke, M raised his eyebrows, glanced at Rushia, who gave him a noncommittal look.

'Exactly, sir. I've been a little in the doldrums in the past few weeks. Lee and the story he told about himself somehow jerked me from my torpor. He *interested me*! In fact I intended to do some kind of follow up, check the fellow out. But your message arrived before I could even begin.'

There was another pause. More pictures in Bond's mind, this time of the man, Lee, his power and toughness tempered with charm.

'Knowing the circumstances as I do,' M started again, pausing, brow furrowed, 'if it was anybody else but you, 007, I'd be very suspicious of your story.'

'Mighty suspicious.' Rushia looked at Bond with an almost vacant stare.

'Let's get it straight one more time,' M continued. 'You saw the man and his entourage outside your hotel; you did a little lip-reading and reckoned he was told something about a death connected with Lords though you didn't understand the significance. You were told his name and, because he was such a striking individual, you followed him and listened to his speech of presentation at the museum.'

'Correct.' Bond looked straight into M's cold grey eyes.

'Do you think *he* would recognise you again?'

'I've no idea. His speech was a bit of a performance. As though he were an actor. He used his eyes well, but whether he marked me I couldn't say. I'd doubt it. Doubt it very much.'

'And the bodyguards?'

'If they're very good – trained surveillance experts – one of them might make me if he saw me again. I just don't know.'

'And you believed all that stuff about his Chinese great-grandfather and the marriage to the Blackfoot woman and so on even unto the third and fourth generation?' M spoke in a mock-parsonical manner.

'It was very convincing. I suppose, apart from his very imposing physical appearance, it was the thing that made him unique.'

M grunted. 'Yes. Yes, it *is* convincing, and you've been party to a quite extraordinary coincidence. Very few people actually get to see Mr Brokenclaw Lee. Usually only those he wants to see, apart from his regular retinue. I needn't remind you, Captain Bond, that in our business, coincidence and luck don't play a very big part.'

'A strange coincidence, to use a phrase, by which some things are settled nowadays,' Rushia quoted almost to himself. 'Who the heck said that?'

'I think it was Byron, actually.' Bond was already irritated by what appeared to be a hostile interrogation. 'But I really don't understand what you're getting at – either of you.'

'Well, listen, Bond.' M bent slightly forward, as though about to impart some choice classified information. 'Brokenclaw Lee *is* powerful. He's a gangster, a hoodlum, a one-man Mafia. He's also a mystery. He comes and goes as he pleases, disappears like a will-o'-the-wisp, he is a known killer, owns a very large portion of San Francisco's shady side. He controls practically every gambling den in Chinatown. Prostitution – and there's plenty of that – only operates under his aegis, the drug dealers pay him a fancy percentage, almost every nightclub or restaurant in the Chinatown area either belongs to him, or pays him hand-somely.'

'What about law enforcement? Surely, if this is known . . . ?' Bond began.

Ed Rushia stirred in his chair. 'Gosh, James. *Knowing* it isn't proving it.'

'Well, how . . . ?'

'How what?' The commander thumped his knee with a big hand, fingers spread wide. 'How he doesn't get arrested? I'll tell you how. Because he *owns* people, owns their souls. Know what that means? It means that, whatever the rumours, whatever the truth, nobody'll talk and certainly nobody will stand up in court. The local cops and FBI have plenty of snitches who pass on bits of information, rumour, tales, tittle-tattle, even truth. But not one of them would even think of giving evidence about your pal Brokenclaw Lee. For all we know he has people inside the SFPD and the FBI. I doubt it, but who knows?' For a second,

Rushia had dropped his down-home image and manner of speech.

'A one-man Mafia, you said.' Bond looked from one to the other. 'But even people mixed up with organised crime talk eventually. What about the special witness programmes? People who give evidence are protected, given new lives. I can't believe that Lee hasn't got enemies if . . .'

'Oh yeah. Sure. Sure he's got plenty of enemies,' Rushia drawled. 'But you try to get solid evidence from them. Ole Brokenclaw has two very powerful bits of ju-ju going for him. First off the stuff about his ancestry – Chinese and Blackfoot Indian. His forebears include at least one Medicine Man, or Woman I should say, and possibly more. May sound like super-stition to you, Cap'n Bond, but a lot of very down-to-earth folk half believe the man has supernatural powers. He makes certain the stories about him are gilded and pretty juiced up. I've met an otherwise rational man who believes that Brokenclaw can turn himself into an eagle.'

Bond recalled the power of voodoo, which he had seen for himself at first hand. Thinking about it, he decided that a man with Brokenclaw Lee's personality might well be able to engender a kind of hypnosis and superstition which made followers believe he had unusual powers.

'Second, there is proof on the streets that nobody has ever managed to inform on Mr Brokenclaw Lee and survive,' Rushia continued. 'There's the tale of one particular snitch, name of Tiger Balm Chan. Lee is supposed to have torn him apart with his bare hands. Don't know if it's true, but ole Tiger Balm was a mess when they found him – over an area of one square mile. Found him piecemeal, so to speak.'

'If there's so much information on him, why hasn't anybody tried to prosecute?' To Bond, the essential way of Brokenclaw Lee's life sounded like something from a strip cartoon. He said just that, his eyes fixed on M.

M laughed. 'Strip cartoon? Maybe. I told you, the man's a

will-o'-the-wisp. All his financial power is held by companies which are themselves dummy companies answerable to other dummy companies. In ten years the IRS has never been able to move against him because they cannot prove a thing – even the FBI, and I have a great deal of time for the FBI, cannot keep him in their sights. Over a dozen times they've mounted very complex, round-the-clock surveillance on him. Result? Those surveillance teams had him for twenty-four hours. Never longer. The man and his closest lieutenants just vanish for long periods. The agencies know of five large estates which might well belong to friend Brokenclaw, but he's never been physically discovered on any of those properties, and *nobody*, I mean *nobody*, has ever come up with conclusive proof of his one-man criminal activities.'

'Sounds like a job you'd put me on to, sir.' Bond smiled as he said it, and the smile was met by a freezing look.

'Oh, you are on it, 007. You and Ed Rushia here, both. You see, as well as being a mobster of immense skill and cunning, we are now one hundred per cent certain that he's taken on another line of work. We're certain that he's an agent of CELD, and probably the CCI as well.'

Bond looked at his chief with renewed interest. Up until now, the man Lee had seemed to be simply into organised crime. But CELD was the Central External Liaison Department, while CCI stood for Central Control of Intelligence. They were Red China's answer to the CIA, the SIS, NSA and any other Intelligence outfit you could think of.

'How much do you know about those happy intriguers in CELD and the CCI, Bond? Precious little I should imagine.'

'As much as anyone else in the trade, sir. They're both as ruthless as KGB was at the height of the cold war, to targets both at home and abroad. I've seen the need-to-know files. I'm aware that, in the current climate, especially since the Tienanmen Square massacre, every Western agency has been put on a red alert regarding Chinese Intelligence.'

'Anything else?'

'Yes. Since the Republic of China began to encourage visitors and tourists, there have been successful and unsuccessful attempts to recruit agents from the West. They desperately need Caucasians to work in Europe and the United States.'

'Mmm,' M growled. 'Tien-an-Men Square,' he divided the words correctly. 'The Gate of Heavenly Peace. Some peace. And what have you made of CELD's attempted conversions?'

'I know that some Chinese nationals have infiltrated our territories, that there are some Intelligence officers working out of consulates and embassies. I also read the long file from our own China Desk on their methods of recruitment and subversion. For a people noted for their cunning and deception, the Chinese methods seemed a shade old-fashioned, the kind of stuff the Russians used in the fifties and sixties. Sexual burns, hidden cameras, drug-induced disorientation, financial rewards.'

Rushia made a rumbling noise in his throat. 'You don't consider that those old ways still work, James?'

'They're less reliable, except in the case of certain subjects.'

'Surprise you if I said the FBI and Navy Intelligence know of at least six successful recruitments of Caucasians in the last twelve months?'

'Tell me about it.' Bond was unconvinced.

'Tell *you*? Hell, no. We can show you a pair of them – well, one is Caucasian. Here. Now. Aboard this floating airbase.'

M held up his hand. 'I should tell you, 007, that the US Navy have kindly given us the run of certain parts of this ship. There is only a skeleton crew aboard. We have several cabins, as well as the area which our American cousins call the Brig, and the ship's Hospital. What the Royal Navy would call the Cells and the Sick Bay.'

Until that moment, Bond had assumed they were the only Intelligence people on board, and that this cabin was a kind of safe house, organised for one meeting. 'Who's here, sir? Apart from us, I mean.'

'You'll see shortly. People known to you. But let's not run before we can walk. There are other things you must be briefed about if you're going to stand any chance against this particular evil.'

'You're suggesting that Brokenclaw Lee is behind the disappearance of these Lords and Lords Day specialists?'

'I would have thought it was obvious by now,' M said tartly. 'Yes. Our service was only brought in when Intelligence on this side of the ocean made the connection.' He looked pointedly towards Ed Rushia, silently ordering him to continue.

The American took a deep breath, 'Gee, James, what can I tell you? When the first coupla guys went AWOL nobody bothered. People go AWOL all the time, but when two more disappeared *everybody* got jumpy, particularly as they were interconnected. Then number five went off into the wide blue yonder and all hell broke loose. I'm just fillin' in the blanks for you, mind, 'cos I wasn't around at the beginning, though we had some mighty smart hombres working on it. Guys that look in their rear-view mirrors and do all those things that just make me plain nervous.'

Rushia waved a large hand in the general direction of the desk at which M was sitting. 'The files of the fearless five, the guys who went missing, are there for your inspection, and you'll see for yourself that all five who became the victims in *Trojan Horse* were very smart cookies. *Trojan Horse* is the crypto for the investigation into the missing experts, and you'd better believe they were experts. Between them they could pass on most of the working secrets of Lords and Lords Day. The first thing we did was to check and double-check the backgrounds of each member of the quintet. We particularly looked for weaknesses which could possibly be used as levers for what you consider to be outdated techniques. Just in case these people were turned in the old-fashioned sense. Then we spent a long time looking into their habits. Came up with some names and numbers, as they say. Three of the guys were buddies and spent a lot of time at The Broken Dragon – that's a kinda Chinese eating place-cum-cat house. They were there on the night they went AWOL. Each one of them was last seen at The Broken Dragon. Guess who owns that joint? And guess who was there on at least two of the occasions when guys disappeared?'

Bond simply nodded. Brokenclaw Lee was the obvious connection.

'So,' Rushia held up his left hand and counted off the fingers, 'Lieutenant Lindsay Robertson, Lieutenant Daniel Harvey and Senior Technician Billy Bob Heron all frequented The Broken Dragon with dangerous monotony. We can put Robertson and Harvey there within two hours of them going AWOL, and there is good evidence that ole Brokenfoot Lee was also there. He showed himself, as if on purpose, both times. More, we can put ole Billy Bob at the same place on the night he did the disappearing act.'

'And the other two?' Bond had a feeling that this was all too easy.

'Frankie McGregor, petty officer first class, and James Joseph Jepson III, lieutenant?'

'If that's who they were – are – do we know if they're . . . ?'

'Alive? Oh, it's *are*, okay. Those people're still alive and breathing. Those last two particular gentlemen, Jepson and McGregor, were heavily into that most dangerously addictive of beasts, gambling. They spent far too much time, mostly independently, at an illegal gaming house known as the Coc-Chai. Both there on the separate nights they went AWOL. Evidence was highly stacked on the pair of them taking it on the lam, as they used to say in the gangster movies, because they were in hock to the Coc-Chai, their messmates, their families and, in Jepson's case, one of Lee's moneylenders.'

'And Mr Lee is the driving force behind the Coc-Chai?'

Rushia nodded. 'Sure is. One hundred fifty per cent.'

'So, we have a tenuous link between Brokenclaw and the missing experts.'

M's hand slapped palm down on the desk top, landing with a thump which imparted irritation with more immediacy than words. The action was so sudden and unexpected that both Bond and Rushia turned sharply towards him.

'Tenuous then. But not now,' M snapped. 'Commander Rushia, I think we should have some food brought in and then invite the sixth missing Lords technician to dine with us. I'm sure she'll make Captain Bond here sit up, take notice, and also begin to take the whole of this business seriously.'

'If you say so, Admiral. Aye aye, sir.' Rushia hauled himself out of his chair and strode over to the desk. He was a man, Bond considered, who could never merely walk. Rushia strode, great loping steps full of purpose. He was reminded of horny-handed men following long gone horse-drawn ploughs.

'It'll be dinner for four, in the C-in-C's day cabin,' Rushia spoke into a red telephone. 'And would you be good enough to ask Lieutenant-Commander Man Song Hing to step up here. Good.' He replaced the handset. 'Wanda'll be right up, sir.' Then turning to Bond, his craggy face broke into a smile which made him look a good deal younger than his years. 'Wanda's quite a gal. She'll stir your juices for sure, Cap'n Bond.'

'Captain Bond's juices have been stirred far too often in the past for my liking,' M said wearily.

'I realise there's a great deal of briefing to be done, sir.' Bond sounded more than a shade acid. 'But one thing's been really bugging me, to use the local parlance.'

'Well?'

'You had FBI surveillance on me. You've already told me that it's been arranged for the local FBI people to believe I'm not strictly a good security risk. I accept that this is a necessary part of whatever's going on. But we've had one agent bludgeoned to death. I watched. I saw it all. Also, I followed the poor wretch and he obviously headed into a very dangerous part of town in search of me. Why?'

'Because he was told you might try to make contact with Brokenclaw Lee's people. He approached the place where he imagined he might just find you.'

'In that little square at the end of an alley?'

'That little square, 007, lies directly behind Lee's favourite haunt. Agent Malloney put himself in jeopardy by going into Brokenclaw Lee's heartland. Behind enemy lines, if you like.'

Bond nodded. 'Would you like to put me more fully in the picture about Lieutenant-Commander er, Wanda . . .'

'Man Song Hing.' M spoke the name flatly, sounding like a schoolteacher correcting an idle pupil. 'No, Bond. You will meet a very brave young woman who has, literally, given everything in an attempt to discover the whereabouts of the missing people from the Lords and Lords Day trials. I mean that she's given all a woman can give, and she lives now in the constant, and very probable, fear that she might not have much time before her cover is blown sky high. Why I doubt . . .' He was cut off by a knock on the cabin door and Rushia went over to open it.

Four men, all in casual dress – slacks, T-shirts, jeans and the like – wheeled in a large folding table of the kind you find room service using in the better hotels.

Bond recognised two of the newcomers as members of his own organisation. They were tough, hard people used for baby-sitting important assets or minding visiting VIPs, men known in the trade as Lion Tamers. One of them acknowledged him with a broad wink as they set up the table, laying places for four people and putting out cold cuts and a variety of salads on a second table, together with several bottles of wine, baskets of bread rolls, neat triangles of buttered brown bread and a flat dish spread with thinly sliced smoked salmon. The tables gleamed with starched napery and sparkling silver.

These unaccustomed 'waiters' performed their tasks with the

speed and deftness of well-trained servers who worked in silence and withdrew quickly once all was made ready.

Rushia busied himself with the wine while M came and sat at the table as though expecting the American officer and Bond to serve him. But before they could even begin to tackle the food there was another knock at the cabin door. This time Bond crossed the deck to open up.

He was aware, for a second, of two of the Lion Tamers standing guard, then his eyes were centred on the girl who had knocked on the door.

From behind him, Rushia called, 'Come in, Wanda. Meet Captain Bond, Royal Navy. James, this is Lieutenant Commander Wanda Man Song Hing, US Navy.'

'Captain Bond, sir,' she acknowledged him as she came into the cabin and, in spite of her very obvious Chinese appearance, her voice was low, husky and totally without any of the short-tongued hesitant pronunciations of an English-speaking Chinese.

She was slender and much taller than an average Chinese girl, somewhere around five-ten, with a high waist which, in the lecherous and chauvinist corner of Bond's mind, predicted legs that went on for ever. This, he saw, was correct as, with a smile, she walked past him into the cabin and stood smartly to attention in front of M.

'Lieutenant-Commander Man Song Hing reporting as requested, sir.'

She wore civilian clothes – a calf-length dark pleated skirt, white shirt with a Hermes scarf knotted at the neck and a short dark jacket with grey piping. Her complexion was smooth, more cream than peaches, and her heavy black hair was swept back from her forehead, falling in a neatly shaped curve above her collar. She wore diamond clips on the tiny lobes of her exquisite ears, her almond-shaped eyes were a deep black, the mouth generous and her nose small, giving an overall impression of a face of near-perfect proportions.

'Let me take your jacket, Wanda.' Rushia was behind her, as

though dancing attendance, and she slipped her arms out of the jacket, straightening the cuffs of her shirt as she did so. The white shirt was tight and Bond's throat went characteristically dry at the clearly rounded shape of her breasts pressing against the thin material.

She caught his eye and immediately looked away as though in an act of modesty, a small tongue running across her lips.

M seated himself opposite the young woman while Rushia and Bond helped them to the smoked salmon and wine – a Californian Chardonnay, at which, until a year or two ago, Bond would have turned up his nose. Things had altered greatly since American wines had started to take prizes against even the best French ones.

'My dear,' M spoke to Wanda in an almost avuncular manner, yet his tone was not patronising. 'I know this is going to be difficult for you, but I fear you're going to have to repeat at least the major details of your current assignment.'

'Everything?' Her voice dropped almost to a whisper.

'I'm sorry.' M fidgeted with his tie, leaving his smoked salmon untouched. Bond felt the Old Man was exceptionally embarrassed. 'I'm sorry, but if we're going to deal with this matter, Captain Bond here *has* to know everything. In a few hours he will be facing the same risks as yourself. Though I doubt if he is going to be treated in the same manner as yourself.'

She gave a slightly self-conscious smile and began to toy with her smoked salmon. She had coloured, a pink blush spreading up both cheeks. 'Then I had better begin.' She glanced at the slim gold watch on her wrist. 'I must be back within two hours, or . . .'

'Sure, Wanda,' Rushia spoke kindly. 'You'll be back. We'll see to that, though God knows I wouldn't return if you paid me a million.'

'If I don't go back, he'll certainly become suspicious, then where will Captain Bond be? And yourself, Ed, not to mention Chi-Chi . . .'

'Would someone let me into the secret?' Bond was beginning to be irritated by the riddles that seemed to be passing to and fro across the table.

'Yes, James.' There was no sign of reproach in M's tone. 'All in good time, and Ms Man Song Hing really doesn't have much of that – time I mean. Nor have you. We've a great deal to get through before morning. You'll hear Wanda's story, and no doubt even you will be disgusted by it. But she is our one ace against the evil empire that Lee represents. She has penetrated his court, and become successfully closer to him than any agent who has tried before.' He turned back to Wanda. 'I suggest you tell the story in your own words. Now, while we eat. You need not worry, Captain Bond is also an Intelligence field officer of great experience. You will not shock him.'

'He is cleared for the classified information?' she asked.

'He wouldn't be here if he were not project cleared.' For the first time in her presence, the old, sharp edge of M's personality peeped from his tone of voice.

'Very well.' She addressed herself to Bond. 'I am a third gen-eration American Chinese. I was born an American citizen. My mother died when I was a child and my father was once a wealthy jeweller. From my teenage years I wanted to serve my country in some active way, so I enlisted in the United States Navy when I was eighteen years of age – I am twenty-six now. I am proud of my success, because, to use the jargon of our times, I'm a high-achiever. I studied electronics, and for the past two years I have been one of three Intelligence officers working on the project known as Lords and Lords Day. As you probably know, most of our work was carried out from the Treasure Island base, and I had permission to live ashore. I have a small apartment on Laguna, close to the Marina. I should also tell you that I love my father deeply and would do anything for him. Anything but sell out my country, which, in the end, I suppose he invited me to do, in order to save his own life. It began three weeks ago. I had a twenty-four-hour off-duty day.' She gave a tight little smile, looked up, caught Bond's eyes and immediately looked away again. 'I was having my first cup of coffee when the telephone rang. It was my father, and within an hour I knew we had to use what he finally told me. I was aware that I had to become one of the primary active agents in *Trojan Horse*.'

6

WANDA'S STORY

It was a warm and beautiful morning, clear and with no sea mist. Wanda Man Song Hing sat, dressed only in her terry-towel bathrobe, on the small balcony of her fourth-storey apartment, looking out from the end of Laguna Street on to the Marina. She sipped her coffee from a huge cup with the Paramount Pictures logo stretching across one side.

The sound of a jet, way out over the sea, sent a tiny wave of pain through her. Billy Chinn had given her the cup only a week before he had so tragically flown his F14 Tomcat straight off the deck of an aircraft carrier to cartwheel and explode in the sea. That was a year ago, and she had only recently been able to come to terms with the deep grief of the loss. They would have been married by now, she thought, and then pushed the feelings and images back into the dark tunnels of her mind. At least she had learned to live with it.

She stretched like a cat, feeling luxurious in the knowledge that she had a whole twenty-four hours to herself, and planned to cram into the day a whole bunch of pleasant things – shopping, having a facial, then, tonight, a movie.

She was just reaching for her copy of the *Chronicle* to see what was playing this week, when the telephone rang. Later she was to think that at its first ring she sensed trouble, but maybe that was hindsight.

'Hi.' She gave no name or number. That was one of the many

things they taught you early on in Naval Intelligence, and she had done far more than the basic course.

'Wanda, honey, I have to see you.'

'Dad. What a surprise. I thought you were out of town.' She tried to sound bright, but it had been difficult with her father for nearly six months now. She knew why. That had not taken much intelligence work. Tony Man Song Hing had that worst Chinese trait. He was a gambler and, judging by the way he had behaved in recent months, he was not on a roll.

'I *have* to see you,' he repeated, and Wanda became vaguely alarmed. There was a wilderness of desperation in his voice.

'Where are you?'

'Over at the store.' He meant his small jewellery store off Market Street, where he sold, not precious gems, but imitation stones in cheap settings and simulated pearls made, in his own small workshop, by coating glass or plastic beads with a liquid called pearl essence extracted from herring scales.

'Give me half-an-hour, Dad. Come over here, but give me a little time, okay?'

'Thirty minutes.' He hung up abruptly, and Wanda's stomach turned over. The last thing she needed was trouble with him. The work on *Trojan Horse* was stressful enough, and she had been through endless problems with her father.

As she showered and dressed she thought about the mess he had made of his life. When her mother died, the little store had sold thousands of dollars worth of real gemstones, silver and gold settings and beautiful jade work. As a child she remembered that the stock alone had been valued at five million dollars. One of the reasons for her own success in life had been the necessity to get away from her father lest she simply became his house-keeper.

Tony Man Song Hing was starting to run to fat, his stomach straining over the belt holding up his grey slacks, while his skin had taken on that pewter colour of a man who did not exercise or look after his diet and was hemmed in by worries.

When Wanda opened the door to him she was shocked that he had gone so much to seed since she had last seen him a month or so before. As she embraced him, she noticed that he also had aged as though some terrible curse had fallen on him. His eyes appeared to be never still and, even as they greeted each other, he seemed to be looking around the main room of her apartment as though afraid someone else might be with her waiting to do him harm.

She gave him coffee and his hand trembled badly as he picked up the cup, spilling some of the liquid.

'What is it, Father?' She used her no-nonsense voice which was very effective on lower ranks in the Navy.

He sipped his coffee without speaking, as though trying to summon some new strength. At last he put the cup down and looked her squarely in the eyes. 'Wanda,' he said. 'Wanda, you are my only daughter, and, as a good Chinese woman brought up in love and respect for her parents, I must make a fatherly demand of you.'

She laughed. 'Come on, Dad. You don't even speak Cantonese. You're third generation American, and the nearest you ever got to bringing me up as a good Chinese girl was the parties we had at New Year.'

'Don't mock me, little oily mouth,' he began, aggressively.

'Father,' she laughed again. 'You've been reading too many James Clavell novels. Little oily mouth indeed. You'll start talking of secret stalks in a minute.'

His hand flashed up as he leant forward, slapping her hard across the face. It was the first time she could remember his striking her and she was furious, rising and stepping away from him. 'Enough!' she commanded. 'Out! Out of my apartment.'

But her father stood his ground. 'You *will* obey your father. It is our way, our heritage,' he shouted, his face suddenly crimson. 'You will do as I say. You hear me?'

Wanda stepped away from him, her cheek still smarting from the blow and her mind battered with anger. But, staring wide-eyed at her father, anxiety began to seep through her fury. This was not the father she remembered from childhood. This man was deeply disturbed, pushed past his limit, on the verge of greater violence.

Had Wanda not been such an intelligent young woman, with a discipline honed by her Navy service, she might have thrown her father out then and there in an hysterical outburst. But in spite of the outrage she felt, the cool, still centre of her being, developed during her long training, overcame the more natural emotions. Wanda took a deep breath and when she spoke it was with a new equilibrium. 'Father, what is it? Something's very wrong. Tell me and maybe we can work something out.'

It was as though this sign of compassion hit Tony like some sudden revelation. She saw her father's face collapse, then he folded over, doubling up like a man in pain. When he straightened himself again, his eyes brimmed with tears and his shoulders quivered.

Wanda went to him, enfolded him in her arms and gently helped him to a chair. Through sobs he kept muttering that he was sorry, shaking his head, his body trembling.

After a while he seemed to regain possession of his emotions, but still had difficulty speaking.

'Come on, Father. Tell me what it's all about. Maybe I can help, after all, like a daughter should.'

This brought on a worse reaction than before. Her father moaned and sobbed, his whole body swaying from side to side.

'It can't be that bad. Pull yourself together, Father. Just tell me.' She spoke very firmly. 'Tell me!'

He pushed her away, wiped his face with a handkerchief and asked for a drink.

'More coffee?'

'Something . . . something stronger . . . Please.'

Drinking had never been a problem, so she went into the kitchen and poured bourbon into a shot glass. He took the whole glass straight and sat looking at her.

'Is it debt?' she asked. 'Is it the damned gambling again?'

Slowly he nodded.

'Bad?'

'Very bad. Even if I sold the store, I'd still owe him the best part of a million.' His voice was almost that of an old man. 'I'm a fool, Wanda. I've seen him do it to others. He gives and gives, then slowly hauls in on the rope.'

'Who're we talking about?'

'Who d'you think? Lee. Brokenclaw Lee.'

For the second time that morning her stomach turned over. After all, they had spent ten hours during the previous day trying to formulate some kind of strategy against Lee.

'You owe Brokenclaw a great deal of money. Okay, Dad, you came to me, laying down the law, telling me I should obey you like an old Chinese father. What were you thinking? What did you want of me?'

He looked away, whispering that he was sorry. Eventually, 'I'm a doomed man, Wanda. I've lost everything this time. The store . . .'

'Your life? Will he have you killed?'

He gave an unamused laugh. 'Oh, no. No, that's not Brokenclaw's way, though I might as well be a dead man.'

'What will he do, then?'

'Take my soul. Bind me to him. Make me serve him in any capacity he decides. You remember old San-San Ho?'

'The nice old man who used to run the fruit and vegetable store on Stockton?'

'You haven't seen him lately, have you?'

'I don't go . . .'

'Into the Chinatown. No, of course you don't. San-San Ho lost everything to Lee. And what did Lee do? He made old San-San into a drug courier. The old man died in agony half a year ago, sitting on an airplane bringing him back to San Francisco; died because one of the twenty little rubber sacks of heroin lodged in his intestines split open.'

Wanda showed no sign of grief. She knew well enough what could happen to people who carried drugs into the United States in this fashion. 'So, my father, *what did you expect of me*? How did you think I could help you?'

Her father looked away and gave a small shake of the head. 'No!' Like a spoiled child refusing to give up some precious secret.

'Who knows, I might still be able to help you.'

'Never . . . No. No, Wanda, I don't know what devil got into me. What I was going to command of you is obscene. Obnoxious.'

But Wanda Man Song Hing had already guessed at the disgusting truth. 'You were going to pimp for Brokenclaw, weren't you? You were going to offer him your daughter in lieu of payment.'

'How could I even . . . ?'

'You were desperate.' She was very calm now. 'Desperate times for any man call for desperate measures. Even loathsome measures like giving your own daughter for Brokenclaw Lee to defile.'

'Don't go on, Wanda. It was a madness . . .'

But the germ of an idea was already formulating in her mind. 'When were you going to do this terrible thing?'

He would not meet her eyes. 'Tonight,' he whispered. 'Lee wishes to see me tonight at The Broken Dragon – where I've spent too much time, where I've lost my soul. Midnight.'

It would be utterly degrading, she thought, but this might be the way to Brokenclaw. 'Have you any other things to do today, Father?'

'No. Well, I have to look my best if I am to see him and deliver myself up to him. That's all.'

She took a deep breath. 'I want you to stay here. Not to go out. Just stay here. Don't answer the telephone. Just rest here.'

'If you say so.'

'I might truly be able to help you.'

'How?'

'Maybe by doing what you were going to suggest.'

'Golly, Wanda, I don't know how to advise you. Gee, I can't send you out on that kind of assignment.'

'Ed, it's me, Wanda. You're not talking to some unsuspecting hicksville dummy, so quit the "Golly Wanda" stuff with me. I know what I'm doing.'

'But the guy's got one hell of a reputation. I mean, you've seen the reports . . .'

'I'm willing to risk all that. Yes, I know he's supposed to be insatiable as far as women are concerned. I'm ready and quite able to deal with it.'

Wanda had left her apartment and called Ed Rushia from a payphone. He picked her up in a battered old Chevy half an hour later and they drove out on to 101, crossing the Golden Gate Bridge and parking at one of the picnic and photographic areas which gave them a panoramic view of the bay and the city.

'I'm not at all sure that, even if I went along with it, I can sanction any undercover operation like this,' Rushia said quietly. 'I don't like it, Wanda. Not at all.'

'Then what if I take full responsibility? What if I just disappear? For heaven's sake, Ed, we've spent hours trying to figure out a way to get a penetration into Lee's entourage. If I can do it and come back with some decent information . . .'

'I can't order this and I can't sanction it, either.' Rushia clamped his jaw firmly closed. 'Sure, we need someone in there, but *you*. It's asking too much. You *do* realise what you'd have to do?'

She sighed. 'Yes, I'll have to sleep with him, possibly suffer indignities. I'm going in with my eyes open. It might become very unpleasant and risky, but I accept that. I'll be doing it for my country.'

Rushia grunted, and the pair remained silent for the best part of two minutes. At last he shifted in the driving seat, turning to look at her. 'Doesn't matter what I say, does it? You're going, whatever. Right?'

'Unless you drag me back to base and put me under arrest, yes. Yes, I'm going, whatever.'

'How would it be if I sent you on a ten-day furlough? I do have *that* authority.'

'That would be fine, Ed.'

'Okay, I'll write you up when I get back to base. Apart from that we didn't have this conversation. You just asked me for ten days' compassionate, right?'

Wanda nodded. 'Right,' she said.

The Broken Dragon had two entrances, one at the rear leading on to the dark little courtyard where FBI Agent Malloney would eventually meet his brutal end, the other straight off the crowded street. This was the main entrance, but there were no signs or gaudy advertising telling the world what lay behind the ordinary door.

In spite of The Broken Dragon's existence being public knowledge among those who sought to gamble or use the other, more personal, services afforded by the place, it had only been raided twice in the past five years. The team working on *Trojan Horse* considered that this fact was proof of some kind of police protection, but nobody had ever been able to prove any such thing.

The other possibility was that the police and other agencies felt it better to allow the place to operate freely. There was never any serious trouble directly emanating from The Broken Dragon, so it could be argued that people would find somewhere to gamble and pick up hookers anyway so it might just as well be at a well-run establishment. But, again, if this was the case, it pointed to a certain lack of enthusiasm with regard to putting Brokenclaw Lee away for a very long time, for it was known that of all his supposed illegal ventures in San Francisco The Broken Dragon was one of his favourite haunts.

At a little before midnight, Wanda and Tony Man Song Hing were deposited from a taxi on to the sidewalk in front of the un-prepossessing door that was the entrance to The Broken Dragon. Wanda had dressed for the occasion in a tight, elaborately embroidered silk cheongsam, which showed off her figure to its greatest advantage, but she had been careful to choose one with a side slit that ended modestly below the knee.

Her father was dressed in a powder-blue double-breasted suit, a cream silk shirt with a Sulka tie, cream with diagonal blue stripes. On his feet he wore expensive snakeskin shoes and his fingers were decked with his most ostentatious rings; a gold identity chain was around his right wrist and a large gold Rolex was on the left. He looked the picture of a high roller, prepared to gamble several thousand dollars away at the Dragon's tables, not a man who was about to plead for his soul with the most powerful gangster in town.

Wanda did not spot any overt surveillance on them, but she was a hundred per cent certain that Lee had people who watched the place both front and rear. The many discussions with the other Naval security people of *Trojan Horse* had disclosed evidence that the club was well protected, and they had been advised by both the local FBI and other security agencies that it was hopeless putting in their own surveillance which would be spotted and, eventually, dismantled – a polite word for destroyed.

Once inside the street door, Wanda found herself in a dimly lit vestibule which seemed to have been built of heavy grey stone. In the wall facing them a narrow archway led down stone steps to a thick ornate oak door studded with steel bands.

Her father touched a small button on the door and a grille slid open disclosing the face of a young Chinese.

'We saw it was you, Tony. Come on in. Nice to see you keep good time.'

It was obvious that the upstairs vestibule and the area in front of the door were monitored by concealed cameras.

'I'm always a good timekeeper, Luk See,' Tony said with a smile, as the door was opened to allow them inside. 'This is my daughter, Wanda. Just so you know and don't get any funny ideas about her.'

Wanda thought she detected a note of serious and sinister warning in her father's voice. This was certainly not the man who had wept and pleaded with her only this morning: now that he was on familiar ground, Tony Man Song Hing appeared to have found a new confidence.

'Very happy to see you here, Ms Man Song Hing.' The young Chinese was impeccably dressed in a black sharkskin suit, and Wanda felt that he was busily appraising her body, as were the two other men who obviously guarded the entrance with him. But all three of them faded as the sight that greeted her within The Broken Dragon all but took her breath away.

The interior was huge and opulent, with deep pile carpet under foot and a decor that was both rich and restrained. A black and gold screen separated the entrance lobby from the main rooms which were reached by descending a wide staircase. They were hardly inside before the man her father had referred to as Luk See beckoned to a haughty young girl in a long black cheongsam who came up the steps towards them.

'Mr and Ms Man Song Hing. There is a table reserved for them.'

The girl nodded, hardly looking at either Wanda or Tony. She merely gestured them to follow her down the stairs leading first to a large bar and dining room, the walls of which were covered in lacquered bamboo and hung with Chinese works of art, illuminated by concealed spotlights.

The tables were placed well clear of each other, all gleaming with white cloths and ivory chopsticks. Waiters moved around silently and the conversation appeared to be conducted almost in whispers, for about three-quarters of the tables were occupied.

A waiter appeared at the table, placing glasses in front of them. 'Champagne, compliments of the management.' He spoke without showing a flicker of interest, banging down an ice bucket containing a bottle buried up to its neck. He opened the bottle and poured for them – a little in Wanda's glass for her to taste. She shook her head. 'I'm sure it will be fine.' Long ago she had learned that this ritual should only be left to experts and much of the wine tasting that went on in restaurants was laughed at by the waiters.

'You will not be kept waiting long.' For the first time, the waiter gave a little smile and the hint of a bow as he left them.

'The man at the door . . . ?' Wanda began to ask.

'Lee's chief bouncer. You'll only see him when the big man is actually here. His name is Lee's joke, of course.'

'Luk See?' Wanda gave a small smile. Her stomach was churning with anxiety, while her eyes restlessly tried to take everything in. The light above them radiated from a golden, carved dropped ceiling; at the far end of the room, a pair of great arched doors were watched over by two burly men in dinner jackets, and the only time noise intruded into the restaurant was when these men opened one of the doors to usher someone in or out. For the few seconds that the door was open, the click of Fan-tan counters and the murmur of an excited gaming house was heard.

She also noticed that there were doors leading to the kitchens to the right of the long bar which took up almost the entire wall to their left, though at the near side of the bar she could see another door with yet one more bouncer in front of it. As she took her second sip of champagne, she saw this door open and the man on guard lean back to speak to someone. He nodded, then things happened very quickly.

Luk See came over to the table, gave them a mock bow and, almost with reverence, said, 'The owner requests the pleasure of your company upstairs please. Now.'

Her father rose – a little nervously, Wanda thought – and

gestured that she should accompany him. Shepherded by Luk See, they crossed to the door on the near side of the bar. Its guard opened it for them and, still with Luk See behind them, they went up a brilliantly lit, heavily carpeted staircase.

There was another door at the top, and Luk See pushed past them to knock. A voice softly called for them to enter and they were almost brusquely pushed through the door into the presence of Brokenclaw Lee himself.

The first thing that caught Wanda off guard was the emptiness of the room. After the opulence of the public rooms, it came as a shock to find that what she took to be Lee's office was merely a bare room, its only decoration being an American Indian mask hanging directly above the long deal table that served as a desk. The second most striking thing was Brokenclaw Lee himself – huge, powerful, his handsome face and dancing, charming eyes, seemed to be inviting her to a pleasant evening's entertainment, and when he rose she admitted to being overawed at his height and bearing.

'This is a great pleasure.' The voice was unaccented and beautifully modulated. 'Tony, have you brought your wife with you?'

'My daughter, sir.' Wanda understood well enough why her father addressed this man in terms of respect.

Brokenclaw nodded and smiled. 'I am sorry I cannot offer you any chairs, but this is where I conduct business when I am here, and I find it simpler to deal with business if I sit and the persons to whom I speak remain standing. Allow me to introduce these members of my staff.' He gestured towards two other men whom Wanda had hardly noticed when they entered. 'They are known as Wan Lo and Big Leu.' He gave Wanda his most charming smile. 'I realise that Big Leu looks a little small compared to myself, but among normal men he is considered large.'

Big Leu must have been around six foot one and very stocky, with broad shoulders, long arms and hands which Wanda immediately thought of as boxer's hands. His sidekick, Wan Lo, was short, thin and wiry – a very tense man with eyes constantly moving and his body taut as though always ready for violence.

'Now, Tony, since I have introduced my people, perhaps you will introduce your daughter.'

Her father hesitated, so Wanda herself stepped forward. 'My name is Wanda Man Song Hing,' she said, summoning all the deference she could command. Then quite without knowing why, she added, 'It is an honour to meet you.'

He smiled down at her and offered a huge hand which took hers and held it in not so much a handshake as a caress.

Then quite suddenly, he stopped smiling. Still looking at Wanda, and keeping his voice down he asked, 'Tony, have you brought my money? You were to bring it tonight.'

'No, sir.' Wanda could hear the surge of terror behind the words from her father. Then he repeated, 'No, sir. But I have brought something more precious than any money.'

'Oh. Pray what?'

'My daughter, sir. I have brought you my daughter, Wanda.'

'Really? And what has Wanda to say about this?'

His voice was always calm, soothing, making her think of the purring of a cat. 'I am a good Chinese girl, sir,' she again heard herself say. 'I obey my father in all things.'

'And you come here of your own free will?'

'I do. But I must tell you that others have claim on my time.'

'What kind of claim?' Reasonable, relaxed.

'I am an officer in the United States Navy.'

'That's even more interesting. So, when do you return to your duties, which would, of course, take you from the orbit of your father's commands and influence?'

'I have a ten-day furlough, sir. After that, I am free for one day a week and one entire weekend in every four.' She kept her eyes raised towards Lee's proud features.

'Well,' he smiled down at her. 'I think we can arrange matters so that your naval duties will not interfere with your status as a gift to me.' He let go of her hand and stepped to one side, standing directly in front of her father. 'You appear to have done very well in bringing me your daughter, Tony Man Song Hing. For the moment, I shall suspend judgment on the question of your financial debt. Be here again at midnight in exactly ten days and I shall give you my complete verdict then. After I have sampled what your daughter has to offer.'

There was not the slightest sign of a threat in his voice, just the gentle, reasonable words of a seemingly gentle and reasonable man.

Wanda had hardly realised that her father had left when she heard Lee speak again. 'You two, make things ready. We leave now. This minute.'

She felt the hands of Big Leu clasp her upper arms and lead her to yet another door at the far end of the room. Then something was slipped over her head, softly pressing against her eyes and cutting off sight.

'Would not try moving mask, missy,' Leu whispered in her ear. 'If your hand goes even near mask, I fear life will become total pain.'

He steered her down some stairs, and a minute later she felt the cool night air on her face. A hand covered the back of her head, forcing her down as Leu gave her instructions. She was being assisted into a car. There was the smell of well-polished leather and the seat seemed to enfold her.

A few seconds later, she knew that Lee had joined her in the car. He wore a musky cologne which she had detected in his office. She could not deny a tiny electric thrill as she felt his hand touch her thigh.

As the car began to move, he whispered apologies for the mask. 'I have to take very careful precautions. I'm sure you, as a member of the United States Navy, will understand.'

She nodded, and he told her to try and rest. 'It is quite a long drive and I wish you to be rested when we reach our destination.'

Once more she felt the thrill pass through her, as though she had absolutely no resistance or personal freedom.

Within two hours, the car slowed down and came to a stop. She heard the doors being opened and felt Leu's hands on her arms again, helping her out and propelling her across gravel and into a building which smelled of flowers. She thought the scent was that of night stocks after rain, but under her feet she detected solid tile or, more likely, marble. Then this changed to thick soft carpet. She knew that she was being taken down long corridors and through other rooms. Then Leu's hands steadied her. 'Stay,' he warned. 'Touch nothing. Do not move the mask. Just wait.'

She felt unsteady after the long car ride and the confined darkness, then she felt Lee near her, his hands running over her waist, buttocks and breasts. Suddenly he plucked the mask from her face and she was aware of being in a dimly lit bedroom of vast proportions.

Gently, like a trainer with a frisky colt, he guided her backwards until she felt the side of a bed behind her upper thighs, then her back against great softness and Brokenclaw's hands moving again, his lips on her lips, and suddenly, his body on her body. Slowly one large hand took the neck of her cheongsam and, in one movement, it was ripped from her body. Her last thought was that she had been right to wear nothing under the dress.

7

TALK OF A MERRY DANCE

M looked decidedly embarrassed, moving uneasily in his chair, fiddling with his napkin and grunting. 'You know how much I abhor this kind of sexual entrapment,' he said gruffly. 'But, in this case, I suppose it was the only way.'

'It was the only opportunity, sir.' They had carried on eating. Wanda had remained very calm while telling the story, and Bond had become almost jealous of Brokenclaw. 'The chance came, and I took it.'

'Unsanctioned,' cautioned M.

'Admiral, it was our operation.' Ed Rushia had dropped his homespun manner. 'Now it's definitely sanctioned, as you know, Wanda is in a unique position.'

Bond raised his eyebrows, and thought Rushia could have chosen his words more carefully.

'Look, in a matter of three weeks we've made incredible headway.'

'Yes.' Bond broke his silence. 'What kind of headway have we made? Infiltration isn't any good unless it produces raw intelligence.'

M gave a small nod, 'Oh, that's one of the reasons you're here, Bond. "Cuckoo", which is Wanda's crypto, has provided not only the raw intelligence but the means to bring us even closer to Brokenclaw and the personnel he's undoubtedly holding. All five of them. And I might add . . .' One of the telephones uttered a quiet purr which stopped M, who walked over and picked up the instrument. He spoke only in monosyllables but they could all tell by his tone and demeanour that something was wrong.

'Well, looks as if you were right about Brokenclaw's people in British Columbia.' He looked at Bond. 'They've found Professor Allardyce's body in some woods just outside Victoria, and that would suggest that we must now move with some haste.'

'I must move quickly anyway, sir.' Wanda pushed her chair back from the table. 'Big Leu's supposed to be picking me up at midnight.'

'I'm intrigued.' Bond put out a hand to restrain her. 'Intrigued that friend Brokenclaw, if he really is such a monster, let *you* return, while he keeps the other people from Lords and Lords Day prisoners.'

Wanda smiled at him. 'I didn't think I stood a chance of getting away, especially after that first night. I should tell you, Captain Bond, that his reputation regarding sexual appetite is quite wrong.'

'Really?'

'Yes, he's more insatiable than any speculation could begin to intimate. But, at the moment, I appear to satisfy him, though none of us know how long that will go on. The few people close to him – the very few he trusts – have made it very clear that he soon tires of one woman.' She spoke without any hint of coyness or self-consciousness, but with the quiet voice of a proficient agent giving facts to interrogators.

'Then I take it he trusts you.' Bond's voice in no way suggested that he did not believe her.

'Not completely. But we're getting there. For the first five days I was not even allowed to leave the suite of rooms we both used. But after that he relaxed a little. I was allowed to use some of the other rooms, though never areas with windows. I also met his closest people. He has quite a set-up wherever it is. I come and go blindfolded, and we've got one or two ideas as to location, but it's always cloak and dagger. I only had to keep my wits about me, and before I left on that first occasion, we came to an arrangement . . .'

'We provide her with good chickenfeed,' Rushia chimed in. 'It's all category four stuff, and keeps him happy.'

'Now, I really must go, if you'll all excuse me.' Wanda stood to attention facing M, who, Bond noted with a wry smile, did not look her in the eyes.

'Yes. Yes. Carry on, Ms er . . . Carry on.'

'So what magic information has she wheedled out of our man?' Bond asked, with little conviction, once Wanda Man Song Hing had left the cabin.

'Y'don't trust our little Wanda, do you, James?' from Rushia, stone-faced in a manner that made Bond very uncomfortable.

'It's not that I don't trust her, it's the facts of life. Sexpionage, as the tabloids call it, can backfire. To tell you the truth, Ed, I'm more worried for her than anything.'

'Pretty rich, coming from you, Bond,' M huffed. 'I suggest you just stay silent while we tell you exactly what Ms Man Song Hing has uncovered for us. More to the point, how she has found a way for *you* to get close to this odd fish, Brokenclaw.'

Bond, a shade on his dignity, nodded, folded his arms and waited, glancing from one to the other.

Rushia began. 'First thing you should know is pretty obvious. Brokenclaw Lee is almost paranoid about treachery – treachery to him personally. He has a very few people who work at close range with him and most of them are pretty weird with names like Big Leu and Luk See. There are others. Among his heavies are a couple of charming Chinese called Bone Bender Ding and Frozen Stalk Pu. Try those on for size. But the one thing Wanda was really able to establish is that Lee does *not* trust his masters in China. There's no doubt that he's put a nice package together with most of the details of Lords and Lords Day. But it appears that he does not trust *any* of his own mob to deliver the stuff to CELD.' He looked towards M, as though asking permission to continue. M gave him a small affirmative nod.

'So, James, CELD are sending their own couriers to analyse the material on the spot and take it out of the country.'

'When?'

M answered, 'Very soon, 007. In fact, they're here already.'

'In the US?'

M nodded. 'You see, Cuckoo, as I would rather call her, made certain that she overheard some of the more sensitive conversations. First she heard of visitors expected between 27th of this month and 7th October. There was no firm date. When she gave us this information she also told us that, because of his paranoia about betrayal, the couriers were to be led quite a dance before they actually got to Mr Lee. Incidentally, his is a wise paranoia – the price of freedom, so to speak. It is the motive force behind his ability to appear and disappear almost at will. You have to be alert constantly, have a fine-tuned instinct and a lot of the aforesaid paranoia to do that.'

'The couriers,' Bond prompted. 'They came in from China?'

'From Beijing to Hong Kong, Hong Kong to Tokyo, then JAL into New York. Cuckoo's information was that, as soon as they arrived in New York, they were to call a number here in San Francisco where there would be an exchange of passwords. Verification that they were the right people. After that had been established, they would be told where to go and whom to speak with . . .'

'A sort of treasure hunt,' Bond smiled.

'Gee whizz, James, right on the button. Lee's own expression. Wanda heard him say, "then we start the treasure hunt. At the end we will be certain they are the right people, and that they are loyal to their masters in Beijing, as well as to us". Yep, a nice little treasure hunt.'

'You have surveillance on them?'

M gave one of his rare smiles which lit up his eyes. 'You might say so, yes, James. Would you call it surveillance, Commander Rushia?'

The American made a small puffing movement with his lips as

though playing an invisible instrument. 'I'd call it, very close surveillance with chemical fringe benefits.'

'Please explain, sir.' Bond sounded irritated.

'Well, you see, 007, we knew three things from Cuckoo. One, the time frame; two, the port of entry; three, the fact that there were two couriers, a man and a woman – the man a Caucasian, probably British, the young woman a Chinese.'

'From our own resources – our China watchers – and in a very short space of time, we were able to identify the pair. Which is more than Brokenclaw Lee has been able to do, and we're naturally very proud of this. Shows we're not the dinosaurs the press would have people believe. Anyway, the couple arrived separately at JFK New York on JAL flight 06 a couple of days ago, which, if you look in your diary, means right at the start of the time scale. Lucky for us, eh, Rushia?'

'Not a case of luck, sir. Just excellent work . . .' Ed turned towards Bond. 'We had 'em picked up. Very quietly, no scenes, no fuss, hooray for us.'

'And?' Slowly Bond was beginning to get the picture.

'And, as I told you, they're here.' M was like a magician producing doves from the air.

'Ah. You mean,' Bond said, very slowly, 'you mean literally here, sir. On this ship?'

M nodded. 'They've been spending time with some good friends of yours, who, I think, have now got all the information we require.'

'God help them.' Once, with feeling, then again, for the insurance, 'God help them.' It all fell into place in Bond's head, a logical piece of neat and symmetrical sleight of mind. 'I presume I am to play the Brit.'

'On the button again, James.' Rushia gave a wide grin.

'And who's the lucky one cast as the girl? Not Ed here?'

'Commander Rushia will have you both under his eye all the time and we trust the FBI will also be on hand.' M was still smiling. 'You see, they've got it into their heads that both you and Rushia are suspect. Actually, the commander's work will be to left foot the FBI if they move in too close and frighten off the big players.'

'But, as I asked before, who's sharing the billing?'

'Nice little thing, Bond. First real operation so you might have to ease her along. CIA provided her. Name of Sue Chi-Ho, known as Chi-Chi Sue to her friends . . .'

'Has no enemies either,' supplied Rushia quietly, but M went on.

'She's a Cantonese speaker, worked for US Navy Intelligence, then the Agency took her in. Just finished the course at the Farm.'

The Farm was Camp Peary, near Williamsburg, the CIA's training facility.

'And I've got to nurse her through what could be a very dangerous operation?'

M looked him in the eyes and then turned away as he said, 'Yes, possibly lethal, 007. But I think you'll find she'll be up to snuff. Good girl.' Then he asked Rushia if he could possibly bring Sue Chi-Ho to them.

As the commander left the cabin, M picked up the red telephone and pressed two numbers. 'Everything in order?' he asked. Then, 'Good. Yes, tell him to finish up now and stand by for the briefing . . . Yes, yes, he's here . . . You are sure they're both cleaned out. I want to be assured of every point, after all it was the Chinese who pioneered what they call "Thought Reform" . . . Really? . . . Yes, very interesting, he'll have to write a paper for us some time. I'll call when I'm ready.' He cradled the instrument and looked up at Bond.

'If you decide to turn down this operation, everyone'll understand. I have to say that because we really are in deep water. Don't want to say this to Rushia but we've had Orr go over Cuckoo's debriefs. She's been very thorough. Good memory, and she's provided verbatim reports on all her conversations with

Brokenclaw. Orr says that as well as a suspicious paranoia, the man also shows dangerous psychopathic tendencies.'

'Do I take it that Orr's here, sir?' Bill Orr was the Service's head Witchdoctor, a man with stratospheric skills in psychiatry and its attendant arts.

'He's here, with others, including the US Navy counterparts. All I want you to know now, 007, is that we're dealing, not just with a man who is filching and passing classified information to Chinese Intelligence, but also an out of control gangster, and a very dangerous one at that.'

'I think I'd have to be a bit of a flake not to have realised that already, sir.'

'Bit of a *flake*!' M was at his most testy. 'Bond, I do abhor your constant use of these odd American terms!'

'When in Rome, sir.'

A knock at the door heralded the return of Ed Rushia, who, with an exaggerated show of old world courtesy, handed a young woman into the cabin.

'Miss Sue Chi-Ho. You've met the admiral here, now I'd like you to meet Captain Bond, Royal Navy.'

Bond had risen. Now he stepped forward to shake hands with the slim young girl facing him. 'James,' he said. 'You must call me James.'

'My friends call me Chi-Chi which in some circles is considered vulgar.'

She stood less than five feet in height, slim and as delicate as porcelain, but her handshake was firm, denoting strength. Bond could feel that toughness as their hands met, as though she was able to impart a kind of electric danger directly from her body to his.

'I'm sure that only the most common and insensitive person could find anything vulgar about you, Chi-Chi.'

Their eyes met, and he saw that she was blessed with clear, steady hazel eyes – a melding of brown and green – almond-shaped, for she was undeniably Oriental and looked very young.

He was also pleased to see that there were tiny scimitars of laughter lines at each side of her slightly askew mouth, as though her lips were contained by a pair of bracket marks.

'We are to work together, I understand.' She spoke flawless English with no trace of any American accent. 'I feel we shall have a common bond.' She gave him a brilliant smile which lit up her whole face and seemed to have its wellspring in the lovely green-flecked eyes.

From the desk, M made a loud harumphing sound. 'Captain Bond, Miss Chi-Ho, we have important work to do. You have not yet seen the person you're to impersonate?' This last directed towards Chi-Chi who shook her head and gave him a clear, 'No, sir.'

'Right. Now, if you'll all be good enough to follow me.' He strode towards the door. Ed Rushia raised an eyebrow at Bond and they all trooped out after M with a great show of courtesy towards Chi-Chi at the door.

Chi-Chi stopped as both Rushia and Bond stood back to make way for her. 'I'd like to be treated like anyone else.' Her manner was very much that of the liberated woman, though Bond was glad to note, without those abrasive bad manners so often used to force women's rights down the throats of men who exhibited a particular kind of chauvinism. 'I am one of a team,' she continued, much to M's irritation as he waited outside the door. 'I don't wish you to think of me as a woman.'

'That's a very tall order, Chi-Chi.' Bond tilted an eyebrow.

'Huh!' she grunted and marched through the door, though Bond thought he detected a tiny flash of pleasure from both her lips and eyes.

'Guess you'll have to watch yourself, James,' Rushia muttered. 'You've got a little ball of fire there.'

'Happily, I agree with you.' Bond gave him a smile of profound satisfaction. 'And she'd better learn that we're two of a team.'

They followed M through one of the companion ways and down metal steps into a corridor which led to the ship's hospital

– a series of spacious cabins with ample room for any medical emergency. At last he plunged through one of the doors and Bond found to his astonishment that a number of very old friends were seated around a large conference table.

'Surprise, James, my dear.' The first greeting in the form of a hug and kiss was from the doughty, tall, elegant, leggy Ann Reilly, assistant to the Armourer, Head of Q Branch, and nick-named Q'ute by every red-blooded man in the Service.

'Well.' Bond disengaged himself from Q'ute who, he saw with some pleasure, still affected a somewhat severe style to her sleek, straw-coloured hair. 'Old home week, eh?' as he went from person to person shaking hands, reflecting that it was good to know he had a familiar and well-tested backup.

Bill Tanner, M's Chief of Staff was present, together with Bill Orr, the Witchdoctor, and a short, quiet man with piercing eyes who was known to the cognoscenti as the Scrivener. His real name was Brian Cogger and his specialty was what they called 'paper', namely forged documents. It was said that the Scrivener could create a new personality for you in a matter of hours, and his work would fool even the most diligent scrutiny.

There were also four American specialists present, and they were introduced in turn. But the most overpowering figure sat at the head of the table – Franks, as he was called.

Nobody knew his real name, but he answered to Franks or, more often, the Grand Inquisitor. Even James Bond was a little in awe of Franks, who could eventually break down anyone under interrogation – his methods ranging from the cosy fireside friendly chat to the more sinister deep examinations which he could only carry out together with one of the service doctors, usually the Witchdoctor.

As soon as they were seated, it was Franks who took command, not even deferring to M.

'This is all straightforward,' he began, and everyone turned in his direction. 'Known facts – five officers and other ranks concerned with the highly classified joint Anglo-American project

Lords and Lords Day, have been abducted. Late today I was also informed that Professor Robert Allardyce, the original brains behind the project, has been found shot dead in British Columbia.

'Fu-Chu Lee, commonly known as Brokenclaw Lee, a local gangster of supposed American Indian and Chinese descent, is known to have arranged the abductions, and appears to have added to his many nefarious operations that of espionage for CELD, the Intelligence Service of the People's Republic of China. With the help of United States' agencies and a penetration agent ferreting close to Mr Lee, we were alerted to the fact that two couriers were about to enter the United States with a view to contacting Mr Lee, evaluating the product he has on offer and taking it back to the People's Republic. My brief was to interrogate the two persons identified by our own Service's China watchers. We have had them here for a matter of forty-eight hours, and it is my understanding that you, Captain Bond, together with you, Miss Chi-Ho, are to take their places.

'It has not been an easy interrogation, and Doctor Orr here will bear me out in this. I tried straightforward methods and found that the two subjects were well prepared. The Chinese have evolved very clever anti-interrogation techniques as you all know. The truth is buried deep in the unconscious of both these people, but I believe we have finally managed to drag it out – with the use of the latest derivatives of the sodium pentathol family. Even then it was like peeling the skin from an onion. Like surgeons we went through five major cover stories before we hit the real thing. Agreed, Bill?'

The Witchdoctor nodded, frowning slightly.

'Captain Bond and Miss Chi-Ho, I would like you to take a good look at the subjects before you embark on the operation. They will sleep now for at least twenty-four hours. I need not remind anyone that we are flagrantly breaking United States' law here by holding them and refusing them access to their respective consulates or ambassadors.' He looked up, sweeping his eyes around the assembled company. 'I just felt everyone should be aware of what we're doing in case we have to account for our actions at a later date.'

Franks glanced at his notes again. 'The two subjects are, first a Caucasian male about your age, Captain Bond, carrying what appears from the information we have managed to get from the UK, his own British passport. He *is* known to us and has worked in the Far East for various countries. His allegiance now seems to be to the People's Republic of China. His name is Peter Argent-bright, which proves that all that glisters is *not* silver, and he was born the son of a perfectly respectable doctor and his wife, now deceased, and brought up in his place of birth, Lymington, in the county of Hampshire, England.

'The woman is, like yourself, Miss Chi-Ho, in her late twenties. Her name is given as Jenny Mo and she is travelling under United States papers, which, though good, we believe to be forgeries. Their immediate superior is a General Hung Chow H'ang. We know of him, do we not, sir?' glancing towards M.

'Indeed we do.' M dropped his voice. 'Hung Chow H'ang is general officer in charge of illegals and works out of the former French Embassy, on Tai ji chang Street, east of Tien-an-Men Square. It's in the old Legation Quarter. There is, and I am speaking from memory, an ornate high red gate with a pair of stone lions. The buildings are pleasant enough and until quite recently it was believed they were used to house special guests of the Party. In 1986 we discovered, through one of our few Chinese defectors, that the former French Embassy is, in fact, one of the main training and organisational houses of CELD. Hung Chow H'ang is an old Party man, skilful, cunning and very good at his job. Lost an eye in the battles around Peking in '48, or '49.'

'Yes, he is.' Franks stopped, looked down and then up again, straight at Bond and Chi-Chi. 'I understand that you are both aware that the man Lee set the conditions for meeting the couriers.'

'A kind of treasure hunt, yes,' Bond answered for them both.

'Indeed, a kind of treasure hunt to establish the couriers' bona fides. There is a telephone number here in San Francisco that you have to call on arrival in New York, and a set form of identification . . .'

'Followed by a merry dance, I should imagine.' As he spoke, Bond realised he was being too flippant.

'A very merry dance, Captain Bond.' Franks was tightlipped, his eyes narrow and his look one of bleakness. 'I have no doubt that the quest for Brokenclaw Lee will be an arduous one and you will both be tested to the full. We can supply you with all you need to begin the jig. The end, however, might prove more than you bargained for. You see General Hung Chow H'ang's orders are specific. When the Lords and Lords Day information is in your hands, you are required to hand over five million dollars to Brokenclaw. Now, we can arrange that. It's no problem, but our China Desk has had a hint that something else may be going down with Brokenclaw and it's possible only one of you will be allowed to leave. This in turn means that one of you is going to be in greater danger, because there are also hints that a third person is making the trip from China. Any scruples about that, Captain Bond, Miss Chi-Ho?'

Neither of them could afford scruples. They were both already committed, so Franks dismissed Chi-Chi and spent a further hour talking to Bond. 'There are things only one of you should know at this stage,' he began, and as he talked, Bond became more concerned about the outcome of the operation which appeared to be loaded with traps and unspeakable dangers.

8

ABELARD AND HÉLOÏSE

It took almost exactly twenty-four hours from the moment Franks stopped speaking for the process to be completed. Bond, Rushia and Chi-Chi were first shown into the operating room, where the two sleeping couriers were laid out on tables, both covered only with hospital gowns. While neither Bond nor Chi-Chi bore any facial resemblance to Peter Argentbright and Jenny Mo, there were some physical similarities. Argentbright and Bond were roughly the same height and build, while Jenny Mo, though a little taller than Chi-Chi, had the same delicate bone structure and their hair was almost identical.

They were taken back into one of the other hospital rooms and the two principals were handed over to the Scrivener, Brian Cogger, who began by taking their photographs, noting down identifying marks, hair and eye colour, complexion and all the other bits and pieces required for official documentation.

Leaving the Scrivener to get on with his work, they rejoined Ed Rushia and settled down to a lengthy briefing with Bill Tanner, the Grand Inquisitor, Franks, Bill Orr and M, plus two of their American counterparts. This took the bulk of their time, starting with a digest of all known facts concerning Peter Argentbright and Jenny Mo. The minutiae on Argentbright was comprehensive, for, as M put it, 'He's been on our books for some time now.' The details regarding Jenny Mo were more sketchy. 'When I talked to you first, we were under the impression that her papers consisted of good forgeries. I was wrong; the details have been run through the magic machines, and the passport, social security and other stuff appears to be genuine,' Franks told them. 'However, I'd best let Mr Grant, here – our adviser from Langley – make some comments.'

Grant was a soft-spoken young man with a thin moustache which gave him a wimpish look, but was not really meant to fool anybody. He was as sharp as a sliver of glass and wasted no time on any preamble.

'There is the possibility, of course, that the young woman we have in the other room, might *not* be the real Jenny Mo. But if she is, she was born a US citizen and seems to have lived and worked in New York until a couple of years ago, then she turned up in the San Francisco area. There is evidence that she is a whizz with figures and dealt with various club and restaurant accounts which, in some cases, have traces of Brokenclaw Lee's ownership. I have people checking on all of this, because if she *is* genuine it is quite possible that you'll come up against people who knew her here, and none of us consider this an amusing prospect. Make no mistake about it, Lee is totally ruthless. If she is the real Jenny Mo, you'll be blown in about ten seconds flat.'

'Yes, that could make things a trifle risky,' Bond understated. 'Might I ask if we're to carry any protection?'

'Depends on what instructions you get.' M was in his most uncompromising play-it-by-the-book mode. He turned to Grant, "How long will your teams take to whittle down the possibilities?'

'On whether Jenny Mo *is* Jenny Mo? Difficult to say. Twenty-four hours probably.'

'Then it could be too late.' M looked towards his Chief of Staff. 'You're running this operation, Tanner. What's our deadline on Captain Bond and Ms Chi-Ho?'

'I want them apparently coming off JAL 06 at Kennedy tomorrow night, sir, which means eleven thirty Eastern time, eight thirty to us. It's not safe to leave it any later than that.'

'Do *we* maintain contact with Commander Rushia?'

'We're working on some kind of link, sir, but it could be tenuous. Q Branch've provided homers for James and Ms Chi-Ho, with a receiving unit for Commander Rushia. We have to work out details of direct contact between Rushia and us.' He paused, his brow furrowed. 'I'd really like some kind of dooms-day link between James and/or Chi-Chi and Rushia as well.'

'See that girl – what's-her-name? The one the Armourer sent over.'

Bill Tanner suppressed a smile, knowing that M always put on his crusty act where Ann Reilly was concerned. In fact they all knew that he had a very tender spot for the girl. 'I'll see to it now, sir.' He excused himself and hurried away to wheel and deal with Q'ute.

M nodded towards Franks, indicating he should continue with the briefing.

'I want to keep this simple.' Franks glanced at Bill Orr, who nodded. 'As I've already told you, we *think* that we've got the full strength out of these two jokers, but nothing on this earth is certain.'

'We took both of them very deep indeed,' Orr added. '*I* believe we have the truth. Mr Franks is not so sure.'

'I'd say around ninety-eight/ninety-nine per cent,' Franks commented. 'The set-up appears to be that Argentbright is to call a San Francisco number on arrival at JFK and use a simple ID sequence. We can give you all that stuff; there appear to be several identification exchanges and I just hope we've got them right, and in the correct order of use. The deal is that when Lee's people are satisfied it's really Argentbright and confirmed that Jenny Mo's with him, they'll give you instructions, and they could be anything from hopping a flight back here to . . .'

Bond coughed. 'I'm not clear how we're supposed to get on to a flight that goes direct from Tokyo to JFK. Particularly as it seems we're required there tomorrow night . . .'

'If you'll just allow me to continue.' Franks was never happy about being interrupted while he held the floor, and Bond noticed that his mood changes were accompanied by the odd movement of rubbing his chin against his shoulder. It was just one fast, odd tic, but Bond recalled that he had read something about that particular twitch and it was not good. The thought flickered through his mind, but Franks had continued to speak. 'If you'll let me finish, I will explain, and what I don't tell you, the Chief of Staff will, once he returns.'

The briefing broke up at two in the morning, when Bond was taken to a cabin and told to get some sleep. His head reeled from the input received from Franks and Orr, which moved from details of the real Peter Argentbright's life to the various options he would have once the operation, now dubbed *Curve*, began to run.

Chi-Chi had been taken away to another part of the carrier, and Bond reflected that he would need some time with the girl before the starting gun which was scheduled for two o'clock that afternoon, some twelve hours from now. Facts paced around his mind, but almost as soon as his head hit the pillow he was asleep.

He dreamed that he was at sea, in a violent thunderstorm which eventually brought him to consciousness again and to the sounds that were thunder in his dream. The carrier appeared to be making way, and the noise that had penetrated his unconscious was that of jet aircraft coming aboard. It was dawn, and a glance at his Rolex showed it was a little after five in the morning.

A few moments later there was a knock at the door and one of the Lion Tamers, who had served the cold dinner in M's cabin the night before, came in with a breezy smile and a breakfast tray.

'M's compliments, sir. He'd be obliged if you would report to his cabin at six o'clock sharp. I'll be around to escort you. Lovely day out there.'

'Are we at sea?' Bond asked, sitting up.

'Not what *you'd* call sea, sir. We've just moved out of the bay a little. They're taking aircraft on board.'

'I thought the ship only had a skeleton crew?'

'Fleshed it out a mite while you were sleeping, sir. See you soon.'

Breakfasted, showered, shaved and dressed, Bond was taken up to M's cabin – the one they had used the night before – arriving at exactly two minutes past six. Chi-Chi, Bill Tanner, the Scrivener and M were already gathered.

'So glad you could join us.' M looked sarcastically at his watch, being a martinet concerning time.

'Delayed by the crowds, sir,' Bond threw back. 'Like Piccadilly Circus this morning. I thought we had the run of the ship.'

'Only this area,' M said sharply. 'We have taken aboard the minimum personnel to carry out phase one of *Curve*. In other words, enough officers and enlisted men to take us fifty miles out to sea, plus three F-14s and one helicopter to ensure your trip to New York. You leave at two this afternoon. On the dot, Bond, otherwise the whole business'll be compromised.'

First they went through the paperwork with the Scrivener who had provided passports identical to those carried by Argent-bright and Mo, plus all the other bits and pieces – credit cards, which they had to sign, an International driving licence for Bond and a Californian one in Jenny Mo's name for Chi-Chi, together with her social security and Blue Cross/Blue Shield cards. Cogger was a painstaking craftsman and there was a whole bagful of pocket litter ranging from cinema stubs and restaurant bills from Hong Kong to Amex receipts from hotels. If the real Jenny Mo was truly out of the picture, they would, Bond thought, be home and dry.

Later, they were separated and taken through their covers during an hour's furious questioning. There was a very early lunch followed by a short session with Q'ute, who explained the homers they were to carry – Chi-Chi's inserted into a belt buckle, Bond's in the heel of his right shoe. Ed Rushia had joined them by this time, and they had what was to be the final run-through, just to make sure everyone was letter perfect.

Their luggage was basically the same as that which had been carried by the original couriers; only some of the items had been changed to make certain they were the correct fit. Bond managed to spend half-an-hour with Chi-Chi, talking, getting to know exactly how she felt about the operation, and, incidentally, finding out how well-trained she was. This short one-on-one period allowed them just enough time to establish the kind of rapport two field agents required at a basic level. Bond led her, rather as a dancing partner, through a brief series of hand and eye contact signals with some one-line codes. 'If I use the American phrase "real soon",' he told her, 'it means that we have a problem and I'm looking for a way out.' There were three or four more of these quick verbal tips, but the conversation proved, to Bond, that under the slim-waisted fragility and the pretty face, there lay a well-trained, very tough young woman.

'If it were a them-or-you situation, would you hesitate before actually taking someone out?' he asked casually.

'You're joking.' She gave him a raised left eyebrow that seemed to have a will of its own. 'I would rather ask the questions afterwards.'

'Okay. If you were armed and told someone to freeze, could you kill if they made even an innocent gesture?'

'You bet your life on it, James. If I tell someone to freeze and have the drop on him, I kill if he even scratches his backside instead of doing what I tell him.'

'Why?'

'Like you, I have been trained in anti-terrorist tactics. People have been killed for not acting when some jughead touches the button on his jacket.'

'You're right. He who hesitates is lost.'

She gave a sensual throaty chuckle. 'You know the real quotation? It is "The man who hesitates is lost; so is the woman who doesn't."'

Bond smiled. 'I think we're going to make an unbeatable team.'

'Like peas in a pod.' She paused. 'The only thing that worries me is this trip to New York.'

'You don't like flying?'

'I don't know if I'm going to like it in a jet fighter.'

'Only difference between that and airlines is you don't get a movie.' He reached out and gently squeezed her shoulder. 'And that, Chi-Chi Sue, is a blessing. You also don't get those little packets of nuts.'

'Thank heaven for that. I thought it was the full coach class business. I feel *much* better now.'

Just after one fifteen in the afternoon, they were both taken to an empty crew room and given blue coveralls with yellow patches on the back, identifying them as baggage handlers. Grant had joined them, and Ed Rushia was already kitted out in a G-suit, having no need for the coveralls. They had a quick final word with the American, who was to leave a little in advance of Bond and Chi-Chi. As he walked from the crew room, Rushia turned and gave them a broad smile. 'Break a leg, you two,' he said. 'Isn't that the correct way to address actors about to go on stage?'

'I believe so.' Bond frowned. 'But we're not actors, Ed.'

'You wanna bet on that, James?' He raised a hand and made a sweeping, theatrical departure.

A technician came in and helped them into their G-suits, then left them alone.

'I feel like an astronaut in this stuff.' Chi-Chi had gone undeniably pale.

'You look like a pretty desirable astronaut then. You can park your shuttle next to mine any time.'

'I might just take you up on that. I was . . .'

She was cut off by the CIA man, Grant, coming into the room. 'Others are on their way down,' he said, not looking either of them in the eyes. 'I have to tell you that we still haven't got a real handle on Jenny Mo yet.'

'Not even an indication?'

'Not a sniff.'

'We'll just have to pray.' Bond glanced at Chi-Chi.

'No.' Grant sounded hard and concerned. 'No, until we get a definite fix that the Jenny Mo we have on this ship is not the real Jenny Mo, you'll both have to assume the worst. I have to tell you, Ms Chi-Ho, that the risk *is* high.'

She shook her head. 'Don't worry, Mr Grant. I just don't want to talk about it any Mo'.'

Bond was amused at the look of pain that passed across Grant's face. Then the others were in the room.

They all shook hands rather soberly, and Bond was reminded of all those stiff-upper-lip, ludicrous scenes from old war movies where the suicide mission volunteers were told what a good thing they were doing for their country and for the world.

'Any new information'll be passed on as best we can, via Indexer.' M looked as solemn as a funeral director. Indexer was their crypto for Ed Rushia. Chi-Chi was Checklist, and Bond, who always wondered how they came up with cryptos, found himself cast as Custodian.

Grant made the final remark. 'Don't forget, all the baggage handlers will be my people. Don't be worried about that, it's been set up and should go like clockwork.' They nodded and passed through to the aircrew briefing room, where two young pilots were waiting for them, checking their route and refuelling points for the last time.

'Okay,' the senior of the US Navy pilots said after handshakes and no introductions. 'Either of you ever fly in a jet warplane before?'

'I'm fully operational with Harriers.' Bond tried not to sound patronising.

Chi-Chi answered with a 'No' at very low volume.

'Right.' The senior man stepped towards Chi-Chi. 'I'll drive you, ma'am. My buddy'll take you, sir.'

They separated in pairs. Bond's aviator looked about nineteen, and the G-suit apart, could well have just graduated from High School. 'You're in the GIB's seat,' he began, then, seeing the quizzical look on Bond's face, interpreted – 'The GIB, sir, Guy In Back, the REO's station.'

'Let me guess. Radio Electronics Officer, right?'

'Near 'nuff, sir. You'll hear all the traffic through the headset, and you'll hear me. With respect, sir, please don't mess with any of the gizmos back there.'

'Wouldn't dream of it.'

'Great. The tech who'll strap you in and make sure you're connected up'll show you the ejector lever. Get *that* one right, please, and if I tell you to punch out, for Pete's sake do it.'

'I'll do it. You're the boss.'

'Okay, sir. Any questions?'

'Let's just get on with the whole business. I have a job to do.'

The young man nodded, and they followed the senior pilot, still talking in a soothing voice to Chi-Chi, out and up the metal steps to the flight deck where a helicopter hovered off on the port side and two F-14 Tomcats, looking wicked and dangerous, were standing close to the starboard catapult area. The catapult crew swarmed around the lead aircraft, mixed with technicians, while the second Tomcat stood back and staggered well out of the way of the first aircraft's engine nozzles.

Chi-Chi and her pilot made for the first F-14 while Bond's man pointed at the second machine.

The REO's cockpit, behind the pilot, was cramped and, once he was strapped and plugged in, Bond realised that it was not the most comfortable of crew positions, though he had little time to think about that. The lead aircraft had started its two Pratt & Whitney turbofans and was manoeuvred into place on the launch ramp.

Everything happened very quickly. The flurry of men fitting

the catapult moved expertly to one side, the great metal baffles rose from the deck to take the full blast from the jets which rose to a deafening roar even within the waiting airplane, then, with a suddenness, the F-14 was hurled forward, leaving a trail of steam along the catapult, dropping slightly then nosing up, gear rising, before it rocketed into the sky.

Bond was still watching it streak upwards as their engines started and they slowly moved into place on the catapult. He could see the catapult officer with his glowing yellow wand off to the right, and could feel the whole craft vibrate as his pilot brought the engines up to maximum throttle. He found himself looking, hypnotised, at the catapult officer who straightened up and raised his wand in a sweeping motion, bringing it down like something out of a *Star Wars* movie, so that the flashing yellow rod was aimed directly below the aircraft, at the catapult. Bond tensed, pushed his head back against the padded seatback and waited, counting to himself . . . One . . . Two . . . and the catapult fired, the gigantic punch in his back, his body pushed almost wildly out of control as they accelerated and were thrown into the air. It was so quick that, mentally, his stomach was left behind, about eight feet above the carrier's deck, while his body was now at a thousand feet and climbing.

Bond preferred the more civilised ski-jump technique of his old friend the Harrier.

They made exceptional time, bumping and buffeting at maximum altitude with engine noise mixed with the wind. There were two stops for midair refuelling, and Bond listened to Chi-Chi's pilot talking to the captain of the great C-130, out of SAC HQ at Offott AFB, Omaha. He had two shots at getting the probe into the refuelling drogue the first time, and there were some distinctly off-colour comments from both pilots.

Bond's driver hit the drogue first time on each occasion, and, like a ritual, the dialogue never varied – 'Just keep it there and let it soak up the good juices,' drawled the C-130 pilot; and when they disengaged, the fighter jock clipped out a 'How was it for you?' To which the C-130 driver sighed and told him that the earth had moved.

At just after ten o'clock, Eastern Standard Time, they locked on to the RAPCON – Radar Approach Control – at the Grumman Aircraft Company's facility on Long Island. At ten thirty they were on the ground and turning off the long runway. Chi-Chi's Tomcat was already parked far away from any of the buildings and Bond could make out the shape of a small Hughes helicopter in civil livery standing off to one side.

Bond climbed down from the rear cockpit, giving the thumbs up to his pilot and rapidly unzipping himself from the G-suit which was taken from him by a technician who greeted him with the words, 'Message from Mr Grant, sir. No joy yet, but the 06 from Tokyo is early. She'll be on the ground and at the terminal in less than half-an-hour.'

'Better get a shift on then.' He nodded at the tech, hurried over to the helicopter and climbed in next to Chi-Chi, both now in the dark-blue coveralls of baggage handlers.

The pilot nodded and the door was closed as the rotors wound up and they lifted into the night sky.

'That was quite a ride, uh?' he shouted at Chi-Chi over the engine noise.

'Sure,' she yelled back. 'I was good. Only vomited four times.'

He looked at her to make sure she was all right and, in spite of the slight pallor, he saw she was smiling.

In the distance the towers of Manhattan glittered against the night sky, and fifteen minutes later, they were over New York's John F Kennedy airport, under local control, and being directed towards the International arrivals terminal on the air side. The pilot touched down just long enough for Chi-Chi and Bond to clamber out. They were greeted by two figures in similar baggage handler's coveralls.

'Indexer sends his regards,' one of the men said, with little conviction.

'The glossary's been completed on time then?' Bond replied with the prearranged question.

'JAL 06's down and taxiing in now. Your personal items are on our truck.' He jerked his head in the direction of the train of baggage trolleys with its little electric truck out in front below the high, jetway where the usual arrivals crew waited for the 747, the engines of which could be heard as it headed towards the end of its long journey from Tokyo. The luggage, which had gone ahead packed in wing pods on the Tomcat that had brought Ed Rushia, was piled on the first trolley, and the supervisor spoke quietly as the Boeing's engines got louder and louder in the background.

'The cabin crew'll deplane all passengers from the front door when it's latched to the ramp,' he told them. 'We've arranged for one of the stewards to open up the rear door when two-thirds of the passengers are off. He's being paid so he imagines it's some scam we're running – drugs or illegals. But once he's opened up the door he's been instructed to go forward and not to let any other crew members back there. We've got a set of steps ready to drive in and secure to the rear door. You just hang around with the lads who'll be doing the unloading. When I give you the okay, get out of the coveralls, grab your hand baggage, and get up there.'

It took around fifteen minutes before they saw the rear door swing back and the motorised steps move forward. Four minutes later, Chi-Chi, carrying a Scribner's Bookstore canvas bag, and Bond hefting a briefcase, both wearing their regular clothes, were at the back of the line of people who were the last to deplane. Bond had flipped his fingers into his breast pocket and pulled into view the top half of his JAL boarding pass given to him by the Scrivener earlier that day. They even thanked the members of the cabin crew at the door as they went out on to the ramp and began that long hike to immigration and customs.

At immigration they split up, Chi-Chi heading for the US Citizens' zone and Bond for the non-US passports. It took about another half-hour for them to get through to the baggage carousels and the usual scramble for luggage, but by eleven forty-five they reached the far side.

Chi-Chi stayed with the luggage and caught a glimpse of Ed Rushia, looking harassed, trying to get some information at one of the baggage desks. Bond headed first for the left baggage lockers, where he found number 64 and unlocked it with the key supplied earlier by the CIA man, Grant. The package was the right weight and he slipped it into his briefcase before getting to the first empty phone booth and dialling the number Franks and Orr had given him.

The distant end answered with a curt, 'Yes?'

'I was given this number to call about some books.' It was exactly what they had told him to say.

'What kind of books?'

'Historical.'

'Ah, they told you wrong. You want a New York number, a 212 area code, okay? You got a pencil?'

'No, but I have a good memory.'

The curt voice rattled off a number, asked him to repeat it and hung up.

When Bond dialled the 212 number, a woman answered with a negative, 'Hello?'

'I'm sorry to call so late, but I understand you have some books for sale on Peter Abelard.'

'Yes. My father had an extensive collection, and I have hand-bound editions of Etienne Gilson's work in translation, Luscombe's *The School of Peter Abelard, The Letters of Abelard and Héloïse*, of course, in the 1925 edition, and most of the other well-known works.'

'And they're all in mint condition?'

'Immaculate.'

'I'm very interested. Would it be too late for me to come over to see them tonight?'

'Your name is . . . ?'

'Peter, Peter Piper.'

'Come as quickly as you can, Peter.' She gave an address on West 56th. 'It's just past the Parker Meridien,' she said. 'I look forward to seeing you. You are coming alone, are you?'

'No, I'll have Héloïse with me.'

The woman at the other end chuckled and closed the line.

'I want you to wait a good fifteen minutes and then take a cab out,' Bond told Chi-Chi, after giving her the address. 'It sounds okay, and she does seem to be expecting you. Ed'll be watching my back, so if there's any surveillance on the place, he'll stop it and hold you off.'

She nodded and Bond gave her a brotherly peck on the cheek, picking up his case and the briefcase and heading towards the taxi rank. On the way he got into a crush of people and found the big Ed Rushia next to him. Talking very low, as if to himself, he gave Rushia the gist of what was happening.

'You sure get around,' Ed muttered before he disappeared into the crowd.

The cab driver was not talkative, but just drove and Bond fiddled with his briefcase, making certain the driver could not see what he was doing – unwrapping the package and transferring his trusted ASP 9mm automatic to the waistband of his trousers, well back behind the right hip.

Manhattan looked like its fabled fairyland self from the bridge. It was only when they got into the caverns of its streets, felt the roughness of the roads, pitted and rutted, and saw the quality of life on the sidewalks at this time of night, that Bond got the flow of adrenaline which always hit him on arrival in this city. It was worse than the last time he had been there and his body tingled with the excitement and static of danger.

The address he had been given was a big, red-brick apartment building. He paid off the driver and carried his own luggage up the steps to the front door, seeking out the apartment number, 4B, on the security panel by the heavily reinforced door. He pressed the bell and a voice – the woman he had spoken to earlier – asked, 'Yes?'

'Peter. Here to look at the books.'

The buzzer was held for enough time to allow him inside before the door clicked back behind him.

There was no elevator, possibly because the building was much older than Otis, so he lugged the cases up four flights of stairs to the smartly painted heavy door with a brass fitting that told him it was 4B.

She was tall and very thin, with a slightly long face and hair which was not naturally blonde. He thought around thirty-five, give or take five years.

'Peter,' he said.

She peered past him. 'Where's Héloïse? You said . . .'

'My people instructed us to come separately.' He was already inside the door. 'They were very specific about it. She's following up to make certain we haven't grown tails.'

'Well, I was . . .'

'What do I call you?' Bond asked, dumping his luggage on the off-white deep pile carpet and taking in the living room at a glance – nicely furnished, two or three good prints on the walls, deep leather chairs, a couple of glass-topped tables, big lamps. There was an exit towards a kitchen to his right and he went down it fast, making sure it was empty. She followed him, bustling a little. 'What do I call you?' he asked again.

'Myra. But I was told . . .'

He turned and glared at her. 'You here alone, Myra?'

'Yes, but . . .'

'No buts. Show me the other rooms.'

She shrugged, then took him back into her main room and through to a master bedroom, her bedroom, he thought, for the ledge in front of a built-in vanity mirror was bottle-scaped with everything from Chanel to Elizabeth Taylor's Passion, plus various unguents unknown even to Bond.

There was one other room which looked as though it was

ready for guests, sporting like Myra's room, a king-sized bed. It flicked through his mind that this might be a shade tricky.

'Okay, Myra. I understand you've a message for me.'

'I must wait for . . .' she began.

'For nobody,' he said firmly. 'You have orders, I have orders. You have a message, for God's sake, she'll be here in a minute.'

'It's only a telephone number.'

'Well?'

It was long distance with the 415 San Francisco area code.

'I use that telephone?' He inclined his head towards the only phone he could see.

'Yes, but please . . .'

The buzzer sounded. Bond smiled at her. 'That'll be Héloïse now. It's okay, Myra.'

But she was already over by the security panel asking her flat, 'Yes?'

'Héloïse.' Chi-Chi's voice was slightly distorted through the speaker.

'Oh, come right up. Come straight up.' Myra's whole mood changed. She held the button for what seemed to be a long time, then turned back to Bond.

'I'm sorry if I was difficult, but it's been so long since I've seen Jenny. I've been on pins and needles all week, just waiting for your call. Oh, it's going to be great to see her again. We were such friends when she lived here.'

9

BEDTIME STORIES

Myra hovered by the door, ready to snatch at the handle as soon as her old friend hit the buzzer. On the other side of the room, Bond tapped out a number on the telephone. But it was not the number Myra had given him. It rang twice, then a voice at the distant end said, 'Curve's Deli, Howard speaking. How can I help you?'

'Oh, sorry, I think I've misdialled.'

'Okay, sir.' The line closed and Bond put down the instrument and began to move towards Myra and the door. There were ten combinations of the misdialled, or misrouted, code that he could have used. The 'Oh, sorry,' prefix meant that Grant's people had to get a message urgently to Rushia and stand by for another call from Bond – Custodian.

The door buzzer gave two quick brrrrps and Myra wrenched at the handle. 'Jenn . . .' she began, then stepped back into the room, her mouth open. 'You're not!!'

'Not Jenny Mo,' Bond said, standing directly behind her as Chi-Chi came in, dumping her case and the canvas bag on the floor.

'I don't . . .' Myra looked around her, eyes wide with terror. 'Who are you? I thought Jenny . . .'

'Get her into the bedroom, over there,' he said sharply, and Chi-Chi moved in, caught Myra's right wrist, spun her around and hissed, 'Move.'

Myra tried to protest, but Chi-Chi merely applied a little pressure and she had no option but to do what was commanded.

'Just keep her quiet in there. We'll sort her out later.'

Chi-Chi said nothing, but indicated with her eyes that she could handle it. When the bedroom door closed he went to the phone again and tapped out the number Myra had given to him. It rang for quite a long time before a gruff, accented voice answered with a grunt.

'I had a message to call you,' Bond said.

'Your name?'

He took a deep breath and prayed that Franks and Orr had got it right. 'Peter Abelard.'

'So you've arrived. Is Héloïse with you?'

'Yes, but she's pretty tired. It's been a long trip.'

'We have your wellbeing at heart.' The voice became strong and not unpleasant. 'That's why we arranged an overnight stop before you come on to San Francisco. You leave tomorrow night, or tonight in your case, for it must be after midnight. American Airlines Flight 15, leaving JFK at nine fifteen. The tickets are being held in your names at the desk. Just be there before eight fifteen to pick them up. You get in here about half past midnight, and you will call this number as soon as you're through the gate. You understand?'

'We'll be there.'

'Good.'

Bond stood, silent and looking at the handset for a few seconds after they had disconnected, then he called to Chi-Chi, 'Bring her out here, we've a whole lot of talking to do.'

Chi-Chi did not have Myra under restraint when the women came back into the room, and it was obvious that the tall girl was confused and upset; her eyes were red and filled with tears.

Chi-Chi sat her down in one of the leather chairs. 'Tell my friend what you've told me.' Her voice had almost a parade ground snap in it.

Myra looked up at Bond, and then away again quickly, as

though very frightened. 'Just tell him,' Chi-Chi commanded again.

'I was expecting my old friend, Jenny,' she began.

'Yes, we all know that. Tell him why you were expecting her.'

She bit her lip. 'They told me that she was one of the people who would come during the period from twenty-seventh of September until seventh of this month.' She was still very tearful.

'And you were to identify her for them? Whoever "they" happen to be.'

'No . . . No . . . No,' in rapid succession, with a wild shaking of the head. 'No, they had no idea that I'd ever known anyone by the name of Jenny Mo.'

Bond thought this was an unlikely story, but he kept up the fiction. 'Myra, who are *they*?'

'I . . .' she began, then faltered and started again, 'I don't really know. People I am indebted to.'

'That's as far as I got with her,' Chi-Chi muttered.

'See if you can rustle up some coffee or something.' Bond moved to sit near Myra, but the girl half rose. 'How stupid of me, I have food waiting for you. I'm sorry to be so damned wet, but – well, I've so looked forward to seeing Jenny, and this is a blow. I thought she was dead.'

'Sit down,' Bond spoke softly, gently, glancing up at Chi-Chi. His eyes tried to indicate that they should play the good cop, bad cop routine. 'Just coffee.'

Chi-Chi nodded and went towards the kitchen.

'These people you say you're beholden to – who are they, exactly?'

'Are you police?' A very small voice.

'No. If you tell us the truth, Myra, nothing bad will happen to you.'

'Then . . .'

'I should warn you, Myra,' Chi-Chi stood in the passageway to the kitchen, 'if you do *not* tell us the truth, we shall know. Then you will wish you had never been born.'

Bond nodded to Myra, as though bearing out the Chinese girl's words, while at the same time showing his own compassion.

There was a long, drifting hesitation, then Myra started again. 'I'd better begin at the beginning, for I was born in China, just outside Peking, as they called it then, in 1948.'

So, Bond thought, she was older than he had suspected. Over forty in fact.

'My parents had spent most of their lives in China. They were American citizens, Baptist missionaries, and you will know that things were chaotic in that strange country during the late 1940s . . .'

'And after,' Bond commented.

Myra gave a little nod. 'When I was born, in the November of '48, there was bitter fighting around Peking. But the memory of my childhood in Peking itself was one of happiness. We lived in a small but pleasant house on the outskirts of the city. My parents taught me and brought me up as a Christian, which I thought odd, because the Communist Revolution was in full flood and I knew that we were different by the time I was seven or eight. There seemed to be no other Americans that we could mix with. In fact, we saw very few white people, though a number of Chinese, most of them officers of the Red Army, visited us.

'When I was sixteen, I was told what had happened. During the fighting between Mao's Red Army and the Nationalist troops at the time of my birth, my parents had sheltered a young Red Army officer. He had been badly wounded and my mother nursed him while my father lied to the Nationalist soldiers who came looking for Communist stragglers.

'When Peking was taken and the Revolution began in earnest, the young officer told my father that he would see to it that we were not harmed. Later, he returned and said it was impossible for him to get us out of the country, but if we made no political trouble, he would ensure that we could live in peace. The house was found for us and there we lived. Both my father and mother embraced Mao's brand of Communism and my father did some translation work for the new government. For this, we were left in peace.

'I understood little of the political implications, though I know that in my late teens I began to feel very uncomfortable about some of the things my father had to do.'

She stopped, as though a host of memories had come drifting back to her, and Bond was forced to prompt her to go on.

'I was twenty-four when the officer who I had been told was the man my parents had sheltered came late one night and spent hours alone with my father. It appeared that he could do little to help us any more. I didn't understand it all, but he seemed to have lost some of his previous power. For several weeks we were confined to the house and there was an armed guard at the door. Then he came again. Apparently there was one way he could save us from being tried as spies and probably executed – we knew many had faced trials and summary death for what was called spying. If my parents would consent to my being taken to the United States, they would be safe. I was to find work in New York and we would be allowed to exchange letters once a month. The officer told me it was not likely that I would ever see my parents again, but at least I would be sure of their safety in their old age if I did as I was told.'

'So you came to America?'

She gave a small nod, biting her lip. 'I think I should have stayed. I was ordered to do anything my parents instructed me to do. I don't think they're alive any more, but I still get letters which appear to be from them.'

'And you obey instructions?'

'Yes. There was no problem with my passport, social security, anything. There was even a job for me. I am a translator at the

UN. I speak several Chinese dialects; German, quite good Russian, and French.'

'Your mother must have been an amazing lady.' Chi-Chi had come through with a tray loaded with cups and a large thermos of coffee.

'Oh, she was. She taught me well.'

'The jobs you were asked to do . . . ?' Bond began.

'There haven't been all that many. I carry a great sadness about my family, but I live comfortably, my work is interesting. I'm modestly happy.'

'The jobs?' he prompted.

'Delivering messages. Picking up letters and forwarding them to various people, both here and abroad. This is only the third time I've had to let people stay here.'

'Chinese people?'

'The first time – oh, six years ago – there were two Caucasians, foreigners who did not speak English well and a Chinese – a young man who was very kind. He comes back to see me quite regularly. He's a good man. Then, last year, there were two Chinese, a man and a woman. They stayed for six days. There were telephone calls and, finally, a rough-looking Chinese came and took them away.'

'This Chinese? The one who comes back to see you. Does he ever give you instructions?'

'No. No, never. We have a kind of . . . well . . .'

'You sleep with him,' Chi-Chi said harshly.

'Yes. Yes, I sleep with him from time to time.'

'Can I make a guess at something?' Bond took a proffered cup of strong black coffee.

'What?'

'I would guess that the young officer your parents saved – the one who had you brought to America – is called Hung Chow H'ang. Right?'

Myra gave a little gasp, 'Yes. How did you . . . ?'

'One of the injuries he suffered when your mother nursed him was to an eye, right?'

'Why, yes. He wears a patch over his left eye.'

'Has he ever visited you here?'

The hesitation was too long. 'He has?' Bond nudged her and she gave a minute nod.

'He's quite an old man now.' She was almost whispering. 'But he visits about twice a year. Always calls a week ahead. Takes me out and buys me dinner. Always correct, but he lies to me.'

'About your parents?'

'He tells me they are fine, but in his stories they are just the same as when I left China.'

'Do you know what you're doing when you pass on messages, post letters and put people up?'

'I think so.' Again the very small voice.

'Then tell me.'

'I think it's something to do with . . . with spying, espionage.'

'It would seem that way. Drink your coffee, Myra. Then tell us about your friend Jenny Mo.'

She sipped nervously at her coffee, eyes restless and cheeks flushed as though she were running a fever.

'She worked in one of the accounts departments at the UN. I got to know her well and we became friends.' There was an extended pause. 'Close friends.' Another silence as though she were trying to tell them more. 'One day, Jenny said she was having problems with the lease on her apartment, so I let her use the spare room here. We shared this place until two years ago, when she was offered a very highly paid job in San Francisco. So she left. I had a couple of telephone calls and several letters, then she wrote to me saying she was worried. She said she thought it was necessary to go to the police . . .'

'She tell you why?' asked Bond.

'You still have the letter?' asked Chi-Chi.

'Yes, I still have it. You want to see?'

'Later, maybe. Just tell us what else happened.'

'Nothing happened. Just this strange letter, then nothing, except the Chinese boy, the one I told you about, the one who still visits from time to time. He made a remark one night when he was here. I thought it odd.' She stopped as though that was all there was to it.

'How odd?'

'Well, he was always nice. Kind and good. But he was pretty casual. I mean he usually wore jeans and a shirt, or a wind-cheater. Then, on this particular night, he arrived wearing an Armani suit. He had a gold Rolex and a heavy gold ID bracelet, two gold rings on his fingers. I was only joking. I said, "Business must be good," and he just laughed. So I told him maybe I would have to go to the police and inform on him if business was that good. I was teasing him. He slapped me, beat me up, but before he left we made it up. He apologised, but he did say that I should be careful talking like that otherwise I'd end up like my old friend Jenny Mo.'

'You follow up on that?'

'I asked him what he meant, and he said he wasn't being serious, only, as I hadn't heard from Jenny in a long time, she must have disappeared. It worried me. Then I had the instructions about you. They simply said that a man called Peter Argentbright, who would identify himself as Peter Abelard, would call and then come with his wife, who would be called Héloïse, but was really Jenny Mo. I thought . . . I thought, well, I thought it *must* be Jenny. It's been so long, and I *had* been very worried. Then, when you came, it was as though she were truly dead.'

'So.' Bond walked over to the telephone, then decided against it.

'Am I in trouble?' Myra asked.

'You mean police? No, but I think some other friends of ours will probably want to see you, maybe keep you in a reasonable place – a house somewhere – and ask you a lot of questions. If you go along with them, you'll be safe, but I believe if you stay here you'll probably be dead inside a week.

'You manage if I go out for a while?' he asked Chi-Chi.

'Telephone?'

'Yes, I don't fancy this one after the last call. I might have screwed things up as it is. Shouldn't be long. Only open up to me – or Indexer of course.'

There was still plenty of traffic on the street even at this time in the morning, and Bond cursed for not having put on a warmer jacket for there was a rising cold wind.

He turned left out of the apartment building and walked a block down to the Parker Meridien. Across the street, Ed Rushia, in a chauffeur's cap, nodded at the wheel of a stretch limo. Bond smiled to himself. Ed was certainly an operator. They had told him to hire a car and back up. He had obviously done just that and hired a stretch limo.

The night porter was on duty outside the 56th Street entrance to the imposing hotel, and as Bond approached him, he stepped forward.

'I help you, buddy?'

'I need to use one of the public telephones.' He slipped a ten into the man's hand.

'Oh, okay, sir. Thank you. You want I should get you a cab?'

'I'll be just fine,' and Bond disappeared into the brightly lit interior. A minute later he had swiped a credit card through one of the telephone booths and dialled the same local number as before.

'Curve's Deli, Joe speaking. How can I help you?'

'Custodian! Patch me through to whoever's the senior officer.'

There were a couple of clicks, then a voice he recognised as Grant's answered. 'Custodian? Where the hell're you calling from?'

'Public booth. Listen, we could have a serious problem. Our hostess seems to have been expecting the real Mo girl, but we're not certain if it's Eeny, Meeny, Miney or Mo, if you follow.'

'I don't, but go on.'

'Our hostess seems to have been working for the people at the old French Legation, but swears she didn't know what she was really up to. I would suggest you make arrangements to have her dried out once we've left. We're off to sunny California tonight.'

'Jetsetter!' Grant was actually trying his hand at a joke. Pity it was so limp.

'You're in touch with Indexer?' Bond did not even have a smirk in his voice.

'Of course.'

'Then use whatever means you can to put a photograph of the Mo woman on the wire and get it to him.'

'Then what?'

'He knows where I am, and you know, right?'

'Right.'

'Are we alone, or does Indexer have company?'

'He says not, and he's usually accurate.'

'I'll call back from the apartment and order pizza or something. You can send a lad down with them. Just get Indexer to intercept and bring the items up.'

'Will do.' Grant hung up and Bond left the hotel.

'Okay, sir?' The doorman would remember him, but that couldn't be helped.

'Sure. Fine. My phone's out and my girl just stood me up.'

'Women!' said the doorman, as though this was the cause of all the world's problems.

'Everything normal?' he asked when he got back into the apartment. Chi-Chi or Myra or both had made more coffee, and there was a plateful of sandwiches.

'Fine.' Chi-Chi smiled at him, as if to say together they could conquer the world. 'Myra's worried about getting arrested.'

'Don't lose a wink over it, Myra. I've been arrested a hundred times. Nothing to it.' He picked up the apartment phone and called the contact number, spending several minutes ordering three jumbo pizzas with all the trimmings while the women sat open-mouthed.

'Myra has enough here to feed an army.' Chi-Chi held out the plate which looked as though someone had tried to make a model of the Leaning Tower of Pisa from bread, smoked salmon and cheese.

'An army doesn't live on smoked salmon alone. Armies like us need other things – camp followers, nurses, air support.'

Chi-Chi raised an eyebrow at this piece of whimsy and Bond thought to himself that she had incredible control over it.

'Will they put me in jail?' Myra asked, anxious and getting quite close to hysteria.

'Not if you're a good girl and eat your sandwiches. Try to relax, Myra. I want you with all your wits about you. Another friend's coming up shortly.' He took his fourth sandwich and munched on it happily. 'We could always play Trivial Pursuit while we wait. Do you have Trivial Pursuit, Myra?'

She shook her head, but did not speak.

'How about Mahjong?'

'Yes, if we have to.'

'We don't have to do anything, Myra. Just stay calm and wait.'

The downstairs buzzer went about half-an-hour later.

'Pizzas from Curve's Deli.' Rushia's growl came out covered in static.

'Come right up,' Bond answered.

He had the chauffeur's peaked cap pushed on to the back of his head. 'There's your eats.' He gave the big smile to the women. 'Do yourself proud here. Very nice.'

'You got the other thing?'

He nodded. 'I'm to slog around passing messages for you, and I've got another little job if you can manage it.'

'I hope you've got somebody watching that limo.' Bond took the photograph. 'Around here it could be on bricks by the time you get back.'

Rushia chuckled. 'I sure fooled them. I let the air outa the tyres.'

'Myra,' Bond walked over to where she sat, holding the photograph out to her, 'you recognise this girl?'

She had a very thin hand which shook slightly as she took the photograph and peered at it as though it were a holy relic.

'No. No, I don't recognise her. Should I?'

'Only if it happened to be your old friend Jenny Mo.'

'Oh, that's not Jenny. She was rather intense-looking and wore big, black-rimmed glasses.'

'Good.' Bond handed the picture back to Rushia. 'Just have this destroyed, my good fellow. Oh, and we'll be heading for JFK tomorrow night. Nine fifteen to the city of Saint Francis.'

'Make a nice change. I'll fix it, even if they have to offload some poor tourist.' He ran a long finger down the side of his nose. 'A word in private, your honour.'

They stepped over to the door.

'Got a couple of Mickey Finns here for the lady.' Ed spoke out of the corner of his mouth, a parody of every Hollywood jail movie.

'How fast, and how long?'

' 'Bout two minutes and twenty-four hours.'

'Okay. Would you tell whoever's going to clean up that we will be away by seven tonight.'

'Anything else I can do? Massage your back? Wash the dishes? Sing a coupla choruses of "Oh dear, what a calamity"?'

'Just keep doing what you're good at, Ed.' Bond took the pills in their little silver foil packet and showed him out of the door.

'Time for sleep,' he announced when Rushia had finally gone. 'Get Myra to bed, then call me in. You're pretty wired – strung up – Myra. I've got a couple of pills that will make certain you'll rest.'

She looked up in alarm. 'You're not going to poison me! No!'

'NO!' Chi-Chi said firmly. 'Come on, let's get you to bed,

Myra. Nobody's going to poison you. We all need rest, and you're going to have problems sleeping.'

Twenty minutes later, Chi-Chi came out of the master bedroom. 'Give me a glass of water, James. I think she'll let me do it.'

'I wish it was an injection. Safer. But make sure she swallows them. Should take two minutes max.'

It took under sixty seconds, Chi-Chi told him when she came back. 'Went out like a candle in a hurricane.'

'Well, we've certainly had a long bedtime story tonight. I wonder how much of it was a fairytale?'

Chi-Chi smiled up at Bond, resting a hand on his shoulder. 'I suppose we'll find out eventually, but now, husband, how about bed?'

'You hussy.' Bond smiled down at her. 'But can I take a raincheck? I have one hell of a headache.'

She pouted. 'Oh, I really thought we worked well as a team.'

'We do, but I'll feel safer if I lie across the door with a gun in my hand.'

'Okay, but you don't know what you're missing.'

'Oh, I think I do.'

Myra was still dead to the world when they left the apartment shortly before seven that night. Both had managed eight hours of sleep, Chi-Chi having taken over from Bond to, as he put it, lie across the door. They had eaten, showered and changed. Just before leaving, Bond stripped down his ASP 9mm and unlocked the shielded false bottom of the briefcase – his usual way of carrying arms illegally through airport security.

They had called for a limo from the nearby firm of Ryan & Sons whom Bond had used on other visits to New York. They were discreet, punctual and always friendly. They also did not know his real name, though all the drivers recognised his face. Tonight they had drawn the Ryan son, George, who pleasantly spent the ride out to JFK telling them the city was going to the dogs, how parts of the roadways were caving in, how a friend had been mugged and how the police didn't seem to do much about it. 'Look,' he pointed out of the window, 'see that guy there with the TV on his shoulder? Betcha he never bought that. He's stealing that and nobody'll do anything about it.'

Bond was glad to see Rushia's car not too far behind them. He leaned forward. 'George, you mind if I close the partition?'

'You go ahead, sir. You do what you like. I won't peek!' The driver gave a jovial chuckle.

Bond leaned back, his shoulder touching Chi-Chi's shoulder: 'Now, tell me the story of your life,' he said with a smile.

'Didn't they give you my dossier? It's all in there.'

'They told me you were a Cantonese speaker . . .'

'And a few dialects. You see, they should have given you my file.'

'Okay. So you tell me.'

'Fourth generation American. Joined the US Navy to see the world and saw nothing but the inside of offices. They gave me a commission. My father was very proud, but the man I was going to marry was humiliated – it was some foolish business to do with class – and he would not go through with the contract.'

'And you still love him?'

'Until quite recently, yes. Now I see how foolish I was even to grieve. I know that it was my vanity crying, not my heart.'

'They tell me it takes three years to get over a really broken heart and accept the facts.'

'You are a chauvinist pig, James. For men, maybe only three years; for women it can be much longer – if ever.'

He laid a hand on her arm. 'You may be right, my dear. A very wise man once told me that if a woman stopped loving you, there was nothing you could do about it except put your hands in your pockets and walk away. I believe the same is also true for women.'

'It's a blow to pride, to vanity. But that's all one now. You still want to hear my life story?'

'You're only giving me the later parts.'

'Okay, maybe I don't want you to know about my terrible teenage days when I ran riot with friends, smoked pot, stayed out all night in line for a Who concert, lost my virginity at sixteen . . .'

'Beat you by almost eighteen months.' Though Bond said it lightly enough, he was slightly concerned about Chi-Chi. He had known many good women operatives, but they only remained good if they did not carry around a great load of what he liked to think of as 'emotional baggage'. He hoped that Sue Chi-Ho did not have a cabin trunk of emotions chained to her ankle. At last he said, 'Well, you got through that. We all go through it.'

'Some never come out the other side.' She turned down the corners of what Bond appreciated as a wicked little mouth. 'I had ten friends – *ten* who never made it. From pot to hard drugs, to theft and death.'

Bond nodded. Looking at her now he realised, as though for the first time, that beneath the fragility she was as hard as tempered steel. 'The drug problem's going to be the downfall of many empires, just as lead poisoning was the trigger to the fall of the Roman Empire. But, as to your own adolescent difficulties, you *did* get through them. If you kick all the bad habits, the only problem is if adolescence stays with you, makes you moody, short-fused and, well, downright immature. You're certainly not that.'

'Thank you.' Was there a hint of uncertainty in her voice?

'So you were commissioned?' he prompted.

'Naval Intelligence for two years. Then an Agency talent spotter gave me an audition. The rest, as they say, is history.' She quite suddenly looked up at Bond, her eyes mirroring a hint of anxiety. 'This business? It is going to be all right, James, isn't it?'

'As long as you remember to call me Peter, and don't forget you're Jenny . . .'

'And married to you, yes.' She ran the tip of her tongue along the lips which Bond was finding more attractive every minute. He looked up to see they were just turning on to the airport ramp.

At the American Airlines desk, the tickets were ready for them. 'There's no charge, sir,' the clerk told Bond. 'They've been paid for.' They checked in their luggage, only retaining the briefcase and the Scribner's canvas bag – a relic of the old days when the now defunct business was one of the best book stores in New York.

They passed through the security and Bond made his excuses, going to the nearest restroom. Inside one of the cubicles, he worked the combination lock on the briefcase, removed the shielded false bottom and retrieved his pistol. In under two minutes he had reassembled the weapon, slipped a magazine into the butt, cocked it, activated the safety and slid it into his waistband, pushing it down firmly behind his right hip. Chi-Chi was waiting patiently for him and together they started the long walk down to the gate.

Back on West 56th Street, two unmarked cars and an ambulance drew up at the apartment building some ten minutes after Bond and Chi-Chi left. They got hold of the superintendent claiming there had been an emergency call saying a woman was unconscious in 4B. The super unlocked the apartment for them, and Myra, still unconscious, was taken down to the ambulance on a stretcher, causing the usual little morbid crowd to gather.

What the crowd did not see was one of the men from the accompanying cars loitering in the apartment until the ambulance rescue squad people had left. He went rapidly back into the bedroom and, using pillows and blankets from one of the closets and a wig he had brought for the purpose, constructed the outline of a body asleep in the bed. He was the last man out.

An hour later, as Chi-Chi and Bond were walking to the AA departure gate, a car drew up across the street from the apartment block. The driver stayed where he was and his passenger, a greying, respectable-looking man wearing a long raincoat over his suit, walked over to the building. He did not spend time calling the superintendent, but inserted a pick-lock into the door, and had it open in thirty seconds.

He carefully closed it behind him, then quietly went up the stairs to 4B, where the door yielded to his expertise in less time than the one downstairs. He wore gloves and opened up quietly, reaching under his raincoat to reveal a wicked-looking Skorpion machine-pistol, fitted with a noise suppression unit.

Slowly he crossed to the master bedroom, opened the door and fired four short bursts of 9mm rounds into the 'body' with a sound like a small child idly running an old glove along a row of railings.

He did not wait to look at his work. He had been told to kill quickly and efficiently and get away without being detected. Within minutes he was crossing the road to the anonymous car which drove away with great care.

Neither the driver nor his murderous passenger even noticed the battered Buick that had seen better days pull out and follow them about two cars back in the traffic.

They had almost made it to the gate and Chi-Chi was just wondering aloud if the movie would be any good, when the two men came up on either side of them. The one next to Bond had Oriental looks, and was a very large man, the one who began to keep pace with Chi-Chi was shorter and Caucasian.

'Just keep walking past the gate, Mr Abelard,' the big one said.

'And please don't make a fuss, this is for your security.' The smaller man's accent could have passed for British.

'My name is Ding,' the large one continued without breaking his stride. 'My friends call me Bone Bender Ding. My partner, here, beside the lovely lady is called Fox, but he answers to other, less salubrious names. Mr Lee felt it safer to send his private jet down for you both. That will make certain that nobody's on your tails, if you'll excuse the expression, ma'am.'

'And what if we prefer American Airlines?' asked Bond.

'Oh, Mr Lee would be very upset, sir. Also it would become unpleasant and Mr Lee cannot abide unpleasantness. Now, straight down to the end of this walkway. We have a car there ready to take you out to the jet.'

10

FLIGHT OF DECEPTION

Ed Rushia was already in line, at the gate, waiting to board AA 15 when he saw Bond and Chi-Chi pass down the long walkway. An unobservant moron would have noticed them, he thought, for their companions were highly visible – the very large, silk-suited Chinese with the arms of a gorilla and the smaller white man whose eyes constantly moved as though looking for trouble. He acted immediately, heading for the nearest payphone and using an Amex card to dial the number Bond had contacted so successfully during the night. The usual response came from Curve's Deli, and he immediately asked to be patched through to control.

In fact, the mythical Curve's Deli was located in a large room some seventeen storeys up in an old apartment building on Lexington Avenue. The floor was bare wood, the walls could have done with several coats of paint and there was an all-pervading smell of damp. But these things were overshadowed by one wall which dominated the place. A series of long tables held a tall bank of sophisticated radio and electronics gear plus a portable automatic switchboard. There were four high-backed office chairs set at intervals along the entire working area and one man sat in the centre of this array while another lay asleep on a camp bed tucked into the opposite corner.

John Grant, the CIA officer who, with two other agents, had assisted on the aircraft carrier, was in charge of monitoring what they had dubbed *Operation Curve*. This New York electronics room was capable of patching through a plethora of information between the various protagonists and Grant's team, which still sat tight with M's people on the Nimitz class carrier, now back and anchored off Treasure Island in San Francisco Bay.

It was Grant himself who was on duty and took the patched through call from Rushia.

'They're not boarding,' the Navy Intelligence man reported with unusual brusqueness.

'Yes, I know.' Grant was so clear on the secure line that it was difficult to believe that he was over three thousand miles away. 'We've got a van out at Kennedy. They've just reported in. The homers have moved down to the end of the walkway. There's also information concerning a private corporate jet parked off the end of the terminal spoke. Hang on, Rushia, there's something else coming in.'

Rushia waited, glancing back to the boarding gate for AA15. The line was moving and he would have to get a decision whether to board or not.

'Their luggage has been off-loaded from the American Airlines flight.' Grant's voice was a shade more tense.

'You've got guys in there?'

'We've got 'em everywhere . . .'

'Well, what do you want me to do? Go and grab a bagel, book a flight to Jallaboo or take the AA15?'

'They *have* to be heading this way. Take the AA and check in as soon as you reach SFO.' SFO is the airport designator code for San Francisco International.

Rushia signed off and ambled back to the gate while Grant continued to give instructions to the New York officer. 'You say the corporate jet's a Gulfstream II?'

'Grumman Gulfstream II, that's the jet version, in the livery of a corporation called Silver Service, Inc.'

'Okay, I'll start the checks on Silver Service. You get your hooks on to that corporate's flight plan and make damned certain he sticks to it. I don't care if you have to go through the military satellites, the COMSATS, anything, but I want that bird tracked through every cloud. I want to know if it wanders one degree off course and I want to know if the captain farts. You've got enough staff?'

'Only Dogface Two, and he did the day shift. I'm going to need about four extra sets of hands in here if we're to do the job right. We've sleeping facilities for eight so I figure that we're a tad undermanned.'

'You've got six extra pairs as from midnight. I'll see to it.' Grant shut down and made two rapid telephone calls, then left his own Number Two in charge – a former field agent built like the proverbial brick wash-house and known to all as Mac. In M's cabin, Grant found the old admiral talking with Bill Tanner and Franks. The doctor, Orr, and Q'ute had already left for London.

'Your man and the girl've been cut out by a couple of Brokenclaw's stalking-horses,' Grant announced.

'Serious?' M clamped his pipe firmly between his teeth.

'From the description, it's probably a Chinese heavy known as Bone Bender Ding who'd rip out his own mother's tongue if the money was right. The other's a little guy called Fox. Ex-Special Forces and answers to various nicknames – "Gory" Fox; "Fatal" Fox, take your pick; he's as pleasant as an asp in your pants.'

'You *do* have them under surveillance?'

'I'm having them tracked all the way sir. But I don't have to remind you what you already know of Brokenclaw Lee. He appears to have the ability to move entire mountains without anyone even noticing until it's done.'

M sucked at his pipe. 'Grant,' he tried to sound diffident, though it did not quite come off, 'we're damned grateful for what you fellows are doing, y'know. Damned grateful. Bond can be a difficult cuss at times, but he's my best agent. Nobody else can touch him when it comes to jobs like this.'

'And *this*,' Bill Tanner said quietly, 'is like old-fashioned intelligence work. I was just thinking that we desperately need agents to cope with the turmoil of transition in Europe, and here we are, half a world away, dealing with stolen plans. It's like a pre-World War I scenario.'

M made a noise which sounded like an embarrassed clearing of the throat. At the same time he glanced at Grant who was looking furtive. 'What's your Chief of Staff's clearance, sir?' he asked.

'Stratospheric, though I'd hoped to keep the darker side out of the way. You think it's gone too far for that now?'

'I think within forty-eight hours we'll know exactly how what you call the "darker side" is going to fall.'

Tanner was quite used to being educated further and given classified information long after an operation had begun to run. It was known in the trade as 'need-to-know'. 'There's more than just Lords and Lords Day?' he asked.

'Possibly, Tanner. Quite possibly. Though the Lords device is about as classified as anyone can get, because the whole safety of the United States' and our own fleets depends on it. I fear there's a lot of woolly-headed thinking going on about the world's future. The Forces of the Western Alliance have a long way to go yet. But, be that as it may, there *is* the possibility of a further threat connected with this man Brokenclaw Lee.'

Tanner steepled his fingers and waited. It was the old inter-rogator's technique, waiting things out until the suspect became talkative, uneasy with the silence.

At last, both M and Grant talked. When they had finished, Bill Tanner wished that his old friend Bond knew what he could be getting himself into. Calmly he put his thoughts into words.

'Oh, he knows.' M sounded like a man whose stocks had just fallen to an all-time low. 'Bond knows.' He cleared his throat again. 'Ahemm, but . . . well, the girl has no idea.' He tapped the desk with his fingertips, then spoke to Grant. 'The other girl, whatsername? Bradshaw?'

'Myra Bradshaw, yes. Our people are holding her in a place we keep for that purpose in Virginia. High up, overlooking the

Shenandoah Valley. She'll be safe enough and we can dry her out slowly. Just a pawn, I think.'

'And the attempted murder?'

'We have those guys – well, the FBI has them. Straight contract killers. Both known. Unlikely to talk. Come to that I doubt if they know who ordered the killing, and the thing that does surprise me is that it went ahead at all. You'd have thought Lee would've had surveillance on that apartment building.'

'Maybe he did,' Tanner mused. 'It's always possible that either he couldn't stop the attempted hit or he wanted it to go ahead simply to discourage others.'

'Mmmm,' Grant grunted.

Tanner still thought he would not like to be in Bond's shoes when there were so many imponderables.

The interior of the Grumman Gulfstream was luxurious even for a corporate jet. The passenger area was lined with a light-blue watered silk, and, while the normal configuration for a Gulfstream called for nineteen passengers, the interior of this particular aircraft had been drastically altered to take only eight. The seats were covered in soft grey leather and were on swivels which could be locked for take-off and landing. They were also high-backed with built-in headrests containing personal stereo headphones. On the right arm of these extravagant chairs was a bank of controls so that the seat could be adjusted to conform to any position, allowing the user maximum comfort.

Ding and Fox had shown nothing but courtesy to their charges who were asked to choose whatever seats they liked, while a young uniformed Chinese girl offered them drinks. There was no hint of threats, no indication of menace. 'Mr Lee wishes you to have the best he can offer,' the ugly-looking Bone Bender Ding smiled, nodding like a Buddha.

Bond and Chi-Chi chose seats together towards the back of the cabin. The stewardess brought a martini for Bond and a white wine spritzer for Chi-Chi. The martini was just as he had ordered it and prepared to his usual formula. 'Three measures of Gordons, one of vodka, half of Kina Lillet, shaken not stirred, until it's very cold. Then add a thin slice of lemon peel.' The Chinese girl merely smiled and bowed and he thought the chances of getting the real thing were pretty remote, but sure enough, when served, the martini passed even Bond's most exacting standards.

It was almost three-quarters of an hour later that they reached the threshold of the active runway and the captain announced that they should prepare for take-off. Already, Ding had come back from his seat in the forward part of the cabin and apologised for the hold up. 'Even Mr Lee cannot override the airport handling delays, I fear,' he said with a look which bade Bond not to be too irritated.

Finally the little executive jet hustled off the runway, pulled back into a rather extreme angle of climb and levelled off at somewhere in the vicinity of thirty-thousand feet, at which time the captain turned off the discreet 'seat belt' sign and the stewardess came back with a large menu.

'Please order anything,' she smiled and bowed her head. 'We have excellent chef on board.'

'Mr Lee certainly knows how to enjoy himself.' Bond leaned over and spoke softly to Chi-Chi, who looked at him and shrugged, 'Eat, drink and be merry for . . .'

'Don't finish it,' he said a little sharply. 'I'm not superstitious except for that little phrase and any quotations from William Shakespeare's Scottish play.'

'Scottish? Oh, you mean Mac . . .'

'No!' He laid a hand on her arm. 'Humour me, Jenny. These are my only superstitions.'

'You'll have to hear mine, one day,' she said. 'They outnumber yours a hundred to one. But this menu is splendid.'

'Let's hope the food's as good as the menu. While I was still at school, which was not for all that long, I made a vow that I would one day only allow the best food in the world to pass my lips.'

'Was it *that* bad? School, I mean.'

'On Fridays we had fish. It was known as the piece of cod that passeth all understanding.'

She gave a wan smile and buried her nose in the menu.

Chi-Chi ordered caviar followed by grilled *rognon de veau* with new potatoes and *petits pois*. 'I shall also make a pig of myself and have the *fraises des bois* with a great deal of cream,' she added with a cat-like smile.

Bond said he would join the lady with the caviar. 'But make certain there is a lot of toast.' He glanced at Chi-Chi. 'Good caviar is easy to come by. The trick is to get enough toast.' He then ordered lamb cutlets with the same vegetables as Chi-Chi. 'And while Madame is enjoying the strawberries, I'll have an avocado with a lot of French dressing – vinaigrette that is, not the pink stuff that sometimes passes for French dressing in this part of the world.'

The stewardess looked shocked. 'But, certainly, sir. It will be vinaigrette. There *is* no other kind of French dressing.'

The meal was extraordinarily good, Bond's cutlets being tender enough for him to cut with a fork alone, while the wines served with each course were, as he said later to Chi-Chi, 'Quite remarkable. There can't be many bottles of the Lafitte-Rothschild '47 left in the world.'

After dinner, Ding came back again to ask if there was anything else they needed. 'They're being a little overly solicitous, aren't they?' Chi-Chi whispered.

'Just a bit.' He hardly moved towards her, yet he spoke in almost a whisper. 'Don't worry, Jenny, I'm sure everything's going to be fine.' He looked down the cabin. Both Fox and the large Chinese seemed to be settling down to sleep.

Turning his head back to Chi-Chi, he suggested that they should also get some rest. 'We don't really know when we'll have a chance to sleep again.'

She merely nodded, not looking at him, and closed her eyes.

As he tried to catnap, Bond was aware of the aircraft doing a series of long, steady turns, as though it was under ATC instructions.

Just under seven hours after he had given instructions to the New York station on Lexington Avenue, Grant was called back to the makeshift communications room which the CIA had set up on the carrier. He had been down there for long periods in the interim, checking on the company called Silver Service. Now both M and his chief of staff accompanied him, arriving to find Mac hunched over the equipment, a series of maps spread out before him and headphones clamped over his ears. He hardly looked up when Grant tapped him on the shoulder and asked what was going on.

'Tell you in a minute, John.' Mac had pushed back the right side of the earphones, now he settled the headset back in place. He was repeating everything being relayed to him from New York.

'He's locked on to the Salinas VOR now, okay . . . ? Cleared by 117.3, okay . . . ? Yes! Yes, I know that's Salinas tower . . . Salinas tower, Gulfstream 44 landed. Okay, yes. Yes, get back if there's anything else. I don't suppose we have anyone out there to cover it. You might call the tower direct and find out. Yes. Good, then do it.' He pushed the headset back and swivelled his chair round to face Grant, M and Tanner.

'Well?' Grant asked.

'Clever. Very clever. His flight plan routed him to hit the coastline around forty miles south of SFO. About an hour ago he complained of turbulence at 31,000 and asked permission to descend to 20,000. Seemed okay, nothing unusual about that. Then, just before he reached the coast, he Maydayed. One engine overheating and losing altitude. No way could he make SFO, or so he said. SFO directed him to the only possible alternative.

Salinas. They landed about three minutes ago. You heard me tell the boys in NY to contact Salinas tower direct.'

Grant shook his head. 'All we can do is get Rushia and a team into a vehicle with tracking facilities and head out there to search for the homer signals.'

Tanner asked if they yet had information regarding the company with which the jet was registered.

Grant nodded. 'I was about to fill you in on that. Very solid little recording company. Specialise in heavy metal nine-day-wonder bands. A bit of an iffy set-up, but they're not breaking any laws. They'll sign up some greasy long-haired group who shove the decibel level to a point where it'll terminate pregnancy, then issue a couple of CDs which just make money for the company. Then they throw away the group, or band, or whatever they want to call it.'

'Exploitation?' M was asking if their FBI friends might get Silver Service on some exploitation law if necessary.

The CIA man shook his head. 'Doubt it. They also have around four to five *very* successful bands who make big money. Anyway, we don't know the tie-in yet. They own a small studio in New York and another in LA. New York's going to run a trace on the company. See who owns it, who's behind it. If their corporate jet takes Custodian and Checklist on a jaunt to meet Mr Lee, the betting's on Mr Lee holding a lot of stock in Silver Service, Inc.'

One of the telephones rang and Mac answered with a series of noncommittal grunts and sighs. 'Well, that just about settles it,' he said, not even looking at Grant as he cradled the instrument. 'Salinas tower says there was a damned great limo there within fifteen minutes of the Gulfstream landing. Carted the passengers away. They thought it was for another corporate they're expecting within the hour.'

'What about . . . ?'

Mac overrode Grant, 'The airplane? Salinas switched on every light they could to assist the landing. Seems their port engine *has* gotten problems. There was a lot of oil loss and smoke as they came in. They – Salinas tower – say there's no doubt it was a genuine emergency landing.'

Grant grunted. 'And I suppose they radioed for a limo while wrestling with the controls.'

'Bit fishy, eh?' from M.

'Like swimming in a vat full of tuna sandwiches.'

There had been absolutely no panic on board the Gulfstream when the emergency began. This was no reflection on anyone's bravery or courage, for the knuckle-dragging Bone Bender Ding had come to the rear of the cabin and told them that they might well experience some alarming manoeuvres within the next few minutes. 'We have a small piece of deception going on.' Ding's smile showed two rows of gold teeth and, Bond thought, a narrowing of the man's eyes which gave him an undeniably sinister look. The face said, 'I enjoy inflicting pain and death.'

'This is a precaution only.' The eyes had become very thin slits by now. 'There is a small possibility that your arrival in the country has been detected, so Mr Lee insists that we play a game in order to throw off any possible surveillance. You understand me, Mr Abelard?'

'I can only thank Mr Lee for his foresight and protection.'

Ding's smile spread wider across his face. 'You will be able to thank Mr Lee personally before long.'

During the twenty minutes or so that followed, they sat, seat belts fastened and the seats themselves locked into the upright position.

At last, Bond heard the whine and thump of the gear coming down and the captain's voice – strangely English – told them they should evacuate the aircraft from the rear door as soon as they came to a standstill.

They roared into a brilliantly lit small airfield and Bond fleetingly saw the name Salinas painted in black along the small clutch of buildings below the tower.

Things happened very quickly after that. Within seconds they were out of the plane – there was a lot of heavy black smoke surrounding the starboard engine – and Ding was urging them on, running towards the left of the buildings.

Bond saw that the crew members and the stewardess were leaving the airplane via the emergency hatch towards the nose, but, strangely, Fox had lagged behind as fire and emergency vehicles hee-hawed their way towards the Gulfstream.

Behind the small airport's limited buildings a black stretch limo had switched on its lights, moving slowly as though to intercept them.

'In!' Ding ordered. 'In quickly. Back of the limo! Now.'

Bond stood back allowing Chi-Chi to climb in and he followed, pushed from behind by Ding. 'Is okay,' the Chinese said to the uniformed driver through the sliding glass partition. 'Foxy coming with baggage. Only take three – four minutes.'

It seemed longer, but Fox appeared on a small electric baggage cart and the driver climbed down to help load the baggage into the trunk. Then with no further delay they were driven away, Fox joining the chauffeur up front, riding shotgun.

Once away from the immediate vicinity of the airport it became very dark and impossible for Bond to get any bearings.

'Long ride now. One-two hour.' Ding's voice came to them in the darkness. Something else accompanied the voice, making Bond's nose twitch. The massive Chinese had a bad case of body odour.

Blackness closed in and soon they were driving on winding narrow roads, climbing upwards through mountain country, Bond thought. Chi-Chi, he was pleased to note, had gone to sleep and shortly he felt her head fall softly against his shoulder.

The roads seemed to level out and they met only occasional cars coming from the opposite direction. Then a thin mist began to float in around them, the driver slowing and taking all sensible precautions.

The mist thickened from time to time, forming a wall from

which the headlights reflected, throwing their glare back into the rear of the limousine. It would thin out for a few miles, then, with no warning, suddenly appear ahead, almost an unearthly curtain of heavy greyness that made Bond turn away in a reflex. His intuition told him that they had gone north, then climbed to the west, finally turning back on a northerly heading. But nothing was certain because of the murkiness that had accompanied most of the drive.

Finally they were through the worst of the mist, though it still lay around them in small wispy pockets. The driver moved his right hand from the steering wheel and Bond saw him pick up a cellular telephone into which he spoke a couple of brief sentences.

He had hardly replaced the instrument when, from straight ahead, a sudden blaze of light exploded in the darkness. Some of the lights had an almost blinding effect as they seemed to be directly facing the car, but the driver did not slow or even falter.

Now the lights were all around them and Bond thought he could see the large bulk of a building. He did glimpse tall metal gates, open, flanked by high dark walls, then they were driving through what appeared to be a tunnel of trees. The white façade of a large house suddenly appeared in the headlights and a couple of seconds later the limo drew up under some kind of canopy. Ding was quickly out of the car, holding the door open for Chi-Chi who seemed dazed with sleep. Bond followed, his feet crunching on what he suspected was gravel, and they were hurried through a heavy, iron-bound door.

Before the door closed behind them, Bond could have sworn that he heard the sound of the sea in the distance and his nostrils twitched, sensing what he thought was the scent of the Pacific in his nostrils.

They were standing in a hallway which would not have been out of place in Bond's beloved western highlands of Scotland. For a fraction of a second, he realised that out there in the fog he had experienced the same tingling dreadful sensation which he had once had on a visit to Glencoe, the site of both the horrific massacre in 1692 and the birthplace of the father he had hardly known. But any further reflections were quickly banished.

They stood on a deep-pile carpet laid across a highly polished oak floor. A wide staircase faced them and oil paintings of rough and barren landscapes hung, one above the other, almost to the top of the high walls, which were covered with thick, heavily patterned paper of gold with a repetitive red design like a Greek urn. The staircase looked to be made of old mahogany, the bannister rail polished to the sheen of glass, as were the several doors which led off the hallway. From the ceiling a great heavy brass chandelier was suspended from a thick chain which must have hung down almost seventeen feet. The chandelier was circular and, at a rough guess, contained fifty electric candle bulbs. The instant impression was of being in a very old house, certainly older than anything Bond had ever seen in California, but the atmosphere was undeniably early seventeenth century, if not earlier. It also had the feel of a well-run house, for everything, from wood to the gilt picture frames down to the brass fittings, gleamed in the light.

All this was taken in as soon as the door shut, for hardly had the sound of its closing died away when one of the tall doors to the left opened.

'Peter Abelard, welcome. Was the surgery successful?' Bond recognised the identification code.

'Completely. I am a fully restored man.' It had gone through Bond's mind that the people in CELD had an odd Chinese sense of humour, considering the fact that the real Peter Abelard had been castrated in the twelfth century because of his love affair with Héloïse.

'And to you, Mrs Abelard, or do I call you Héloïse? Or simply Ms Mo?'

'Jenny will do . . .' Chi-Chi faltered, and no wonder.

Brokenclaw Lee seemed even taller and more imposing than when Bond had last seen him in Victoria. Now that he was close to the man, his features appeared to be more pronounced – the strange yet fascinating meld of Chinese and American-Indian bone structure and colouring. The voice was unchanged, soft, pleasant with a genuine welcoming quality. He wore dark trousers and a red, heavy velvet smoking jacket, while his face seemed to shine with no trace of stubble around the chin. Here was a man who knew he looked like a powerhouse, and so presented an image not only of authority but also of richness, from his clothes to his hair and the well-barbered chin.

'But come in, Peter, my dear fellow, and Jenny, come in, come in.' Without changing his pleasant tone, his eyes lifted behind Bond's shoulder as he spoke to Ding. 'We have something which needs your special talents, Ding. Unfortunate, but these things happen.' He continued to talk as they entered the large room from which he had emerged. It was like time travel, walking from the seventeenth century of the hall into a room of the present – tall, light and airy, decorated in light blues and creams, furnished with a stylish, almost Scandinavian touch.

'Peter, I'm so glad to see you and Jenny, but your arrival has coincided with a slightly unpleasant domestic problem. It would appear we have been harbouring some kind of spy in our midst. Ding, would you take her away and we'll deal with the matter in due course? I'm sure our guests will understand.' He turned towards Bond and Chi-Chi, his eyes dancing and his face composed, but as imposing a figure as ever. This one, Bond thought, would be very difficult to deceive. Then he looked across the room and froze.

At the far end, between two sets of heavy cream velvet drapes and below a large watercolour showing a lake and mountains in a gauzy mist, stood a large wood and metal chair on which a figure was slumped, the arms and feet shackled to the solid arms and legs of the chair.

'Take the wretched girl now, Ding.'

With a moan, the girl in the chair raised her head. Her face was covered with bruises. There was blood around her mouth and one eye had been closed. It was Wanda Man Song Hing, whom Bond had last seen in M's cabin on the carrier.

11

WELCOME

The arrivals terminal of San Francisco International can be a crowded and confusing place to the uninitiated, but at a quarter to one in the morning, Ed Rushia wished the place was seething with people coming in from half-a-dozen flights, not merely the two hundred or so from American Airlines 15. He was, as they used to say in his home town of Jewel Junction, Iowa, between a rock and a hard place.

First, his job had been to watch Bond's and Chi-Chi's backs. They had disappeared into the night on some little corporate jet, so how should he now proceed? Second, he had, like his British colleague, been set up – the target for FBI scrutiny. There were good reasons for this, no doubt, but he felt uneasy about it.

He came into the ground side of the terminal carrying the small bag containing one change of clothing, his toilet gear and a paperback that he had tried to read during the boring flight. Better to travel light. After all he was now back in his home base and could change properly if they ever allowed him to make it back to the small apartment in which he lived. His young wife would be there waiting for him, probably worrying herself sick about him, even though she was used to his long absences.

There was one uniformed cop near the sliding glass exit doors, and Rushia made up his mind within seconds of walking into the street side of the terminal. Get a cab, go down to the Embarcadero, then call the carrier from there.

Outside it was chilly, the usual dampness in the air at this time of year. There was a short line for cabs and he quickly joined it, aware, with that instinct bred into good Intelligence officers, that someone had come up behind him, from the rear, as though he had been waiting for his arrival.

'Indexer?' a voice said softly in his ear.

'You talking to me?' He turned his head and saw the face belonged to a youngish man who looked uncertain and anxious, his eyes darting everywhere.

'We'll take the cab together. They want to see you. The operation's bust wide open.'

Rushia grunted.

'If you want sleep, I wouldn't bank on getting much tonight.' The stranger smiled happily, as though thinking that if he had to go for a couple of nights without sleep, why should he be concerned about others having to do the same?

There was no conversation as the cab took them through the night streets, across to the Naval facility. From there they travelled out to the carrier by helicopter. Twenty minutes later, Commander Ed Rushia stood in the makeshift CIA control and communications room aboard the ship. Much had altered since he had last been aboard. More communications and electronic gear appeared to have been installed and there was a new tension among the men who were controlling *Operation Curve* from this floating airbase.

He was also surprised when M, not the CIA Officer in charge, gave him the briefing, running through the events which had occurred by the time he arrived.

'To be honest, we haven't a clue where Checklist and Custodian have been taken.' The Old Man looked more grizzled and tired than during the previous meeting. A large scale map was lowered in front of him, sandwiched between a pair of heavy plastic plates. The surface of the plastic was covered in lines and circles marked in various colours.

'We know they managed somehow to stage an emergency right at a point which made Salinas their only possible alternate.'

He raised a pointer to show the small airfield. 'Once there, the local people were convinced it was a genuine problem. They also reported that a limousine picked up at least three, possibly four, passengers. The Gulfstream's captain, his second officer, a steward and a chef are still at Salinas waiting for mechanics to arrive from their home base which apparently is Los Angeles. We've flown out a CIA officer posing as an FAA inspector to try and get more firm explanations. He'll interrogate the crew, but they're probably just going to tell us they were obeying orders.

'Now if our two people were moved from Salinas by limo, we figure they could have been taken anywhere within a forty mile radius. They could also be back here in the Bay area. We do know the homers they had concealed on them were still operating in New York. We can but presume they're still sending signals, but these could be weakened if they're hidden among buildings. Mr Grant'll tell you what we feel should be done.'

Grant also looked tired and washed out. 'It is true they might well have been brought back into the Bay area,' he began, 'but it seems far more likely that they've been taken to some kind of safe house outside the immediate vicinity. If I were a betting man, I'd say the natural place is somewhere near Big Sur. We now have six electronics vehicles square-searching the Bay area, tuned to the homer frequency. As you tracked them some of the way in New York, we're putting you in a helicopter at first light. The chopper's being fitted with a pretty powerful array at this moment. You'll scan an area of forty by forty miles with Big Sur as the furthest western point.'

'You got a chopper that'll do that?' Rushia growled, poker-faced. 'Forty by forty comes to around sixteen hundred square miles in my book, leastways it used to, though I haven't any idea what it might work out if you went metric. I mean . . .'

'Ed,' Grant's voice exuded enormous patience, 'there will be refuelling points. The crew will be experienced in square searches, so leave all that to them. You just sit there and twiddle the buttons, trying to get a fix on one or both of the homers. Okay?'

'Time was when Homer was all Greek to me.'

They gave him a spare cabin and he drifted off into an uneasy sleep. At one point he dreamed of his childhood in Jewel Junction and thought he heard his father calling him to get out of bed. 'The doctor's nearly ready, Ed. Come on!' But he woke to find one of the CIA juniors shaking him and saying, 'It's past five thirty. The chopper's nearly ready, Ed. Come on!'

He rolled out of the bunk, washed and shaved, then drank scalding coffee brought to him together with hot cornbread rolls and butter in little foil packets. 'And I expected butter in a lordly dish,' he said quietly to himself. Then he thought of his wife and muttered, 'Well, she's a lordly dish and no mistake.' Good ole Ed Rushia, he reflected, just keep up the homespun, a bit eccentric cover and everyone'll treat you right.

In the helicopter crew room, they gave him warm flying clothes and a heavy white rollneck sweater. He put the big protective helmet on and thought he must look like a Martian, but once inside the helicopter, in front of the scopes and scanning equipment, the good ole boy in Commander Edwin Rushia drained away like sand in an eggtimer and he became totally focused on finding Chi-Chi and Bond.

James Bond's eyes snapped open, and he came from deep sleep to full consciousness in a matter of seconds. Silently he cursed, knowing he had done the unforgivable and dropped asleep when he should have been keeping watch.

It was four thirty in the morning, and already traces of dawn had started to show through the drapes on the two high, arched windows. With his waking, alertness returned and the memories of the previous night came hustling into his mind sharp and clear.

On the other side of the bed, Chi-Chi slept, curled on one side with her face turned away from the two pillows that lay down the length of the bed between them. He smiled. That was about the only bright recollection from a few hours ago. His first real thought was of Wanda.

'What kind of spy?' he had asked of Brokenclaw as Ding strutted across the room, undid the shackles and hoisted the girl over his shoulder like a butcher carrying the carcass of a beast. There had been a little moan from Wanda and a tiny smear of blood had spotted the back of Ding's jacket.

'The kind of spy that neither you nor I wish even to know of our existence,' Lee shrugged. There was neither anger nor foreboding in his voice which remained even and soft. 'Her father owed money to one of my gambling houses. He sought to buy his own freedom from debt by giving me his daughter as a plaything. In China it would be taken as giving me her hand in marriage; in my other life, it would be to add more women to my teepee. Now I fear her father will have to pay in full.'

'But, the girl, what was she up to?'

Brokenclaw made a gentle gesture, raising his right hand as though to dismiss the whole business. 'I knew she was in the US Navy. What I did not know was that she belongs to Naval Intelligence . . .'

'Oh, my God!' Bond feigned extreme agitation.

'Oh, my God, indeed. They have a whole operation dedicated to finding those who have given me the information you are to carry back to Beijing. It seems they are desperate. Already she's told me British Intelligence is involved.'

'Then we must . . .'

'We must remain calm and enjoy ourselves. Forgive me, I am being a bad host. Can I offer you anything? Food? Drink?'

Bond looked at Chi-Chi. 'I think you can possibly offer rest. Both of us are tired.'

'Of course, your journey has been long and arduous. I'll personally show you to your suite. You can sleep late tomorrow, then we can deal with the information you have to smuggle back to Beijing Hsia. Personally, I'm going to be a little busy for a few more hours. We really have to be more sophisticated with the interrogation of the girl.' He shook his head sadly. 'Nothing is ever really accomplished by mere crude brutality.'

'You should dump the oily piece of female rubbish in San Francisco Bay.' Chi-Chi spoke with venom, bringing a tone of genuine distaste into her voice.

'Ah, Jenny Mo, or is it really Argentbright? An odd name. You might have done such a thing at the old Legation, but we are trying to be more economic these days. She is a beautiful girl, therefore she can be used; she can make money for us. We will simply suck her dry of all she knows about this operation against us, then put her to work in which she excels. It can be all so simple. I have learned that nothing should be wasted if it can be recycled. This also applies to people.' He extended his hands to both of them. 'Come, I'll show you to your suite. Tomorrow we will go over the information, and make arrangements for its safe transference back to Beijing Hsia, before we begin the real work. Come.'

He strode, not to the door through which they had entered from the hallway, but to a smaller exit which stood in the right-hand wall between high pine bookcases. They discovered that the door led to a short, brilliantly lit, passage, then in turn to narrow stairs which ran down some fourteen feet under the house. There were corridors to left and right and the walls were hung with both Chinese and American Indian art. Brokenclaw took them past the first bisecting corridors and stopped at a door which he opened, standing back to allow his guests to enter a large suite of rooms furnished in almost overpowering modern luxury.

The main room contained a large leisure complex which took up almost an entire wall – a large screen TV, stereo equipment and video machine set into shelves which appeared to have been sculpted rather than built, the shelves and equipment all in a light grey which reflected the general decor of the entire room, light greys and whites. There were soft leather armchairs, a large glass table, the thick, tinted glass resting on two long drums of marble. Everything from cushions to the telephone were what is known as state-of-the-art – a term which made Bond wince, but he winced easily at many other cumbersome assaults on the English language, such as 'at this moment in time' or 'take on board', and appalling new words like 'mindset'.

The bedroom was decorated in the same shades, but here they took on an almost feminine lushness. A tall four-poster, hung with lace and frills, matched the gauze-thin curtains falling in swirls almost from the ceiling to the floor. Their luggage was placed neatly on folding racks near a long walk-in closet which took up an entire wall. Underfoot it felt as though you might have to cut your way through the carpet with a machete. The bathroom, which Brokenclaw showed them with some pride, was marble and gold with a massive whirlpool bath as the centre-piece.

Chi-Chi gasped.

'I designed this guest suite myself,' Brokenclaw purred, 'like many other things in this house. The refrigerator is well stocked and there is fresh fruit on the table there. Now I trust you will sleep well. When you wake, simply press nine on any of the telephones and order what you will.'

Bond followed him into the main room, and at the door Brokenclaw smiled his friendly all-embracing beam. 'If you require any stimulation,' he came close, his voice dropping to a whisper, 'just press the button marked M on the bed console. It unveils a superb set of mirrors over the bed.' He winked, and, for a moment, the proud face became that of a lecherous school-boy.

When the door was closed, Bond walked around examining the TV and stereo equipment, then, as though he had suddenly had a thought, he went over to the telephone and ripped a sheet from its small message pad. At the big glass table, he swiftly scribbled a note, taking it straight through to Chi-Chi who he found had started to experiment with the many bottles of scents, bath oils and the like. He pursed his lips, handing the slip of paper to her. 'Just a note regarding the cameras. We'll have to ask Mr Lee about them in the morning.'

She nodded after reading it, then tore it up and flushed it away in the bathroom, giving him a look as if to say, 'I'm not a fool, not even a trained fool.'

Bond nodded, and they began to talk of the imagined journey from China to Hong Kong, then of the arrival in New York and their time with Myra.

'What a highly strung girl she is.' Chi-Chi was starting to undress. 'As highly strung as I will be if I don't get some rest. I'm going to take a shower and go straight to bed, darling, or I'll be no good for anything in the morning.'

Bond nodded. 'I'll go and take a quick brandy, then join you.'

'There's to be no *joining* tonight, my dear!' Chi-Chi gave him a coquettish look that spoke volumes. 'And isn't Mr Lee a nice man? No wonder Beijing Hsia thinks so well of him,' she played to the hidden microphones, and went on undressing as though it were the most natural thing in the world. Bond's note had warned her of possible *son et lumière*. Brokenclaw Lee, he thought, was the kind of man who would have a room wired not only as a safety precaution, but also to amuse the voyeuristic traits in his own make-up.

'Magnificent man,' he answered, sweeping the bedroom with his eyes, trying to figure where the cameras were hidden. Then he went into the main room, poured himself a liberal glass of brandy and sat down in one of the comfortable leather armchairs. Bond was a man who detested all the phoney mumbo-jumbo that sometimes goes on when you order brandy in restaurants. The business of warming vast glasses had nothing to do with the taste of good brandy.

He allowed the liquid to stay in his mouth for a second before swallowing the first sip. It always did him good, focused the mind. At this moment all he could think of was Dr Johnson's famous remark, 'Claret is the liquor for boys; port for men; but he who aspires to be a hero must drink brandy'. Well, Bond did not aspire to be a hero, it was just something that came with the job.

He took ten minutes over the drink, his eyes lazily inspecting the main room for signs of hidden cameras, not that it would be much use nowadays with the advent of fibre-optics, but his main concern was keeping the ASP 9mm hidden when he undressed.

Back in the bedroom, Chi-Chi seemed to have dealt with her shower in record time, for she appeared to be fast asleep, bundled cosily in the bed, all the lights off except for a dimmed reading lamp on the side left unoccupied.

He tiptoed through to the bathroom, removing his jacket and at the same time extracting the automatic. Covering it with the clothing, he placed it carefully on one of the pair of bathroom chairs. Swiftly he stripped, showered, dried himself and put on the towelling robe that hung ready for him. A chute was set into the wall with a notice telling guests to put any washing into it. The clean laundry would be returned within an hour. He also caught sight of a piece of torn paper lying by one of the soap dishes. The paper had a swiftly scrawled message on it which he did not stop to read.

He picked up his clothes and carried them back to the bedroom, slipping the pistol into the robe pocket under cover of the clothing which he now carefully hung on a patent press. He then unpacked his shaving gear and took it, with his soiled clothing, back into the bathroom, dumping the clothes into the chute. In doing so, he palmed the note and swiftly read it.

Chi-Chi had written—

> I will stay awake for one hour, then wake you. We can do one hour on and one off to be sure of no nasty surprises. Don't be cross about the pillows. I read about it once. I think it's called 'bundling'. Love xx

He smiled to himself, disposed of the note, then went back into the bedroom and took off the robe, placing it on the bed so that the pocket with the automatic was close, then slid between the covers.

Chi-Chi had placed three pillows down the centre of the bed, separating them. He wondered where she had read about bundling. As he recalled, it was an old custom in Wales and, he thought, New England. In houses where a courting couple could find no corner to be alone to discuss their future, their families would allow them to use the one large bed for an hour or two – fully dressed – with the bed divided by a long, and usually solid, bolster to prevent matters from going too far.

He fell asleep almost immediately. Chi-Chi woke him gently after what appeared to have been about five minutes. He lay in the dark, glancing at the illuminated face of his watch from time to time, but – unusual for him – sleep had overtaken him. But now he was awake and alert, not knowing what might have happened during the hours of darkness.

His mind roved around the previous day's experiences, in particular the virtuoso manner in which Brokenclaw had outsmarted any possible surveillance on them by switching to the corporate jet and the 'emergency' landing at Salinas. Had his companions controlling the operation from the carrier been able to keep watchers on them the whole time? He suspected not, and wondered where they had now placed Ed Rushia, the closest backup. Then there was Wanda and the interrogation which might easily have taken place overnight. Bond was convinced that Brokenclaw had no idea that his guests were not Peter Argentbright and Jenny Mo, straight out of Beijing Hsia. He knew that Hsia, the way they pronounced it, stood for 'cage'. Other pronunciations turned the word into 'control' or 'to govern'. Further variations meant 'artful' or 'clever'. He could only presume that the term meant CEDL headquarters in Beijing, just as the facilities in and around Moscow, used by KGB, were known as Moscow Centre.

So Brokenclaw had welcomed them as the real thing on their arrival, but Bond was concerned. It might not take very long to break Wanda. Then the dragon would be truly out of the cave. The way Brokenclaw Lee had spoken could mean only one thing – deep interrogation, and the Chinese were past masters at that. Indeed, the Chinese had written the book on Thought Reform as they liked to call the techniques of control. Interrogation was simply an extension of Thought Reform, now honed to a fine art, with the use of drugs and other chemicals.

He stared up at the ceiling, gradually getting more clear as a new day came over the Eastern horizon, and, unbidden, another of Brokenclaw's lines from the night before came back with stunning suddenness. 'Tomorrow,' the big Chinese Indian had said, 'we will go over the information and make arrangements for its safe transference back to Beijing Hsia, *before we begin the real work.*'

M and Franks had warned him of the possibility of this *real work*, but he was certain Chi-Chi had no knowledge of it. The thing had been one of the imponderables.

After another ten minutes' thought, Bond decided he should make a reconnaissance – find out where they really were.

Quietly he got out of bed, picked up the robe which contained the automatic, collected a clean shirt, socks and underwear from his case and went into the bathroom.

He shaved, showered, vigorously towelled himself and dressed, using clothing, as before, to effect the transfer of his pistol to its normal position behind his right hip.

In the main room he wrote a short note in full view of any cameras that might be watching. It was addressed to Jenny and merely said he had gone out to find their generous host.

She still slept peacefully, and he placed the note on the side table, where she would see it as soon as she woke.

Back in the main room, he was walking towards the door when another thought struck him. Turning, he retraced his steps, going to the high main windows, feeling around under the drapes for a tassel, then pulling. They swept silently back, and the sunlight of a beautiful morning stabbed into the room.

He turned and peered out, then took a couple of paces back, not believing what he could see.

They had landed at Salinas and driven for an hour and a half, two hours maximum, therefore they had to be in California and quite close to San Francisco. Yet he was looking out on a formal garden laid out with conifers and roses. At the limit of the garden, a meadow sloped away. There were horses grazing peacefully, and the ground dipped to a densely wooded area, where the lush trees rose to a skyline that could not possibly be in California. For he recognised it, both from photographs and from the memory of seeing it at close quarters himself some years ago.

How could he be in California when he was looking out at the unmistakable Blue Ridge Mountains of Central Virginia?

12

CHINESE BOXES

Bond just stood at the window, actually rubbing his eyes, not believing the unexpected view. It was unmistakable, even to the distinctive blue haze which gives that particular chain of mountains its name. He frowned, trying to think logically. They had entered the house at the front directly into the ground floor, and gone into Lee's study. From there they had been taken *down* to the guest suite. He remembered counting the stairs, and worked out that they were at least fourteen feet below the ground. So, unless the house was built on the split-level principle, there should be no view at all from these windows.

Turning, Bond walked quickly to the door, opening it to find his clean laundry, carefully wrapped, reposing on a small folding stool. He paused to pick it up, leaving it in the bedroom before returning to the corridor to retrace their footsteps up the stairs and into Brokenclaw's study.

The sunlight streamed into this room also, and there was the same view. The Blue Ridge. No argument. Yet something worried him. Either his eyesight was playing tricks or the glass in the windows did something to the peripheral vision. He stepped back to take a look from well inside the room.

'So you're an early riser also. A lovely morning, Peter, eh? You like the view we have from here? Spectacular, isn't it?' Lee had emerged from a door to his left.

'Incredible!' Bond heard the note of surprise and bafflement in his own voice.

Brokenclaw gave a low chuckle. 'I did not expect to find you about yet. You should have slept, rested.'

'Jenny is still asleep.'

'Well, come and breakfast with me. You hail from an old British family, I understand, so you'll enjoy my breakfast ritual here.'

Bond was ushered through the door to his left, conscious that it also stood between bookcases and was directly opposite the door which led down to the guest suite and its many corridors.

This door also led to a similar short passageway, then down a long flight of steps. He was convinced that they were going below ground. Then Brokenclaw opened a door at the foot of the stairs on the right, and Bond found himself in a long, low dining room. The floor was made up of polished boards which looked very old, the walls were panelled, and the ceiling appeared to be held in place by great beams, again old and irregular. The furniture was Jacobean, Bond would have staked money on it. A polished table with at least thirty matching chairs took up the centre of the room, while along one wall stood a tall, elaborately carved chest, which served as a sideboard. On the chest were silver chafing dishes, and the table was laid for three.

In the wall opposite the long tall chest gaped an open fire-place, complete with its iron basket and a set of fire tongs, poker and shovel. Above the fireplace hung the only picture in the room – a large engraving showing, as it said in lettering inside an ornamental oval at the top of the picture, the *Great Frost Fair on the Thames in London, 1683–4*.

Two mullioned windows, leaded, with diamond-shaped panes, gave light from the far end of the room, and even from just inside the doorway, Bond could see the view was of the same Blue Ridge Virginian mountains.

Brokenclaw stood by the makeshift sideboard, plate in hand. 'Come, Peter Abelard, there are good things here – bacon, saus-age, eggs, kedgeree. All you would expect in an old English country house.'

There was a knock at the door and an emaciated-looking Chinese entered, carrying a large tray loaded with two silver coffee pots, sugar basin and cream jug.

'Ah, Peter, this is one of the few trusted men I allow to come here. He is known as Frozen Stalk Pu – a reference, I believe, to his amazing virility. He does not look much, but I do assure you he can do things to men that would turn your hair grey. This is Mr Abelard, Pu.'

Frozen Stalk Pu gave a little bow, placed the tray on the table and retired.

At Brokenclaw's pressing invitation, Bond helped himself to bacon and two eggs. It was not his usual, or indeed favourite breakfast, but eating with the man might solve some of the puzzles.

Brokenclaw had seated himself at the head of the table, and as Bond took the place to his right, Frozen Stalk Pu entered silently, placing two large racks of toast in front of each of them.

'You are quite a legend at Beijing Hsia,' Bond began. 'They say that you are half Chinese and half Blackfoot Indian. Can this be true?'

Lee swallowed a mouthful of food, nodding. 'It is true. What some people do not realise is that my ancestry is almost royal, on both sides – Chinese and Blackfoot.' He continued, telling the same story that Bond had heard in the museum of British Columbia.

As Bond had experienced at the first hearing of the story, there was something almost hypnotic about the way Brokenclaw spoke. Then he noticed two other things – when he sat close, watching Lee eat, the strange twisted hand became more apparent, also the tale of his mixed ancestry was repeated as though learned by heart. He recalled a remark Lee had made in Victoria – 'I have heard it said,' Bond clearly recalled the almost conspiratorial smile which had crossed his face, 'I have heard it said that I am a fraud, that I have invented these stories, that I am nothing more than the child of some itinerant Chinese tailor and a Blackfoot girl who sold her body in Fort Benton. None of this is true.'

As he remembered this, Brokenclaw repeated those same words, as though they were a ritual part of his story, learned and programmed into his mind.

Bond nodded. 'You are, obviously, rightly proud of your heritage, Mr Lee. You've certainly proved that to those of us who work in Beijing Hsia. But what of your Blackfoot ancestors? Do you still maintain contact?'

Lee nodded. 'Most certainly. I doubt if I could live with myself if I did not spend time among my other people. I need to recharge my batteries like the next man. There are members of the old Blackfoot Confederacy who live apart. High in the Chelan Mountains, in Washington State, there is a peaceful camp where they live out their lives in the old way. I go there often. I like to breathe the smoke from my teepee, reflect on life, talk to my ancestors. Few people know I visit this camp, but I can tell you that those quiet tranquil people would fight to the death for me because I am one of them and I have relatives among them.'

He stopped abruptly and went on eating until Bond, changing the conversation, asked if there were any worries about the girl, Wanda.

He shook his head. 'Not exactly worries. But I have to admit we did not get very far with her. She is well trained. I've had her taken away so that we can work on her at our leisure. But it is clear they know certain things. For instance, they know I have precious information regarding this new piece of technology which can detect any kind of submarine over vast distances and at great depths. They know that you and Jenny are either coming, or have come, to this country as couriers. This is why, my dear Peter, we really have to get all that business cleared away quickly. Today if possible.'

'Hung Chow H'ang briefed us about this amazing coup you

have pulled off. How did you manage to infiltrate their scientific team?'

Lee's smile was the sly look of one who has been very clever. 'I did not infiltrate. Setting up and putting in penetration agents is too time-consuming, too drawn out. I preferred the more simple approach.'

'Oh?' He knew his query sounded genuine enough.

'I merely kidnapped some of their key people and had them interrogated. *Those* men – US Navy personnel – are not brave, nor do they have the mental defences like, say, the clever Wanda. It was like stealing candy from a baby.'

'Kidnapped them?'

'A very simple business. Yes.'

'Kidnapped, interrogated and then disposed of?'

'No, Peter.' He sounded quite shocked. 'You only dispose of people who cannot be recycled. Remember? I have these officers here, in this place, just in case we have further need of them. Mind you, there might well come a point when we have to think seriously about their futures. But we have everything, even though our final ploy – an attempt to bring their leading scientist here – did not quite work out. He was required for corroboration only. We have the goods, Peter. Incidentally, have you brought the money?'

'I have the means to collect it.'

The smile faded on Brokenclaw's face. 'The means? I understood from Beijing Hsia that you would bring it with you.'

Bond slowly shook his head. 'That is not quite how we work. My instructions are to let Jenny check over the information and, providing she is satisfied, turn it into microdots which I shall personally return to Beijing Hsia. While she does the complicated photography, I go and collect the money. Or, at least I hope I can collect the money. You see, sir, I understood we were to operate with you in the San Francisco area. Looking from the windows this morning, I'm not certain that I know where we are.'

Brokenclaw Lee threw back his head and gave a huge laugh, his burly shoulders shaking with mirth. 'Ah, it works,' he still chuckled. 'It always works on strangers, and it is all part of my methods for avoiding detection. They say that Brokenclaw Lee can come and go as he pleases, he can make himself invisible and fly away like an eagle. Yes, Peter Abelard, or Argentbright, come with me and let me show you. Come to these windows here.' He rose and led the way across to the leaded mullion windows at the end of the room.

Bond joined him and looked out on the sweeping expanse of the Virginian Blue Ridge. Occasionally he detected movement, a car's windshield reflecting sunlight. Also the sun had begun to shift, moving higher.

'You see Virginia, yes?' He could feel Brokenclaw's smile.

'Of course.'

'Let me show you something else.'

Bond was aware of the big man's hand moving to a point in the panelling between the two windows. There was a click and he glanced down to see that a small console with knobs, buttons and switches had slid from the wall. 'Keep looking,' said Brokenclaw.

Outside, there was a sudden darkening of the day, as though the sun had gone behind thick cloud, then he saw the clouds themselves, drawing in, covering the landscape until it was as black as night. Lights twinkled in the far distance, then there was complete darkness. It was an eerie experience.

Then, just as the night had come quickly across the view so there were streaks of pink on the horizon, washing the sky with light. A new dawn was coming up, but with unusual speed, and, as the daylight returned, Bond realised that they were not looking at the Blue Ridge Mountains any more.

He gasped audibly, for they now stood at these leaded windows looking out across London – *his* London, only it was not *his* London, but a London of an earlier time, the London reflected in the engraving over the fireplace. A London of the seventeenth century, complete in all its perspective, real enough to touch; there was even movement on the Thames which seemed to be flowing almost past the house.

'You like that little trick? My time and place machine?' Brokenclaw was fiddling with the buttons again, and in seconds the view of the Blue Ridge Mountains reappeared. The sense of time, place and dimension was startling.

'How?' Bond asked.

Brokenclaw laughed. 'How? Oh, with a great deal of technology.'

He began to explain to Bond that they were in fact within a house that did not exist at all.

'But I saw it. I saw its bulk last night when we arrived.'

'You saw *a* house. But not *this* house. Did you notice the name of the company on whose executive jet you travelled?'

'Silver something . . .'

'Silver Service.' Chi-Chi, dressed in a robe, had entered, Frozen Stalk Pu at her elbow.

'Lady walk about. I bring her straight to you,' Pu said.

'Good,' Brokenclaw gave another of his beaming smiles. 'Go and bring coffee and more toast for the lady, Pu. You will take breakfast, Jenny? Yes, I may call you Jenny?'

'Of course, and of course. I guess I must be disorientated. I could have sworn I saw the Blue Ridge Mountains from the windows of the guest suite.'

'Come on in, darling.' Bond crossed to her, kissing her cheek. 'I left you to sleep.'

'And I awoke and found you gone. So I came looking.'

'Just in time. Mr Lee has been explaining why you can see the Blue Ridge, but I still don't understand him. He says we are in a house that does not exist.'

'Silver Service, Inc. That was on the side of the Gulfstream,' she said, as though contributing something of immense value. 'Am I right?'

'Completely.' Brokenclaw was still smiling the sly, want-to-know-a-secret smirk. 'Silver Service, Inc. is a company which can never, never in a hundred years be tied to me. I own it, naturally, but nobody can ever prove that, if only because my name does not appear in any of its records. Like a number of companies I own, much is done on trust. Trust, and, well, I suppose you could say, fear.'

They moved back to the table as Frozen Stalk reappeared, carrying fresh coffee and toast. Lee gave orders to have the chafing dishes checked and asked what Ms Mo would like to eat. She said that toast would be just fine. 'Toast and some preserves.'

They all took more coffee and, when Pu had left, Brokenclaw carried on his explanation.

'The house you caught a glimpse of in the early hours of this morning, certainly exists. Silver Service, Inc. makes compact disks – for the young market, for those who have to have loud, discordant music with unbelievable lyrics. The company manages to get through about forty new bands in a year. The run-of-the-mill bands do not last long. However, it also owns, lock, stock, barrel, electronic keyboards and drum machines, four bands who manage to keep turning out albums which please their public so much that they make millions of dollars a year – millions for themselves and millions for Silver Service. The house you saw last night belongs to that company, who rents or sells it to members of one or another of the bands in vogue. If it has been sold, then the company simply buys it back when the band ceases to be financially viable. At the moment, it belongs to a young man called Halman, an odd name and I think not his own, Marty Halman, drummer for a band called Ice Age. He lives in that house, often with several concubines, and a very expensive and serious nasal habit. I believe he's in residence at the moment, and I fear that Ice Age, who have been chart-toppers for nearly eighteen months, will soon be no more. But, while they last, they make a great deal of money. When they are gone, the house will be bought – I use the word loosely – by another member of one of Silver Service's top groups, or bands.

'The house has appeared during TV interviews; it's even been raided by the police – that was before Mr Halman moved in. It is secluded, though within easy reach of San Francisco. Why, we even moved out the unrepentant Wanda to Sausalito in the early hours of this morning.'

'But we came in through a great iron-bound door into that magnificent hall,' Bond protested. Already he had some inkling of what Brokenclaw was telling them, but he would play the naive, amazed member of the audience if only to humour the magician.

'And if you went to find that door, you would merely see part of Mr Halman's end wall, with no windows, just the gable end. Of course, the door is there, and I can make it appear at the press of a button, but it is covered by steel and brick. A great slab of steel with a brick façade. A press of the button and the slab moves outwards and upwards. Rarely do we open that entrance during the daytime. We have other exits at the end of each of the long corridors underground.'

'But the hallway, and . . .' Bond continued to play being baffled.

'The hallway exists, but the stairs lead to nowhere. The hallway and my study both exist, but they are as Chinese boxes within the strongly built house where Mr Halman resides. In other words, they are surrounded by quite a large portion of the building you saw last night. The main house is a great deal larger than our false hallway and my study. In fact, by the use of great construction skills, it is almost impossible to detect that our hallway and my study are within the house at all. They are bounded by corridors of their own, even moderately sized servants quarters, and, with some cleverly placed false windows, it would take even a very experienced architect a great deal of time to discover there is "missing space", as we call it, within the main house.

'The rest of *my* building is underground. The views from the windows are achieved with great technical skill. Within the box, that is part of the house, there is a cyclorama, and our somewhat large and expensive home underground is also surrounded by a similar cyclorama. You know what a cyclorama is, Peter?'

'Yes. A device usually found in theatres.'

'A curved screen. A large structure. In this case a very large, long curved screen made of cement and covered with the same material used for making wide screens in movie houses.'

'So those incredible views are somehow projected on . . . ?' Bond began.

'In simple, laymen's terms, yes.' Now Brokenclaw was smiling like an indulgent parent. 'But there's a great deal more to it than that. The detail and movement are recorded by what is a further step in laser technology. You know of the laserdisk principle, I presume?'

They both nodded, Bond thinking that this set-up alone must have cost millions.

'Well, what you see when you look from the windows and the system is running is really a super, three-dimensionalised laser-disk throwing the images, in great clarity, and in three dimensions on to the cyclorama. If you bothered to stand there for a long time, possibly with a stopwatch, you would see almost the same cycle repeated – car movements, cattle and horses grazing – about once every two hours. However, there are further enhancements. The projections at dusk and dawn can be changed to conform to fifty-nine different patterns, while we can pick random sequences which will alter the weather over a twenty-four hour period. The whole is, naturally, computer controlled.'

'Naturally,' Bond murmured.

'It is all very effective, and I do have some specialised tricks – like the one you saw of seventeenth-century London, Peter.'

'Oh, I'd like to see that.' Chi-Chi was as fascinated as Bond by the idea of a house underground, below two areas that were virtually Chinese boxes within the main structure. Brokenclaw could, of course, come and go as he pleased if this place was his central headquarters.

'Well, I'll show it to you, Jenny.' Brokenclaw rose, obviously enjoying the display. But, as he stood, there was a brisk knocking at the door.

'Come,' he called, as pleasantly as ever.

Bone Bender Ding stood in the doorway. 'We have the spy bitch's father here, sir.' His face was wreathed in the most unpleasant gold-toothed grin that Bond had seen for a long time.

Brokenclaw turned to Bond and Chi-Chi, 'Please excuse me, this will not take long. Just eat your breakfast and I'll show you how we discourage people from turning against us. Bring him in,' he ordered, his voice giving no sign of anger.

Tony Man Song Hing, for they knew immediately who this man must be, was almost hurled into the room, falling in front of Brokenclaw sprawling on his knees. He was out of breath and there was a fresh, bloody bruise on the right side of his cheek. He was a small man and next to Brokenclaw he seemed even smaller.

'Tony, I am very disappointed with you.' It could not have been a more pleasant tone.

'What . . . ? I don't understand . . . Why . . . ? What have I done . . . ?' the words tumbled from the little man, his voice rising in panic.

'What have you done? You're trying to tell me you don't know?'

'Of course I don't know. I don't owe you money any more; we settled that ten days after . . .'

'Ten days after you so kindly presented me with your beautiful daughter, yes. I thanked you then, Tony Man Song Hing. Now, it is time to curse you.'

'If she has not pleased you . . .'

'Oh, she pleased me for a time. Then we discovered that she had a small, short-wave transmitter hidden in this house. In *my* house, Tony. I knew she was a United States Naval officer. I did not know she was an intelligence officer and that she was spying. Your precious daughter was spying on me, Tony . . .'

'I had no idea . . . What . . . ?'

'Tony.' He shook his great head and his voice took on the same soft and mellow tone he would doubtless use when making love. 'Tony, how can I believe you?'

'You must! You must believe me!'

'I'm sorry, but I cannot take that risk. She is a spy. We will deal with her. You introduced her to me, so you must pay also.' His eyes lifted to look at Ding standing in the doorway. Behind Ding, Bond could make out the figure of Frozen Stalk Pu.

Very softly, Brokenclaw Lee said, 'Throw him to the wolves.'

Tony Man Song Hing began to blubber and scream as Ding, assisted by Pu, grabbed him, pulling him from the floor and dragging him from the room. The cries and screams echoed from outside for almost thirty seconds.

In the silence that followed, Bond felt he had to make some remark gauged to show his contempt for anyone like Man Song Hing. 'That is a good description, sir. Throw him to the wolves. Your men are undoubtedly as ferocious as that poor dying breed of animals.'

'My men?' Lee looked at him with a blankness which was almost bone-chilling. 'A description? That wasn't a description, Peter Abelard. That was reality. I have a pack of seven wolves. As you say, they are a dying breed, a threatened species. I meant what I said. My wolves are hungry. My men will strip Mr Man Song Hing then cover his body with various animal fats which attract my little pack. After that, they *will* throw him to my wolves. You'd like to watch?'

'No, I think not. Not this time anyway.' Bond thought Chi-Chi was going to vomit.

'Well, now. I suppose Ms Mo – Jenny – here should get dressed, so that we can start you off, looking through the intelligence I've gathered for you.'

There was a slight pause, then Chi-Chi took the cue, 'Yes, if it's as good as you say – and I don't doubt that it is – I'll have my time cut out getting it made into microdots for the transference back to Beijing Hsia. They will be pleased to see it there.'

'Yes, I set great store by the analysts at Beijing Hsia. I meant to ask, how was old One-Eye H'ang when you last saw him?'

'In excellent spirits,' Bond filled in, as Chi-Chi left the table and began to make her excuses.

'Yes, it will be good to see him again.' Brokenclaw had gone to stand near the empty fireplace. 'I presume that it will be you, Peter, who will be smuggling the microdots out of here; I mean, Jenny is so good with numbers and the computers that I imagine she will be the one who stays to assist with the real work, with what old One-Eye has so humorously called *Operation Jericho*.'

'Yes. Yes,' Bond said hurriedly, hoping that Chi-Chi would remain calm.

'So, you will want to get away by late tonight I shouldn't doubt?'

'If we can complete the work.'

'And if you can get the promised payment, which, of course, you will. What a pity, Peter. You'll miss old One-Eye H'ang. He doesn't arrive here until tomorrow night.'

James Bond felt that the earth was about to swallow him up. Chi-Chi just went chalk white, swaying slightly in the doorway.

Brokenclaw was not even looking at them. 'Yes, it will be very good to talk again with One-Eye. It has been a long time.'

13

BLACK MAGIC

James Bond did not dare to follow Chi-Chi back to the guest suite. She was good, but the sudden knowledge of the imminence of Hung Chow H'ang's arrival and of another operation on the boil might just throw her into speaking questions aloud. He simply hoped that he could give her some comfort as they went through the farce of examining the Lords and Lords Day intelligence. Neither Chi-Chi nor Bond were in any way qualified to judge the importance of the technology.

When M and Franks had spoken to him about the further possibility of Brokenclaw being involved in *Jericho*, he had suggested that Chi-Chi should be briefed, but time was pressing and the likelihood of the matter arising seemed so remote that M had actually said, 'If, by any unhappy chance, it does come up, you'll have to busk it, 007.'

Franks had commented that, for the Chinese, the operation was so remote and vague that he would put hard cash down on Brokenclaw having no knowledge whatsoever. 'Mind you,' Franks had said towards the end of the briefing, 'if it were the Japanese, the picture would be different. There's already been a leak from the Japs. A complete document, circulated on the Hill and under analysis at Langley, seems to suggest a covert operation against the economy of the United States.'

There it had been left, and Bond cursed himself for not having at least given her the sketchy improbabilities during their journey. What he had to do now was give his imprimatur to the material Brokenclaw had produced, and so force the question of money which appeared to be Brokenclaw's obsession. There was little doubt in his mind that Mr Brokenclaw Lee was, like so many wealthy men, preoccupied with the acquisition of more money. A Biblical text ran, unbidden, through his head. 'Unto every one that hath shall be given . . . but from him that hath not shall be taken away even that which he hath.' He always remembered that text. It was the kind of thing he imagined tax inspectors the world over had embroidered on samplers and hung over their desks.

Brokenclaw, who had excused himself at the same time as Chi-Chi, now returned, carrying a large leather file which he held up proudly. 'Here is the information asked for by Beijing Hsia. It's coded Black Magic, around two hundred pages in all, but I should imagine Jenny and yourself will authenticate it quite quickly.'

'I should imagine so. We know what to look for.'

'Good. Now, Peter, what are the actual arrangements for you regarding the money? You said that you had the means to collect it. What does this entail?'

'Nothing difficult, if we are as close to San Francisco as you say we are.'

'We are between Big Sur and Monterey, well back from the PCH, in pretty barren country, though we have some trees which afford protection for transport. You have to go to San Francisco to lay your hands on the money?'

'We have an arrangement with a bank. They will pay me, and me alone, with a banker's draft made out to whoever you like.'

'Where in the Bay area?'

'I need to get near to Fisherman's Wharf. It's not far from there.'

Brokenclaw smiled as though supremely happy. 'Then there is no problem. One of our vehicles is a helicopter and Ding can accompany you. We have a working arrangement with a firm called Chopper Views. They maintain two helipads near the Wharf.'

'Then, it's only a fifteen-minute walk, maybe half-an-hour.' Bond shrugged, giving the impression that the whole business was of no consequence. 'If we don't get all this stuff dealt with today, I can go down in the morning.'

'No! No!' Lee shook his head, his voice, as ever, betraying no sign of agitation. 'No. I'm certain you'll get it all done today.'

The heartening thing, Bond reflected, was that Lee gave no indication of suspicion. He had completely accepted both Bond and Chi-Chi on trust through the passwords and codes. And why should he not? They had seemingly arrived by the correct route, called the designated numbers and established their bona fides correctly. The crunch could only come when H'ang, the unsuspected insect in the liniment, turned up and saw either one of them. He was also cheered by the thought that he had still managed to remain armed, another indication that he was completely trusted.

'You can go through these at the table here or in my study. I forgot to mention that the soundproofing throughout is remarkably good.'

'Then, I think it should be the study.' Bond was already heading for the door and Lee was behind him, moving with the great agility one often sees in very big men.

As they reached the study, Chi-Chi appeared, dressed very simply in faded jeans, a white T-shirt and a short denim jacket. Every garment was well worn and anyone could believe that this was just the kind of thing she would wear at the offices inside the old French Legation in Beijing.

'Jenny,' Brokenclaw glowed with pleasure. 'Peter has suggested that you work in here. It should not take long.' He placed the leather folder on the table.

Chi-Chi glanced at Bond. 'I think we should have some clean paper and maybe a calculator. I have been remiss. My own very specialised calculator was left in the Beijing office.'

Bond was almost elated to see that she had regained her composure.

'What kind was it exactly?' Brokenclaw's soft and soothing voice had taken on the unmistakable tones of lechery.

So, Bond thought, that is only one of the reasons he wants me out of the way for an hour or so.

'It was an HP-28S, an advanced scientific calculator. Very difficult to get hold of. I feel most annoyed with myself,' Chi-Chi answered Lee's question.

'I'm sure one of the *Jericho* operators'll have one, or something similar. Come, we can be quick, but you'll see how ready we are to put *Jericho* into action.' He turned back to the door that led down to the dining room and Bond saw the tiny shadow of concern cross Chi-Chi's face.

'Though it is most apt,' Brokenclaw hovered by the door, 'do you not think it amazing that old One-Eye H'ang has used what could either be a Jewish or a Christian symbol for this incredible operation?'

Chi-Chi did not pause in her stride. 'Didn't you know, sir? When General H'ang was very young, before he joined the Red Army and fought in the Revolution, he was raised by Christian missionaries, and it was also a pair of Christians who nursed him when he was wounded before the taking of Beijing.'

'So? Yes. Yes, of course. The unfortunate girl in New York, Myra, was daughter to the couple who nursed him so long ago. I had forgotten. But come.'

He led the way back down the stairs and past the door to the dining room. At one point Bond gave Chi-Chi a little nod, meant to reassure her, but she returned a clear signal of anxiety and perplexity.

They were now in an even deeper level underground, though there was no hint of dampness or even of being below what was in all probability rock strata. The walls were hung with thick paper and this had been covered with white emulsion. Lights set into the ceiling kept the corridor as bright as day.

Finally, Brokenclaw stopped at a door in which there was a thick glass viewing panel. He peered through the glass and they saw him nod to someone within.

'Here we are.' He turned to Bond and Chi-Chi. 'Our *Jericho* laboratory.' He held back the door to allow them to enter.

They were in a brilliantly lit operations room watched over by four white-coated technicians – two women, one of them Chinese, one Caucasian, and two men, one black and one white.

Facing them was a bank of electronics gear at which the black man was sitting; the other members of the team sat at a leather-covered table which had computer VDUs embedded and angled below the table line. Bond also caught a glimpse of keyboards tucked away on sliding trays below the table level.

This monitoring position faced a wall of clear thick glass, and from it you could look down on a long, sterile room in which up to forty men and women sat at computer terminals, each with its modem and telephone. Around the periphery of the room ran a perpetual electronic tape printing out stocks and shares prices. It was very like the interior of a major stockbroker firm's main office, the only difference being that these people sat calmly at their terminals. There was none of the usual chaotic shouting, bustling and confusion. Only occasionally one of the people in the monitoring room would flick a switch and say a few words into a microphone.

The large black man who sat at the electronics equipment appeared to be in charge, for it was to him that Brokenclaw spoke. 'Andrew, I'm sorry to bother you. These are good friends of ours, Mr and Mrs Abelard. Peter, Jenny, this is Andrew, in charge of operations at the moment. What's on for today, Andrew?'

Andrew gave a big smile. 'We're giving a couple of hotel chains a small fright. Just for the hell of it. Practice.'

One of the three overlooking the room below spoke softly into a microphone, 'Okay, twenty-two and twenty-six start selling. Offload all the stuff you bought when the market opened. Just dump it. You have to remember that we're playing with monopoly money, but the clients out there have the real stuff on their minds.'

'We really only wanted to see if anyone had an advanced scientific calculator.' Brokenclaw sounded almost apologetic.

'I've got a Texas Instruments calculator. You want to borrow it?' from one of the controllers.

Chi-Chi replied, saying she would only need it for a short time, and the small calculator was handed back towards her.

As they left, one of the other controllers was saying, 'Watch it thirty-two, your gilt-edged are starting to drop. Buy up all you can get your hands on. Do it now, quickly. We can dump them again later; they'll begin to rise as you buy, then we sell and the bottom'll drop out for a while.'

'They seem very efficient.' Chi-Chi managed to remain composed during the return to the study.

'They're well trained. They've all worked on the stock market, and I had them recruited for their skill.' Brokenclaw gave a sinister little chuckle. 'They also have motivation. Everyone in that lab has a reason for hating the Stock Exchange. They'll shout with joy when Wall Street comes tumbling down.'

'I bet they will,' muttered Chi-Chi.

Lee left them together in his study, saying that when they were finished with the Black Magic material one of them should just press six on the telephone and they would be put straight through to him.

They sat, side by side, the Black Magic papers between them, and the pads and pens which had appeared during their absence, directly in front of them.

Chi-Chi glanced through the first five sheets lying open between the leaves of the leather folder, then wrote quickly on her pad, 'What in hell's going on?'

Bond also riffled through the first five sheets, looked at what she had written and added—

Operation Jericho was not supposed to be even on the cards yet. It's a long term plan for tapping into the New York Stock Exchange and causing an unnatural economic disaster over a period of days or weeks. It is aimed at bringing about a complete collapse of the dollar which will in turn hit most of the world's other major currencies. The Japanese thought of it first, but it seems One-Eye plus our man are going to do it quite soon.

She nodded, passed over some of the other documents from the file, jotting down—

What are we going to do?

Bond scribbled in reply—

Stay cool. Pretend to go through this stuff, but don't spin it out. The sooner you start making these pages into microdots the sooner I get out of here and bring in the Fifth Cavalry.

Bending over the pile of Black Magic pages, they went through the motions of working, making occasional notes, muttering to each other, Chi-Chi doing imaginary calculations and Bond occasionally calling her attention to points of interest.

There was little doubt that Brokenclaw had gathered together a gold mine from the five kidnapped Navy men, though Black Magic contained scientific data much too advanced for either of them. Bond already knew some words and phrases from the little he had learned of Stealth Technology, and these cropped up between lengthy mathematical equations. The words Radar Cross Section, Visual and Acoustic Signature Reduction, Frequency Emission and Leakage, Laser Enhanced Sonic Signal and the like were familiar, though he could not have written a report on what he read.

They worked on Black Magic for just over an hour.

The helicopter made wearisome passes across the wide search area, and Ed Rushia was pleased to get out and stretch his legs on the two occasions they had landed for refuelling. Now, having drawn a complete blank on picking up any of the homer signals, they circled over the Big Sur area. Still no joy. The instruments remained silent and the earphones picked up no beeps.

They were at the end of the search, having flown back and forth for nearly three hours.

'Negative, Commander?' the helicopter pilot asked on the internal RT.

'Blank.' Rushia's weariness penetrated his voice. 'Let's move up the coast towards Monterey.'

'Not in our search area.'

'No, but it's a quick way home.'

The helicopter turned north. Below, the bleak and rocky terrain looked endless but for the ribbon of the Pacific Coast Highway.

Suddenly Rushia strained his hearing. The noise had been only a tiny peep, but the DF needle had swung a fraction to the east. 'Go East,' he commanded. 'Gently. Cut back speed.'

Two minutes later the signal returned, very weak, hardly audible, but nevertheless there. He looked forward. Tucked into the foot of a rocky outcrop there were trees, a small secondary road, and a house, big, solid and set plumb on a grassy slope. He could see a couple of cars parked openly on a turning circle at the front which faced East, and another drawn up near a big clump of trees on the southern side. Obviously a lot of work had gone into building and landscaping this house, hemmed in by rocks and bleak terrain. As they did the final pass, he even saw what appeared to be a dog pound on the other side of the trees to the south of the house.

The DF needle quivered, and the little red 'guide light' weakly winked on and off while there was an unmistakable morse J & K – the two homer call signs – faint in the headphones.

'Photographs!' Rushia ordered. 'Photographs. Then let's get the hell out of here.' He had found them, but heaven knew what was shielding the signals. They sounded, he thought, as though they were being transmitted from the centre of the earth.

Rushia made contact with base, being the carrier with the *Curve* operations team aboard, calling out co-ordinates, and passing on all positive information that he, Indexer, had tracked down Custodian and Checklist.

Within fifteen minutes of Rushia's report reaching the carrier, a piston-engined Lockheed SA 2–37A quiet reconnaissance aircraft lifted off from Moffet Field – the centre for much secret aerial and electronic 'watch and listen' work – heading for the co-ordinates Rushia had given. The SA 2–37A is younger brother to the old YO-3A which was used extensively by the US Army, CIA and NASA for some time during the Vietnam War and proved invaluable for gathering information on enemy troop movements. There are not many of them left in service but the SA 2–37A looks like an ordinary, small, one-engined private airplane, yet is fitted with high-definition cameras, and all the sensor and heat-seeking photographic equipment you will find in larger, high-fly reconnaissance aircraft.

The SA 2–37A did its work quickly. Its two crew members, seated side by side, were both experienced men and within two hours, M, Grant, Tanner and Franks were looking at the resultant photographs with the help of a Recce Pix expert. The various colourings showed clearly that this was no ordinary house, for the various strata of different temperatures picked out the long, symmetrical underground areas.

'They've got a whole, well-organised bunker down there,' Grant said, running his finger along the pink and red areas.

'And on the blow-ups you can see they have an exit near this dog pound thing.' Tanner circled the area south of the copse which they had already realised was a cleverly camouflaged helicopter pad.

They found another exit to the north, between two rocky mounds.

'What's the drill on getting a full-scale raid on this place underway?' M's face had taken on the colour of granite.

'We can risk an unofficial assault, using only my people.' Grant's brow furrowed. 'But it'd be easier to make it a Special Forces deal.'

'You think Comrade Lee's got the Naval people down there as well as Bond and the girl?' M's eyes did not leave the various photographs spread out on the desk.

'There's room here for some kind of security area, and the heat signatures look like five, maybe six, people.' Grant again traced his finger round the underground area. 'Or this one here, though I don't understand it. If the heat signatures – the red dots – are correct, there seem to be around thirty or forty people, plus a lot of electronic . . . Oh, God!'

'Yes?' M answered abruptly.

'*Jericho*!' Grant spat out. 'We know the Chinese have this harebrained scheme based on the Japanese report.'

Franks craned forward. 'They can't possibly have *that* in place and ready to start up. There's not been time.'

'There's been time if the Chinese were working along similar lines long before the Japs.' Grant sounded concerned. 'I think we should go in. I'm going to get a Presidential instruction if necessary, though we can probably do it through the local cops. They have a Marine Special Forces fast reaction team in training over at Alameda. Let me get the business going.' He turned towards the bank of telephones just as the red instrument began to cry its long series of single chirps.

This was M's contact phone. He grabbed it and said, '*Curve One* . . . Yes, where?' Putting his hand over the mouthpiece, he quickly shot back at the others, 'It's Bond. He's at the bank.'

14

A TRIP TO THE BANK

After the hour of feigned work on the Black Magic material, Bond pulled one of his spare sheets of paper towards him and wrote—

> Don't worry, my dear. Stick around and you'll see some fireworks. I've been living by my wits on this one so far. Usually something unpleasant happens and I think we've almost reached that point. Don't despair, as a rule I live to fight another day, and it would not be the first time that I've saved a lady in distress. Love J.

Chi-Chi smiled, took the paper and wrote—

> If you save this fair lady, your reward would be pleasing to both of us. Love xxx

Her face lit up with what Bond would categorise as devilment. He carefully folded the paper, adding to it the other scraps on which they had jotted notes to each other, then placed them in the inside pocket of his jacket. Chi-Chi pressed nine on the telephone. A voice she thought was Ding's answered, and she asked for Mr Lee.

'You are satisfied, then?' Brokenclaw appeared in the doorway a few seconds later. The man had the unnerving knack of arriving soundlessly in a room.

Bond gave him a happy smile. 'Very satisfied. In some ways I wish we could wait for old One-Eye H'ang, but I know the analysts at Beijing Hsia are waiting to get their hands on this. It's better than we could ever have hoped for. You are to be congratulated, sir.'

Lee beamed. 'All seems to be working towards a conclusion that will please everybody, and after One-Eye arrives tomorrow, we will, with his help, start putting the fear of God into these Americans who still think they rule the world. It might take months, but with the talent we have gathered here and the skilful way they have accessed so many of the stock market computers, it can only be a matter of time. We will have the Huge Crash of 1990, and this time there will be no recovery.'

'If there's no recovery, your own considerable private fortune'll also suffer.'

There was the sly smile again and the soft, hypnotic voice. 'I think not. Switzerland and Luxembourg are still safe. Over the years I've built up many ways of escape, just as I've constructed a worldwide network of contacts, informers and businesses. You need not feel worried about me, Comrade Argentbright. I shall be living a pleasant life of retirement while you still work the treadmills at Beijing Hsia.'

Bond allowed his manner to become cold and distant. 'I fear that I'm not impressed with what used to be known in my old country as champagne Communists.' He tried a leer. 'Incidentally, who's the bank draft to be made out to?'

Brokenclaw shrugged off the Communist insult. 'The bank draft must be made out to Black & Black, Inc.' He gestured elegantly towards the door. 'Ding and the helicopter pilot are waiting for you. At least I can be sure you will return with my well-earned money.'

'I shall indeed return, sir. But you *must* make sure your man Ding knows that he may only follow at a distance. It is absolutely forbidden for him to come into the bank with me. The question of your payment has caused Beijing much grief and they've set up a one-time operation which *cannot* be compromised. So Ding waits outside. Otherwise, I shall return empty-handed and await General H'ang's instructions when he arrives.'

Brokenclaw did not seem in the least concerned by these remarks. Once more Bond thought of him as a horrific monster – the manners, voice, gestures were always polite, he carried himself with an imposing assurance and remained calm and reasonable even when condemning a man to death – as in the case of Tony Man Song Hing. He thought briefly that something must be done about Wanda. Where did Lee say she had been taken? Sausalito, that little artists' colony on the far side of the Bay in Marin County where, it was said, people basked in an alternative lifestyle, drinking wine while stretching out in jacuzzis and learning self-awareness by fanning themselves with peacock feathers.

Bond embraced Chi-Chi, whispering that he would soon be back. He was halfway down the corridor, following Lee past the dining room, when he realised that she had whispered 'I love you.'

Some you win, he thought, then turned his mind back to Sausalito, Wanda and the sleight-of-body that he must now embark upon if Brokenclaw Lee's organisation was to be smashed this very day.

Ding stood at the furthest extremity of the passageway beside a young white man who was dressed in black trousers and a white short-sleeved shirt with sunglasses clipped to the breast pocket. They had passed the *Jericho* laboratory some five hundred yards back, so Bond reckoned that the whole underground complex running south of the house covered an area of around three-quarters of a mile.

Brokenclaw gave rapid orders to Ding, speaking in fast Cantonese, Ding interrupting with single sharp 'Ais', making it obvious that he understood. Bond prayed that Lee was passing on the facts of life to his burly bodyguard. The last thing he required was Bone Bender Ding's presence in the bank where the *Curve* team had set up a method of contact, and a means to bring Chi-Chi and himself out from undercover. 'I'll be all set and ready for you,' Grant had said during the briefing. 'I'll have three of my best guys working on it.'

Finally, Brokenclaw nodded, the gesture signifying that they should move quickly. There were the usual stairs at the end of the corridor, this time leading to a door on which electronic bolts had to be deactivated from a small keypad in the wall before it could be opened. Passing through into the sunlight, he saw that even with the security locks, well-trained experts could blow the door in a matter of seconds.

Bond followed the pilot and Ding took up a position to the rear as they made their way over a long, grassy mound dotted with rocks. To the left, the ground sloped upwards, craggy, high and uninviting like a cliff towering above them. He could smell the sea close at hand and there was the hum of traffic in the distance.

When they reached the wooded area, some hundred yards from the exit, Bond saw that in fact there were only some forty tall trees forming a rough circle. Inside the circle the way was barred by a high fence, cunningly decorated with evergreens, so that even from a few paces away the circle of trees appeared to be a dense copse.

The pilot pushed through one pair of trees and pulled down on a branch which opened a small door into the copse. Inside, they were in a fully operational hangar, on the floor of which was a large painted white H.

A French-built variation of the AS 350 Ecureuil – Squirrel – helicopter sat on the H with a team of three mechanics nearby.

The pilot spoke with the mechanics for a moment, and one of them walked over to what looked like an ordinary household fuse box set into the curved wall. As the pilot beckoned to Bond and Ding, so, from the corner of his eye, Bond saw the mechanic operate a lever as though turning on current. There was a soft whining sound, and looking up, he saw the roof above them slowly separate into two halves, opening up like the dome of a planetarium.

By the time they were all settled into the machine, Bond and Ding occupying two seats directly behind the pilot, the dome had fully opened. The motor started and the rotors began to turn slowly.

The pilot adjusted his headset, waved the mechanics off and opened the throttles. Gently the helicopter rose clear of the camouflaged hangar.

At around a thousand feet the pilot began speaking, obviously making contact with the Bay Area ATC. The machine slid sideways and Bond caught a good view of the large house and grounds, mentally memorising its position in relation to the PCH which they could see clearly some five miles away. The house was well protected, almost ringed by rocky outcrops and with the high rise of jagged rock sweeping up behind it.

They banked and began to track the coastline towards Monterey and San Francisco itself. The sun was high and warm with no sign of cloud or mist obscuring that most pleasing view of San Francisco Bay as they came in across Golden Gate Park and the Presidio, with the long unmistakable outline of the Golden Gate Bridge to their left and the great landmarks of the city standing out like some giant diorama – Telegraph Hill with Coit Tower sprouting from the summit, the tall, needle-like TransAmerica Pyramid, the Embarcadero with the piers reaching like oblong fingers clutching towards Oakland.

Leaning back in his seat, Bond had to fight down the desire to pull the ASP and force Ding and the pilot to take them out towards Treasure Island and the moored carrier, but that would have served no purpose. They were over the water now and could clearly see Fisherman's Wharf, crowded with tourists and eating places. He even caught a glimpse of Ghirardelli Square, one of the main points of reference that he was now about to use.

They descended over the sea, coming down on to another white H, and Bond saw that there was a little Bell helicopter waiting to take on joy-riding passengers. Then, with a start of surprise, he saw, pulled up near their landing place, the long stretch limo in which they had travelled from Salinas. Frozen Stalk Pu leaned against the hood, smoking as he watched them land.

Once the helicopter had settled on its pad, the pilot indicated he would stay with the machine until they were ready to leave. 'How long this all going to take?' the pilot asked Ding in a slow effort at pidgin English.

'How long?' Ding flexed his hard muscles. 'You ask how long Mr Abelard, Ai?'

'It depends. Shouldn't be more than fifteen to thirty minutes.' Bond made it as casual as possible. Then Ding nudged him.

'In car,' the large hoodlum ordered.

'You *do* know the instructions?' Bond asked quietly.

' 'Course I know. We no come into bank. Just wait. That what the Brokenclaw one tell me.'

They had arrived at the limo and Frozen Stalk was holding the passenger door open in an exaggerated manner. 'I take wherever you wan' go, sir.' He gave a toothy grin as he spoke.

Bond reasoned that these two were on their real home turf now and were out to show him who could give the orders. He took one pace back from the car.

'Okay, I want to be certain neither of you even try to get into the bank with me. If you *do* try, then I fear your master is going to be extremely angry. There might even be broken heads. It's essential you don't show yourselves, so I think I'll walk and you can follow me in the car.'

Ding and Pu looked at each other, and then at Bond.

'Suggest you get in car.' Ding pushed hard against Bond who had to turn his body slightly to avoid the Chinese coming in contact with his back and therefore feeling the hard lump of the pistol.

'I warn you, if you make any mistake, it will not go well for you. Particularly if I do not return with the money.'

Ding nodded his understanding. 'We watch, that is all. Now, where you wish go?'

'You drop me off at Beach and Hyde, near the Cannery. And, even if the cops try to move you on, you stay parked on Beach. Got it?'

'Not going to financial district?' Pu chimed in.

'No, there's a small bank very close to Beach on Hyde. If you stay at the corner on Beach, you'll see me go in and you'll be ready when I come out.' Bond wondered if his instructions would allow him to come out at all. 'This is a small private bank. Understand?'

Ding shrugged then spoke rapidly to Pu. Bond climbed into the car and they drove slowly up to Beach Street, pulling in exactly where he directed them.

'How long?' Ding asked.

'Fifteen minutes at the most,' Bond lied.

'If you not out fifteen minutes, then we come.'

'You come, and you're dead,' Bond spat, climbing from the car, slamming the door on a fuming Ding and marching off up Hyde Street, crossing the road and heading for the small branch of the Sino-Republican Bank which had only set up for business during the past forty-eight hours and where three of Grant's men waited for him.

The office was obviously closed for a complete interior over-haul and refurbishing. He pressed the security buzzer.

A tinny voice said, 'Who goes?'

'Custodian.'

The lock buzzer sounded and Bond pushed the door open.

The front area was quite bare, but one of the CIA men stood in a doorway at the back leading to a very ordinary-looking utilitarian office.

'The phone's over there.' The welcoming party remained very low-key, the one man staying by the door while the other two sat watching silently as Bond came in and went straight to the phone.

Before picking up the instrument he told them the bank draft was to be made out to Black & Black, Inc. One of them nodded and began to work while the other started tapping at the keys of a computer. 'And much good will it do the noble house of Black & Black,' the computer operator muttered. 'I've got it here. Hong Kong based, subsidiary of Trivex which is in turn owned by Cummings Technology and I can't figure out who owns them.'

As the computer man spoke, Bond tapped in the number that would get him directly to M. The distant end purred twice, then M was on the line, '*Curve* One.'

'Custodian, sir.'

'Yes, where?'

'At the bank. Checklist's still with our friend. You want directions?'

'No. We know where you are.'

'Where?' Bond was near to that operational point where he questioned the facts and trusted nobody, not even his old chief.

'The house is five miles or so off the PCH, hemmed in by rock, a massive bunker running under the ground from the house, both north and south.'

'How? How do you know that?'

'Rushia picked up your homers from a chopper.'

'Right, sir.'

'We're getting together an assault team. One moment . . .' M was obviously being spoken to by some other person. Bond assumed it was either Grant, Franks or Tanner. Then M said, 'Can you give us details of numbers inside?'

'I have only seen a few people close to Lee, sir. But there are forty or so technicians in the *Jericho* laboratory, as they call it. *Jericho*'s on, sir. There's nothing vague about it. They have it all set up.'

'Good luck to them.' M seemed hardly ruffled. 'There seems to be quite a gaggle of people in the northern wing.' M paused once more for someone else to ask him a question. Bond thought he detected Grant's voice. 'We believe they're holding the kidnapped personnel there. No idea of firepower?'

'None, sir.'

'We also need to know the strength of the exits – the one close to the trees and the other one at the far end, the northern end.'

'The first thing is, do *not*, repeat *not*, attempt to enter the house itself. You've obviously pinpointed the exits from the underground sections.'

'We did a low fly recce. Pictures here, infra-red, the full business. Now what about those exits?'

'I've only been out through the southern one, sir.' Bond told him exactly what to expect and where the tunnels went, including the *Jericho* laboratory. 'If the other entrance is the same, a pair of well-organised charges should take them out; I have no idea of firepower, but the copse is a camouflaged helicopter hangar. They're waiting to take me back as soon as I get the draft.'

M was silent for a second, and Bond caught the sound of someone else talking. 'There's another thing,' the chief was back on the line, 'a kind of dog pen. Wired off area south of the copse?'

'It's probably the wolf pen. Our man keeps a small pack of wolves there; uses them for killing purposes. I have to go, sir.'

'You're not to go back.' The order was as crisp as if the old admiral had given it during a battle at sea.

'If I don't go back, Lord knows what they'll do to Checklist, sir. I *have* to go back.'

'We'll have a Special Forces assault set up for late afternoon, maybe sooner. You'll obey my orders and come straight out to the carrier. There's a car heading for the other side of Ghirardelli Square now. It'll pick you up and bring you back here so that you can make it in with the assault team.'

'With respect, it's a terrible risk, sir. You should also know that they're expecting General Hung Chow H'ang in person, tonight.

He's going to oversee the *Jericho* business. They are all set up for it – another reason I should go back.'

There was a long sigh at the other end of the line. Then M replied, 'Take the draft in case of trouble, but make it out through the back of the building you're in now. Go through into Ghirardelli Square and meet the car on the far side. Go straight through under the Indian restaurant and out on to Polk Street. Ten minutes. Move, Custodian!'

'Sir,' Bond acknowledged unhappily, 'there is another thing you should know,' he added quickly. 'They're holding the girl, Wanda, somewhere in Sausalito, and they've killed her father, Tony. They threw him to the wolves.'

'Got it. Now move! Out! Now!'

'Sir.' As he cradled the telephone, Bond knew he would be leaving Chi-Chi to almost certain death.

'I have to take the draft, but it's a just-in-case deal.' The agent who had been working on the bank draft handed him an envelope, and Bond had the good sense to remove the little package of notes exchanged between Chi-Chi and himself during their Black Magic analysis. 'Shred those,' he ordered, 'and tell me how I get out of the back of this place and into Ghirardelli Square.'

The agent at the door did not move and the one working the computer was still tapping away, muttering that it would take an army of accountants to unravel Black & Black. The agent who had given him the bank draft inclined his head to a small door on the other side of the room. 'Through there, along the passage and out the back door. That'll take you to Larkin Street. Cross the road and go into Ghirardelli through the entrance between the Clock Tower and Sharper Image.'

Bond moved.

Ghirardelli Square is a colourful little shopping mall named after Domingo Ghirardelli, an enterprising Italian merchant who came to San Francisco and prospered in 1849. It is not unlike a smaller version of London's Covent Garden shopping area. Basically the mall is made of renovated old buildings, the largest standing on the site of what had been a woollen mill during the Civil War. Most of the buildings are of red brick and were built in the early 1900s to house Ghirardelli Chocolate Manufactory, some of the original vats and ovens still being in operation. There are pleasant walks, a striking ornamental fountain and several speciality shops, like Bears 'R Us, and a Mickey Mouse store as well as a branch of the famous Sharper Image chain which sells expensive executive toys and other items that people can easily live without. In plain language, a lucrative business.

He crossed Larkin, dodging the traffic, and entered the square, walking quickly round Fountain Plaza with its pond spraying jets of water into the air and the mermaid statue. In seconds he was heading rapidly towards West Plaza which would take him nearer the furthest end and Polk Street.

'Ai! Abelar! You stop, Abelar!' It was Ding's voice, shouting from behind. Bond glanced back and saw the big Chinese moving through Fountain Plaza. People were scattering, and as he reached for the ASP, two bullets ricocheted from the brickwork to his right.

Dodging behind the nearest wall, round the side of the Woollen Mill building, Bond took a deep breath. He held the automatic in the two-handed grip, muzzle upwards, hands tucked into his right shoulder. Another breath and he swung out into the open again.

Ding was moving fast towards him, his gun raised, and as he saw Bond take up a firing stance, he slid to a halt, lifting his hands to fire.

Bond had him cold, but at that moment his only desire was to cripple and stop Ding. He fired twice, low, and saw the large Chinese jump sideways as concrete splintered between his feet.

At least, Bond thought, it would hold him for a few seconds. Turning, he weaved through the walkways, heading for the exit into Polk Street, praying M's car had arrived by this time. As he reached the street, he saw that the traffic had stalled. He glanced to left and right, deciding to make a run for it away from the Beach Street front, but as he began to move, the words, 'Stop! FBI! Drop the weapon!' came from nearby.

Though he was a set-up for the FBI, he knew this was at least his one way out. A call from the FBI to the carrier would put him in the clear.

There was a clatter as he dropped the 9mm, turned, and placed his hands on his head.

'Well, well. Captain Bond. We thought your own people had taken care of you. But it'll be a pleasure to fix you once and for all.'

The taller of the two men had spoken, but both were slowly coming towards him, and he recognised the agents who had called on him at the Fairmont after he had seen Agent Malloney bludgeoned to death. Even their names came back readily to him. Wood and Nolan.

It was Wood who was speaking while Nolan dispersed the small knot of people who had gathered with the usual morbidity of people who watch arrests being made, happy in the thought that 'There, but for the grace of God, go I.'

'I'll come with you gladly, gentlemen. I need to make a phone call. I am allowed one, aren't I?' Then he saw that Wood was looking past him, talking to someone near the building. 'You want this guy, Ding?'

'Want him bad, Mr Wood. The broken clawed one requires him,' Ding hissed.

'Dead or alive?' Wood asked.

'Oh, we take him back alive, I think. Much vengeance to be reaped.'

Nolan had joined the party. 'Where you want him, Ding?'

'Our car. On corner. I take him, okay?'

'By all means.' Wood gave Bond a little push.

'Just tell Mr Lee to keep those little envelopes coming, Ding. We'll need extra for this.' Then, to Bond, 'Act natural, Captain. I guess where you're going there won't be much chance to act natural for a long time.'

Ding grinned and stooped to pick up the fallen ASP which he jabbed into the right side of his belt.

'If ever.' Wood gave him another push, straight into the arms of Bone Bender Ding, who embraced him like a bear, put an armlock on him and prodded his back with his own handgun. 'You move now. Our way this time. The wolves will not go hungry tonight, I think. Ai?'

15

TO DIE LIKE A GENTLEMAN

'Golly, and you let him go back there, sir?' Ed Rushia stood in M's cabin, while both Tanner and Franks spoke on telephones. John Grant had shouldered past Rushia as the tall Naval Intelligence man was coming in. He appeared to be in a great hurry. Now Rushia stared at M with horror.

'No, Commander Rushia, I did *not* let him go back. I expressly ordered him to come in. We even had a car less than a hundred yards away when he was taken. There were shots fired, it seems, and two FBI men recognised Bond – they want him as much as they want you, Rushia. That's the way we set it up – to give you both extra protection if the FBI decided to tail you.'

'Well, if the FBI guys . . .'

'The FBI gu . . . men, lost him. So he's back to square one.'

Rushia rubbed a hand over his chin. 'Guess he hasn't got much of a chance. Jiminy, I feel terrible about this.'

'Commander Rushia,' M barked, 'stop playing the dolt with me. I know you're not a country bumpkin. It might work with interrogations, but it cuts no ice here.'

'No. Guess it doesn't, sir. But the ice man cometh, as the playwright sayeth.'

M raised his eyes to heaven, as though in a silent prayer for strength. 'There's a team of US Marines at Alameda. Mr Grant's gone to try and procure their use for an assault . . .'

'Request I go in with them, sir.' Rushia had lost his homespun manner.

M frowned. 'If there's any special duties you can perform, then I suppose . . .'

Grant crashed through the cabin door without even knocking. 'We've got a problem, sir. The Marines over at Alameda; they're all rookies on a training exercise.'

M, not a man to use profane language under normal circumstances, spat out a single four-letter word.

'It means a delay,' Grant looked flushed, 'but I do have good news as well. We're authorised to use a First Special Forces Operational Detachment.'

'Delta?' M asked.

'I don't know; there are four of those elements. Delta was the first. It doesn't matter which one they send, because they're as good as your own Special Air Service boys, Admiral. Problem is they have to get up here from Fort Bragg. That's North Carolina – say four hours if they get a move on. They're good and we can brief them very quickly.'

M sighed. 'Better than nothing. I wouldn't want to send in any old force. That place needs specialists. Even Bond doesn't seem to know what their strength is.'

Ed Rushia, the tallest man in the room, cleared his throat. 'Would someone put me in the picture, the entire picture. James has become a friend and colleague. Mightn't there be some way I can help until the Special Forces people get here?'

Everyone looked at him, in silence. Then Grant spoke, 'I'm second guessing this Brokenclaw bastard. But maybe there is one thing you might do. It's not one hundred per cent certain, but it's worth doing. As a long shot, it just might save Captain Bond.' He then outlined what he had in mind.

The risks, Ed Rushia thought, were higher than a kite on the Fourth of July.

Bone Bender Ding frog-marched Bond down to Beach Street. The FBI men, in Brokenclaw's pay, had chased away any lingering tourists, and it was surprisingly easy for Ding to get Bond into the limo.

The whole business took less than a minute, and all his instincts told him that any attempt to break free would end in disaster. There *had* to be a moment, a fraction of a second, during which he would be able to act.

Frozen Stalk drove carefully and well while Ding still held his captive in the armlock, his own pistol well back in his left hand, ready to use. It was being done by the book. These people certainly knew what they were about. There was no sloppiness.

When they reached the helipad, the rotors were already idling and there was a quick exchange between Ding and Pu, from which Bond gathered that Pu had to return in the limo while Ding took his prisoner back to Brokenclaw.

Back in the helicopter Bond was pushed into the right hand seat with Ding on his left directly behind the pilot. It was only when they were airborne that the armlock was relaxed and Ding shouted, 'Please do nothing stupid. I shall kill you if necessary, but would rather present you with whole body to the broken clawed one. Unerstan'?'

'Unerstan',' Bond mimicked.

'Good. You now enjoy the friendly skies, Ai?'

'Ai.' Bond was summing up the situation. His own automatic was within easy reach, tucked into the right side of Ding's considerable waistband, but the Chinese had his own handgun, which looked like a nasty little snub-nosed S & W Chief's Special. It was an old but truly tried design and the .38 Special ammunition would blow a sizeable hole in anyone who got in its way.

Stay alert, he told himself. If the ride got bumpy there just might be a chance to turn the tables on Ding and the pilot, who had appeared to take everything in his stride.

They cleared the Bay area, and staying over the sea, followed the coastline back past Monterey until they were at the turning point which would take them low over the PCH and across the rock-encrusted area leading to the house.

Bond's moment finally came as the helicopter went into a steep bank to the left. Momentarily, Ding was tilted back sideways against the doorway, off balance for the wink of an eye. In that split second, Bond's hand shot out and pulled the ASP automatic from Ding's waistband, bringing it back in a ferocious chop down on the wrist of Ding's gun hand.

Ding gave a sharp, angry cry of pain and his pistol fell to the floor of the cabin. In an automatic reflex, Ding leaned forward, straining his arm down towards the weapon. As he did so, Bond brought the ASP's butt down hard on the hoodlum's neck.

For a second, as though nothing had happened, Ding turned his face towards Bond in an evil grimace.

'You do not put Bone Bender Ding unconscious with the blow of a fly,' he said, still grinning as his eyes turned upwards and he collapsed in an untidy heap of comatose flesh.

Bond now prodded the pilot in the back of his neck with the ASP. 'Turn this thing back,' he shouted. 'Just right back over the sea, or I swear to put a bullet through you.'

The pilot nodded, and Bond watched as he began to swing the machine to the left on its own axis. They were lower than he had thought, and must have been about to land by the time his short tussle with Ding was over. Below them the dome of the camouflaged tree hangar was open, and they turned at around two hundred feet towards the house.

'Get her up!' He prodded the pilot's neck again, for during the turn they seemed to have lost another fifty feet. The house was now directly in front of them, and as they began to slip to the right in order to fly back over the sea, like some monster rising from its hiding place, a second wicked-looking helicopter lifted from behind the house. It flashed through Bond's mind that the machine looked like an old Bölkow-Kawasaki 117, and he could clearly see the left-hand door open, with a heavy machine-gun mounting swung forward, the gunner himself in a harness manning the weapon.

'Go left!' Bond yelled, but as they did so the other chopper followed suit. The pilot was in a Mexican standoff, obviously terrified both by Bond's pistol and by the aggressive machine in front of him.

He put down the nose and tried to gain height, but the 117 followed his move so that, in the space of a minute, the two helicopters appeared to be performing a strange insect-like ritual dance. Then the shots came.

The gunner from the door of the 117 put a single burst to their right. The pilot jerked away to his left, the machine tilting dangerously on one side, recovering only seconds before the rotors would have lost their grip on the air.

'He'll blow us out of the sky!' the pilot was shouting hysterically as Bond slid back one of the side panels of the cabin, leaning over to get a quick shot in at the gunner. But the 117 seemed to have disappeared.

He looked around, then was aware of new forces on their own machine – a great buffeting from above as the 117 came down directly over them. Bond turned his hand and fired off a couple of random shots aimed upwards. But there was no reduction of pressure; slowly they were being forced down, the helicopter swaying and bouncing as the down-wash from the 117's rotors tossed them about.

'It's no good!' the pilot shrieked. 'No good! Don't shoot! I can't maintain control.' He had tried to back out from under the massive turbulence but was only forced down further. Bond glanced to his right and saw they were almost level with the circular hangar. Then a sudden surge in the wind from above seemed to throw them sideways. He watched as a rotor blade chopped at one of the trees then buckled.

There was a furious grinding. The world spun. Then the sound of metal disintegrating, the smell of oil and gasoline, followed by what seemed to be an endless drop into a cavern which swallowed them up in darkness. The last thing he noticed was the hands on his Rolex showing almost ten thirty.

From far away came the sweet noise of the dawn chorus, the morning songs from thousands of birds. Then the noise diminished. Now only one bird sang, its notes tripping up and down in loud waves. After that the song stopped and he realised it was someone speaking to him, a sweet sad, sing-song voice saying, 'James? Oh, James! Please wake up! Please forgive me!'

Gingerly he opened his eyes. His head hurt and his vision took a few minutes to focus.

Chi-Chi was leaning over him, and the first thing he noticed was that she was stripped to the waist, her gentle, small breasts only inches from his face.

'Thank God,' she said. 'You're awake. Please, James, forgive me.'

His throat was dry and he asked for a drink. She moved and returned a second later with a small plastic cup of water. She was sobbing and he saw that her hair was tousled.

He swallowed the water and hauled himself on to one elbow, looking up at her.

'Just say you'll forgive me,' she continued.

'Forgive you for what?'

Her mouth opened then closed as though she were having problems speaking. 'I told them. I told them everything. You. Me. What the operational team know. I couldn't hold out. I couldn't.' As she turned away, he saw the blood and the deep red welts across her back.

'Who did that?' In spite of the dizziness and general disorientation, a spark fired fury in his belly. 'Who did it?'

'Lee. Who else? Soon after you left he tried . . . He tried to . . .'

'Yes, I thought he might, but . . .'

'I managed to resist. I think I hurt him a little. My knee had an argument with his groin. So he went away.'

'And?'

'And then he returned and said he now knew I was not Jenny Mo, and he was certain you were not Argentbright.'

'You denied it?' He was feeling a little stronger and the room had stopped spinning.

'Of course, but he said he would have the truth, one way or another.'

He saw her wrists were marked with deep bruises. 'What did he do, Chi-Chi?'

'He said . . .' she faltered. 'He said that if I did not give him all the information I knew, he would kill me on the spot.' She gulped a sob. 'I told him to kill me.' Once more she gave a sob and began to weep gently, the tears flowing down her cheeks, the delicious little nose crimson. 'He said they did not have time to waste with drugs. He said he knew the best way to deal with me.' A shuddering sigh. 'They stripped me; hung me with leather thongs around my wrists and whipped me. I screamed. I even became unconscious. But, James, the pain went on and on. I just told him so that it would stop. I'm sorry.'

'There's no need to be sorry, Chi-Chi.' He put his arms around her, taking care not to touch the bruised and bleeding back. 'The person has yet to be born who doesn't give in. If the brutality hadn't worked, they'd have tried some other way.'

She moaned as he cradled her like a small child.

'What else happened? Do you know?'

'They have the Navy people here. He put me in a cell across from them. They're in a bad way in a special area, a very narrow passage running off the north underground wing. There's a wall, and it opens up when you kick a brick on the lower left side. They have a lot of guards. I was there for a while, then the big one, Ding . . .'

Bond nodded.

'. . . Ding came down. He seemed very angry. He grabbed at me and said I was going to nurse you, that you were lucky to be alive, that he had been in a helicopter accident with you. The pilot was killed, he told me. Then he dragged me to you. We're in a secure room in the north wing passage, near the other prisoners.'

Bond was sitting up, now. Almost back to normal. 'How long?' he asked. 'How long have I . . . ?'

'I've been with you for two hours, maybe more. I was frightened you would die. I think they've already spent quite a while trying to bring you round. They said you were concussed, and when Ding came, he had obviously been hurt. He had been bandaged and treated before he was sent to me. Brokenclaw said that if I did not keep you alive, he would burn me on your funeral pyre. They said it was essential for you to be alive.'

'Very necessary. I prefer to have you alive, Captain Bond.' They had heard no door open, yet there was Brokenclaw, standing in the cell-like room. In one hand he held the bank draft for five million dollars. 'I presume this is useless?' He did not raise his voice and the way he asked sounded as though he thought it oddly amusing.

'Quite useless. Just as all your plans are useless now, Mr Lee.'

'Oh, I don't think so, Captain Bond. There is time. Incidentally, you haven't met the man who was supposed to have been your controller from Beijing. He arrived a little earlier than expected. May I present General Hung Chow H'ang.' He stepped to one side to reveal a short, old man. He was slightly stooped, moved slowly and wore a black patch over his left eye.

'It is interesting to meet you.' H'ang spoke almost unaccented English and his voice somehow seemed to belie his age, for it was strong, almost young. 'You are not unlike my man Argentbright. Interesting. Argentbright-Abelard-Bond. Who cares about the name? We still have the secrets of the Anglo-American submarine detection weapon known as Lords, and its antidote, Lords Day. I can leave now. Be gone within the hour with them. Believe me, Captain Bond, I can get away quite undetected.' He gave a little chuckle. 'Incidentally, it was my helicopter that brought you down. You are lucky to have survived. But it's for the best. You see, we have to know if your masters have any information on where we are, also on our *Operation Jericho*. These two things, we don't know. But you'll tell us.'

'Not a chance.' Bond's voice was stronger.

H'ang did not flinch. Quietly he turned to Lee. 'Ah, yes, we require Captain Bond to tell us all things.'

'It will be done, General. I'm going to see to it personally.' Lee gave Bond a courteous little bow. 'I'm terribly sorry about this, Bond, but we have little time for the kind of finesse you would use in an interrogation. Speed, time, as the lawyers say, are of the essence, though I really don't think you have a great deal to tell us. Ding and poor old Frozen Stalk had their eyes on you all the time, except when you were in the so-called bank, and I've had that searched now, so I know it is empty – no telephones, nothing. A dead drop presumably, and you just had time to leave some message there, so we will have to put you to the question.'

'You'd have scored a lot of brownie points had you been with the Spanish Inquisition.' Bond looked him straight in the eyes, unblinking.

Brokenclaw gave a throaty laugh. 'I think you'll find there is a pretty irony in our method of inquisition. You should appreciate it.'

'Really?' He sounded more interested than afraid, though warning sirens of an unspeakable horror to come were already sounding in his head.

'Yes.' Brokenclaw looked relaxed and quite at ease, as though he had all the time in the world. 'Your code names. Well, General H'ang's code names really, Peter Abelard and Héloïse. A nice touch. You are familiar with your history books, Captain Bond? You remember the story of Abelard and Héloïse, and what happened to them? You know all that?'

'Not intimately, no. Just a kind of rough outline.'

Brokenclaw chuckled. 'Oh, yes, it was rough. But in the eleventh century, they *were* rough and ready. They were not squeamish. Peter Abelard was a theologian who scandalised the church, not only by his philosophy and theology, but also by his affair with, and possible marriage to, Héloïse. He was declared a heretic, and unhappily, the beautiful Héloïse was the niece of a very influential priest, Canon Fulbert of Notre-Dame. Poor Héloïse, she ended up in a nunnery. Abelard was disgraced and spent the rest of his days in the Abbey of Saint-Denis.' He gave a broad smile. 'I like the disgrace part myself. Peter Abelard was castrated, Captain Bond. Neutered. Lost his manhood. I'm sure we've talked of this before.'

'I believe it was mentioned.'

'Then, Peter Abelard, I suggest that you answer all our questions. Tell us what we need to know and tell us quickly; tell us what information your masters have about us, about where we are, about *Jericho*. We do not ask much.'

Bond returned Brokenclaw's smile and shook his head.

'What a pity, James Bond. What a great pity, because when we have done what must be done, there will be no abbey in which you can hide. In fact, there will be little of you left. When you see what we have ready for you, then I think even you will change your mind.' He leaned back into the passageway and snapped his fingers.

Two armed men, Chinese and wearing some kind of grey uniform, came into the little room.

'Say your farewells, Peter Abelard. Say farewell to your Héloïse. I fear that if you remain stubborn, she'll not see you again.'

'James.' Chi-Chi moved close to him. 'Tell them. What can it cost now? Please tell them.'

Rising from the floor on which he had been lying, he took her in his arms. Holding her close, he whispered, urging her to try not to worry. 'If I tell them, they'll do away with both of us anyway.' And with a last, close embrace he kissed the fragile-looking girl and turned to his captors.

There were more men than he had ever seen before in the long corridors and the main rooms. They all seemed to be armed, and many wore the grey uniform of the men who held him. He saw that some had badges of a claw riven in half on the breast pockets of their jackets. What was it M had said? 'We're getting together an assault team.' Well, he had better be bloody quick about it, because friend Brokenclaw obviously had something original and unpleasant in store.

They hustled him along the passages and finally up the stairs at the southern end of the huge bunker to the exit through which he had been taken for the ride into San Francisco. Outside, near the tree-camouflaged hangar, more men worked clearing away the debris of the helicopter. He winced when he saw what remained. They had certainly bent that machine more than somewhat as Damon Runyon would have said.

As they passed the hangar, Bond knew without a doubt what they were about to do. The general walked with the aid of a cane, limping along next to the gigantic Brokenclaw. Bone Bender Ding was there also, his head bandaged, and he thought Frozen Stalk Pu was one of the others, mostly uniformed.

Finally they reached the place. At one end, on a hard standing, there was a large, low, oblong building. Running from this building was an area of around thirty feet, fenced in with heavy chain-link secured at regular intervals to high concrete poles.

As they walked the length of the chain-link fence, Bond glanced back. The oblong building was a cage. Strong iron bars ran the length of the structure on the enclosure end, and inside he caught his first sight of the wolves.

Seven of them, Brokenclaw had said, and he could well believe it, as he saw the creatures padding to and fro within the cage, restless, as though sniffing the air for food.

They reached the far end of the enclosure and Brokenclaw brought the party to a halt.

'You are certain, Captain Bond, that you will not relent? My wolves have yet to be fed today. It will be unpleasant to be unmanned by them. But I suppose what will follow may not be too bad. After the exquisite pain, the ripping of your most private self, you'll long for them to finish the job.'

'Let's get on with it, shall we?' Bond was determined that if this was to be his end, then he would meet it in as dignified a manner as possible. He remembered an old instructor saying to him, 'Bond, always remember you are a gentleman. So, live like a gentleman and for God's sake die like a gentleman.'

Brokenclaw gave a sharp order and two of the other uniformed men helped the pair of guards to strip Bond until he was standing completely naked. It was only then that Brokenclaw approached him. Frozen Stalk Pu was with him, carrying a small bucket.

Brokenclaw gestured towards the bucket. 'A particularly pleasant animal fat,' he explained. 'My pets are very partial to this nourishment. It's a gourmet meal for them. In fact anything daubed with this stuff becomes a delicious treat.' As he spoke, he pulled on a pair of surgical gloves. Then he plunged his hands into the bucket, bringing out a large glutinous lump which he began to smear around Bond's loins.

'I'm sorry if the smell offends you, Bond, but my pets like their treat. There, I think that's enough. You are certain you don't wish to tell us what we want to know?'

'Quite determined, thank you. In fact, all I'll say is that it's been very unpleasant knowing you.'

'Thank you.' Brokenclaw made it sound as though he had been paid a great compliment. 'I should tell you that at any time before you lose consciousness, if you change your mind we can call them off. They obey me very well considering they are creatures of the wild.' He turned to the guards and nodded.

There was a small gateway set in the chain-link fence at the far end of the enclosure through which he was pushed.

They took him to within ten feet of the cage, and he could see the wolves getting excited. Some appeared to be slavering. One barked, expectantly.

Four stakes had been firmly driven into the ground and Bond was pushed down, his back against the earth, between the stakes. He felt his wrists and ankles being secured, he thought with strong leather thongs, which were in turn affixed to the stakes. His body was now spreadeagled, the thongs pulled tight, on the ground directly in front of the cage. He could smell the fat which was smeared on his body and hear the wolves start to growl as they became more excited.

'This is your last opportunity, Captain Bond. You're sure we cannot make you change your mind?'

'Go to hell where you belong, Brokenclaw Lee, son of a Chinese tailor and a Blackfoot whore,' he shouted.

For a second, he had the pleasure of hearing Brokenclaw lose his composure and shout in outrage – 'Kill!'

There was a rattling noise and, lifting his head, Bond saw a section of the cage slide upwards.

Then the wolves came bounding and howling into the arena.

16

AWESOME

Commander Edwin Rushia, United States Navy, had done many strange and dangerous things in his time, but never anything like this.

'It's just on the off chance,' M had told him.

'If they did it to Wanda's father, they could just as well do it to Bond,' Bill Tanner said. 'Mind you, with all the delays, we could be too late anyway.'

But he was not too late. They had kitted him out in camouflaged fatigues and given him an M40A1, the Marines' sniper's rifle complete with long-range sights. This last was only handed over after he had assured them of his skill with weapons.

Grant had questioned him thoroughly on this point. 'If you're not any good, you could be risking everything.'

Rushia, who was only a couple of years Grant's senior, looked at him in a quiet, reflective manner before saying, 'Son, when I was a kid in Jewel Junction, Iowa, I'd go hunting with my old Daddy. When I tell you I could take the eyes out of a rabbit at fifty yards, maybe you'll believe me.' So they also gave him a 9mm DA 140 automatic, a development of the famous Browning Highpower.

'Feel like a guerrilla,' Rushia commented.

'You look like a gorilla,' Bill Tanner drawled. He had come to like and respect this slow-speaking, humorous and intelligent man.

They had also provided a pair of small ultra-light binoculars and a compass.

Rushia gathered one or two things that were his own idea and stuffed them into a backpack, before being handed the main weapon.

When the doctor, whom Franks had dredged up from the depths of the ship, handed over the package, carefully wrapped in tinfoil, Rushia had taken hold of it gingerly as though it were a bomb.

'For heaven's sake, don't let any humans near those,' the doctor had said. 'There's enough chloral in them to put an army out for a couple of weeks. Better to overdo it than give standard doses. We don't know the stamina of the beasts.'

We don't know if I'm going to get within spitting distance of them either, Rushia thought. Then they went over the maps for the last time, took him up on deck and loaded him into a helicopter.

They flew in very low over the sea, hovering just off the PCH to let him down the rope dropped from the main door. Rushia hit the ground with adrenaline pumping, moving fast into the rocky area sloping away from the highway.

It proved to be five miles of very heavy going. The ground undulated, and he thought that seeing it from the air did not prepare you for dealing with the real thing. It took almost two hours, as he was careful to dodge between rocks and keep his eyes skinned for sentries or look-outs which he was pretty certain Brokenclaw would have posted around the western limit of the property. But there were none, and when he finally reached a rock-strewn bluff overlooking the house, Rushia saw why.

A short distance below him, men worked hard to clear the wreckage of a helicopter. He only hoped to heaven that Bond had not perished in what must have been a nasty crash. Something had to happen soon. It would be dusk in less than two hours.

Carefully he scanned the entire area through the binoculars. The wolf pen was way over to his right, but he thought there was a useful piece of high ground from which he could operate. It took a good half-hour of painstaking movement to bring him to the chosen site – the top of a mound which was heavily scored with rocks and boulders.

Below, about a hundred yards away, he could see with his naked eyes the long wolf pen and the big low cage in which the beasts prowled. They looked, he thought, mightily excited, but, if he were to do the job properly, he would have to risk being seen, or even caught. Hunkering down behind the rocks, he removed the pack and laid everything but the side-arm on the ground. Lastly, he pulled on the pair of surgical gloves they had given him and opened the pack, bringing out the foil-covered package. 'Don't want you licking your fingers after handling that stuff,' the doctor had told him. Now he glanced at his watch. It had taken a very long time to get this far. By his reckoning around five hours had passed since M had first asked him if he would undertake the job. The Special Forces unit must already be on the way, but what of Bond? It might already be too late for him.

Loosening the pistol in his holster, Ed Rushia slowly rose from the rocks and moved quickly down the slope towards the wolf pen. The small gate at the extreme end of the enclosure was fastened only by a simple bolt, and he was through and walking quickly towards the cage in a matter of seconds.

The seven wolves inside the edge itself seemed to become excited, even agitated, as he approached, recoiling slightly at the smell which came from them.

They were magnificent. Big and with long grey coats, occasionally giving a throaty growl as they started to crowd towards the bars of the cage.

Some six feet from the bars, Rushia squatted down, listened for any odd sounds and then unwrapped the package, disclosing the dozen juicy and bloody steaks which had been doctored with chloral.

When he tossed the first steak through the bars there was pandemonium as the beasts fought over the food. So he quickly followed up with the other steaks, running along the outside of the cage and throwing them in, one at a time, so that they would land in different spots.

In all, it took around five minutes, and the wolves were still fighting and grabbing at the red meat. He had done all he could, so Rushia moved swiftly back along the enclosure, through the gate which he bolted, then up the hundred yards to his little eyrie where he made himself comfortable, settling behind the rifle in case it became necessary for him to turn from Navy commander to sniper first class.

Occasionally he viewed the wolves through the scope. They still prowled to and fro, though he noticed that at least one of the brutes had started to stagger as he walked, while another had lain on the floor of the cage. From time to time one or the other of them would emit a howl, a cross between a cry of anxiety and a yawn.

Then he heard the noise floating from the other side of the clump of trees. People were approaching.

Later, Rushia was to say that the total barbarity of the next few minutes left him cold and unable to move. The little party came into sight, the huge figure of Brokenclaw Lee walking slowly so that the elderly Chinese could hobble beside him with the help of a cane, Bond being led by two uniformed men, while another pair followed behind. Then came the two Chinese, one a big bruiser of a man with a bandaged head, the other emaciated and carrying a bucket.

Rushia froze as he saw what was intended, feeling nauseated as Bond was stripped and the massive Brokenclaw daubed him with what looked like grease from the bucket. They manhandled Bond into the wolf run and Rushia suddenly became very angry. The nausea turned to cold hatred and he lifted the rifle, zeroing on to Brokenclaw Lee himself, then lowering the weapon to watch with horror as they pegged his friend on to the ground and moved quickly back to the outside of the enclosed run.

He heard Bond's shout loud and clear. 'Go to hell where you belong, Brokenclaw Lee, son of a Chinese tailor and a Blackfoot whore.'

Then Lee's rejoinder, 'Kill!'

He even heard the section of the cage rattle upwards and saw four of the wolves come bounding out making little half-hearted howling sounds.

Rushia turned the rifle towards the wolves, then lowered it once more as he saw what was happening.

The first beast to come from the cage seemed to slide to a halt and blink around him, his head moving and snout lifting, sniffing the air. Then the wolf took a couple of staggering paces, as though drunk, before he rolled over on his back giving tired little howls.

Similar things were going on among the other wolves. One found the leap from the cage into brightness too much. It skidded to a halt, legs buckling from under it, while the other two wolves just wandered aimlessly, staggering and uncertain of where they were or what they should do.

One was still asleep in the cage, and the final pair came slowly into the arena.

Brokenclaw was shouting something, as though trying to urge his killers into action. Rushia heard the words, 'Not been fed since last night . . .' float upwards.

'Wrong,' he said aloud.

One of the final pair had just stretched out in a warm patch of sun, while the other, Rushia saw with some anxiety, was inching its way unsteadily towards Bond. He raised the rifle again, then began to chuckle. The wolf had reached the junction of Bond's thighs and was licking at whatever Brokenclaw had smeared there. But the licks were desultory and looked like small signs of affection. At last, with Brokenclaw heading towards the gate into the enclosure, the animal just curled up against Bond's legs, laid his muzzle on a thigh and relaxed into unconsciousness.

The cross-hairs on Rushia's scope were spot on Brokenclaw's head as he pulled open the gate and as he pulled so the action appeared to set off the first explosion.

It came like a dull double crump, a column of smoke billowing up from the far northern extremity behind the house.

Brokenclaw turned, his face registering amazement. Then came the second explosion, nearer at hand, less than fifty yards on the other side of the copse. Below him, Rushia watched the sudden chaos – Brokenclaw shouting orders, the old Chinese staring about him utterly bewildered, while the men with weapons started to run back towards the house.

Ed Rushia fired once, putting the bullet almost at Lee's feet, but the big man was moving very quickly now, out of the enclosure and back towards the house, dragging the little old Chinese man with him.

At that moment two big Blackhawk helicopters seemed to rise from the direction of the road and hover at either end of the boundaries, while ropes snaked down and troops abseiled to the ground. As soon as the first waves were out, the helicopters moved upwards, making room for the second wave.

By this time Rushia was on his feet and running down towards the enclosure, arms and legs going every which way as he raced towards the spreadeagled form of Bond.

'You cut that a little fine.' Bond took a deep breath. In spite of his outward calm, Rushia had little doubt that 007 was almost at the extreme point of shock. He cut through the leather thongs, rolled the sleeping wolf from his friend's leg and said, 'Good grief, James, you smell like a polecat.'

'The damned fat they spread on me. Let me out. Let me get to my clothes and for heaven's sake give me a weapon.'

Rushia followed him. Rarely had he seen anyone dress so quickly. When he was fully clothed, Bond grabbed the pistol from Rushia's holster. 'You've got a rifle, so you're okay,' he shouted as he dashed towards the noise coming from the direction of the house.

There were dull crumps which Bond correctly identified as flash-bangs – stun grenades – and the occasional shot was underscored by the quick rattling bursts of automatic weapons.

He reached the far side of the hangar of trees. Smoke was pouring from the southern exit to the bunker, and as he neared it, a uniformed figure, the face covered with a breathing mask, shouted a muffled, 'Halt! Drop the gun! Now!'

'Custodian!' Bond yelled, hoping the assault team had been given their respective code names.

'Okay, sir. Captain who?'

'Bond,' he shouted. 'James Bond. Now let me get in there.'

The mask was obviously fitted with a speaker device, for the Special Forces man could be heard clearly. 'Best not try it without a mask, sir.'

'Well, get me one.' Bond's adrenaline was pumping, and he was aware that most of the firing had stopped.

'James.' It was his old friend Bill Tanner in camouflage fatigues, a pistol in his hand. 'I think they've got the lot.' He was puffing a little as he reached Bond who made an immediate grab for the smoke mask that dangled from Tanner's waist.

'Let me see for myself,' he shouted, slipping the mask across his face and adjusting the straps.

'Put that on.' Tanner shoved a Special Forces armband around Bond's wrist and up his right arm.

When he reached the southern exit, troops were already bringing people out, but he saw neither Brokenclaw nor Bone Bender Ding among them. 'Hold them back, I need to get in,' he snapped at the officer in charge.

'Who's asking?' the man sounded belligerent.

'Custodian!' he snapped. 'Captain Bond, Royal Navy.'

'Okay, you're cleared, sir.' The Special Forces officer sounded no less belligerent, but held back the line of prisoners being herded out.

As he proceeded into the corridor, he looked at every face in the line of men being prodded and shoved into the sunlight above. The deeper he went the more anxious he became. Not only was there no sign of Brokenclaw, Ding, or even General H'ang, but he had not set eyes on anyone remotely looking like one of the Navy prisoners. Nor Chi-Chi. All his instincts told him that it was far from over yet.

In the room that had been Lee's study, several officers and enlisted men were gathered around the table looking at a drawing of the complex maze of tunnels.

No smoke lingered here, so Bond took off the mask and quickly introduced himself. 'Unless you've taken people out of the north exit, you haven't got them all, not by any stretch.'

'We know that, Captain Bond. There are still some down there. Here.' His finger traced one of the offshoots from the main corridor. 'But we haven't identified it.'

Bond's mind raced back. He had been taken from the secure room where they had left Chi-Chi. Yes, the passage was small and had led straight into the main corridor. Chi-Chi had said something about a false wall and a narrow passage. 'I think I know.' He did not even wait for anyone to follow him but dived through the door and dashed down the stairs, heading along the northern corridor. The passages sprouted to left and right then about two hundred yards into the tunnel, he saw the start of an oblong passage leading to the left. It looked as though nobody had bothered to extend it, for six paces inside, it was blocked by what seemed to be a solid brick wall. Chi-Chi had said something about kicking a brick at the lower left side. Looking down it was plain that the brick in question protruded slightly. Bond kicked and the whole wall slid away, revealing a lighted passage. A figure moved thirty yards down, shouting and turning at the same moment.

Frozen Stalk Pu lifted a handgun, but Bond already had two shots away, and Pu levitated for a second before being flung back to sprawl on the floor.

There were cheers from further down the passage. The Naval prisoners, he presumed. Someone shouted, 'That bastard Ding's with the girl.'

Bond's feet hardly touched the ground as he covered the distance to what he now recognised as the secure room where he had last been with Chi-Chi. Pistol at the high port, he lashed out at the door and leaped into the room.

There was a blurred image of Chi-Chi, now quite naked, cowering in a corner, but the next thing he knew was a ferocious kick which sent his pistol flying.

Bond dropped and rolled, coming up to face the grinning, gold-toothed Bone Bender Ding. 'Now you fin' out why they call me Bone Bender,' the giant hissed.

Bond moved in, but Ding was fast and very good. Feinting left, his foot lashed out catching Bond's shin and toppling him to the floor. He was on his feet again quickly, but Ding performed an almost balletic pirouette. His body seemed to hang sideways in the air for a second as both feet slammed into Bond's chest, one after the other.

Bond staggered against the wall; his chest seemed on fire and he had difficulty breathing.

Ding smiled and bounced from one leg to the other. 'One on one bit different for you, eh?'

Bond did not even see the right leg lift and straighten, slamming into his chest again, knocking the breath from his body. Yet instinct warned him of the left leg which he was just able to sidestep and grab, giving the foot a quick wrench. He knew this was mostly luck – against a man like Ding, he was out of his league.

Ding was indeed up and coming in at him again. A right hand smashed forward, the arm straight, knuckles like iron grazing Bond's cheek. 'Chi-Chi, where's the gun?' he whispered. But the Chinese was coming in again, putting the entire weight of his body into a swift curving jump, turning to smash into Bond sideways.

As he hit the wall, Bond heard Chi-Chi whisper, 'Here. By me, James.' Before he could even glance in her direction, Ding was swinging into his Ninja kicks again, the heels of each foot making contact, one to the shoulder and the other to the face. They felt like bullet shocks and he reeled against the wall, just in time to see one foot come up. For the second time, he managed to grasp the foot and wrench it, first one way, then the other, going with the body and then against it.

Ding gave a growl of anger as he slewed over on to the bare concrete floor. He took a few seconds to get back on his feet and Bond only needed a blink of time. The pistol he had taken from Rushia was close to where Chi-Chi was trying to push herself through the wall.

He dived towards it as Ding's foot came whistling within an inch of his head. He saw the big Chinese back away, then gather himself for what would be the final lunge that would send his entire weight and body smashing into Bond. Ding seemed to rise in the air and hurtle towards his target as though propelled by a rocket.

Bond curled into a ball, lifted his right hand and squeezed the trigger twice. He heard the explosions like grenades in the small room. Ding just kept on flying towards him, his mouth blood-flecked and open in surprise. He landed flat against the wall near Chi-Chi. There was a moment when the big Chinese appeared to be nailed there, just hanging like some terrible three-dimensional mural. Then he crumpled, leaving several snakes of blood on the white cement.

Chi-Chi screamed.

She did not stop screaming until Bond put his arms around her and told her it was okay. 'It's over,' he kept saying. 'It's all over.'

'No it's not.' Bill Tanner stood in the doorway.

'Get something to cover the girl, Bill,' Bond said quietly, and a second later, Ed Rushia was in the room with a blanket over one arm and his eyes averted.

Bond draped the blanket around Chi-Chi's shaking body. 'Just stay here,' he told her. 'It's going to be fine. Look, Ed's by the door. Nobody's coming to get you.'

'Please don't leave me, James. Please!'

'Only for a moment.' Gently he untangled himself and went into the corridor. 'What's up?' he asked Tanner.

'Come and take a look.'

They went further down the narrow passage, past the barred rooms from which the original hostages were being taken, and then up steps and out into the waning day.

'He's not here.' Tanner's voice was dull with disappointment.

'Lee?'

Tanner nodded.

'General H'ang?' Bond asked, and the chief of staff shook his head.

'Both of them. They're both gone.'

'They can't have got far.' They had started to walk back towards the house.

'We think he had another helicopter stashed away at this end,' Tanner said dryly. 'There's a small wood to the north, and they're going up now to see if it's like the other hangar. Two of the Special Forces people say they thought another chopper took off in the middle of the whole business. We've alerted the FAA and all the radar stations. They've got aircraft up looking. Fighters were scrambled from Alameda. So far, no joy.'

A figure was approaching from the southern side of the house, and Bond recognised Broderick, the San Francisco FBI Bureau Chief.

'I understand I've an apology to make, Captain Bond,' Broderick began.

'No, no time for that.' Another thought had raced through Bond's mind. 'Anyone know of a house in Sausalito where Lee might have stashed Wanda? Because that's where she is.'

'There's a cathouse out there that we've often thought had

links with Brokenclaw.' Broderick reached for his pager. 'I'll get someone on to it now. Nolan and Wood aren't busy . . .'

'Oh, no,' said Bond, quietly. 'I think you're going to need a man to man talk with Messrs Nolan and Wood. A man to man talk in an interrogation room.'

He was about to tell the FBI officer all he knew about his agents Wood and Nolan, when a youngish, thin man with long hair shambled up to them in the fast dimming light. He was dressed in jeans and a T-shirt emblazoned with a colourful decoration of a skull frozen into a block of ice, underneath which the words 'Ice Age' were displayed in a Gothic script.

'Hey, man,' the newcomer began. 'Hey, that was some real heavy music you were playing just now. Real heavy.'

Both Tanner and Broderick looked aghast. 'I think this is the owner of the main house, gentlemen.' Bond inclined his head towards the figure. 'Mr Marty Halman of Ice Age?'

'Yeah. Man that music was heavy. Awesome.'

Bond smiled. 'Thank you. We thought it was kind of humongously awesome ourselves.'

17

NEW DAYS, NEW WAYS,
LOVE STAYS

The military unit left twenty men to comb the tunnels, passage-ways and the grounds around Brokenclaw's hideout.

Everyone else was loaded into helicopters and ferried back to the carrier where they waited for news. At around nine thirty on that Friday evening, Broderick, the local FBI Bureau chief, went off to Sausalito with some local members of the Marin County Sheriff's Department. They found Wanda Man Song Hing in a sprawling house tucked away behind the boutiques, cafés, shops and art galleries of Bridgeway, the main street which led down to the waterfront with its magnificent view of the San Francisco skyline.

They arrested ten other young girls, four brawny men who were obviously there to protect the place, Mama Tia, the Madame of this particular moneyspinner, and several clients, some of whom had reputations to lose.

In a further development, agents Nolan and Wood were suspended from duty pending serious allegations against them. Only later did Broderick wish he had pushed for their arrest and incarceration.

Wanda was moved immediately to the Naval hospital. She was in shock, had been badly beaten, but, according to the doctors, would soon recover her physical strength. They would not vouch for her mental state until they had time to evaluate her.

Both Chi-Chi and Bond were taken down to the ship's hospital, where Chi-Chi's back was treated for the deep welts made by Brokenclaw's whip, and Bond was X-rayed. Though bruised he had no broken bones. 'I would suggest you take a shower, Captain Bond,' the doctor said. 'To be blunt, you stink like a skunk.' The animal fat Brokenclaw had spread around his loins was still active. 'You need rest,' the doctor added, and he was given a stateroom near the hospital area.

They had brought all his clothes and travelling equipment to the carrier, so he showered, first in scalding water, rubbing himself down with Clinique soap, which he had only recently discovered, and now preferred to anything he had ever used before. Next he showered again, this time in cold water, allowing the sharp needlepoints of the spray to wash away any excess oil in his opened pores. He towelled himself dry, and splashed Penhaligon's cologne over his body. Only then did he realise how exhausted he had become. He slept until a steward brought him coffee at ten the next morning.

Half-an-hour later Bill Tanner came down with the ASP 9mm. 'They found it among some other weapons in the bunker. You okay now?'

'They must have salvaged it from the helicopter wreck, Bill. Yes, I'm fine. How's Chi-Chi?'

'Walking wounded, but you're both expected up in M's cabin for a conference in an hour.'

Bond hefted the pistol in his hand. 'You get me some shells for this thing?' he asked.

Tanner said he would try and, in fact, handed over a small box of ammunition when Bond arrived at the day cabin that M had used throughout as his headquarters.

The *Curve* operations team was all present – M, Franks, the CIA man, John Grant with a couple of his men, the officer commanding the Special Forces unit, Commander Edwin Rushia, Chi-Chi and Bond.

M outlined the situation by congratulating all who had taken part in the tracking down, penetrating and assaulting what he called Brokenclaw's burrow. Then he gave them what he called a Profit and Loss balance sheet.

'On the profit side, we have managed to break up a complex and sophisticated hideout, which the man Brokenclaw Lee has undoubtedly used for a long time,' he began. 'Also on the profit side a very serious operation has been stopped in its tracks. Both my own Service and the CIA have long been aware that the Chinese, following sight of a similar plan which appears to have been formulated by Japanese businessmen, have been co-ordinating an operation which we all knew as *Jericho*. Its aim was to bring down Wall Street by hacking into the Stock Exchange computers, buying, selling, altering prices surreptitiously.

'Nobody realised how advanced this particular piece of skulduggery had become, and after seeing the amount of computerised detail hidden in Brokenclaw's vaults, it would appear that we put a stop to the business just in time. I should add that the ladies and gentlemen of Wall Street and the London Stock Exchange have, at our instigation, taken new security steps which will, eventually, prevent anyone from tampering with the system. We all know that while computers have made our lives easier and can provide instant access to information, they are also a danger, particularly when operated by skilled people who are able to interfere with information stored in corporate data bases. Computer fraud could lead to terrible financial chaos.'

Lastly, on the profit side, he talked about the rescue of the five Naval experts taken hostage. 'They undoubtedly provided huge amounts of classified intelligence concerning the Anglo-American projects Lords and Lords Day. Happily, we're ninety-nine per cent sure that we've recovered *all* the existing material, due to the work of Ms Sue Chi-Ho and Captain James Bond.'

Before passing on to the loss side of the balance sheet, M said he would like to call on his Service's special expert, Mr Franks, to say something about Brokenclaw's manipulation of the hostages.

Franks stood, his twitch becoming more and more pronounced as he talked at some length on how Brokenclaw had elicited the vital and classified information from the hostages.

'We are only in the very early stages of debriefing, as you can imagine,' he started, 'but already a picture is emerging which is both sinister and a cause for future concern.' He said that if Brokenclaw alone had carried out the hostage-takings and the manner of their interrogation, he had been very highly trained. So far, all five of the hostages had admitted to the same kind of treatment.

'There are several unique and vital steps, known well to psychiatrists and ruthless interrogators, which if followed, lead inevitably to the breaking of a victim. Contrary to popular belief, these breaking techniques can sometimes be used to manipulate very quickly. Fiction nowadays claims that the most dependable fast interrogations have to be performed with the assistance of mind- and mood altering drugs. Under some circumstances, the drugs are a hindrance. Manipulation and coercion can be achieved with the body alert and the mind clear, though possibly bewildered.'

He went on to outline the steps required to accomplish this. First, the abduction had to be sudden. No questions would be answered, no details given; and a quick move made into a restrained environment, preferably in darkness. The victim would not know what was happening to him. Next, in order to break the hostage, you had to make him vulnerable. Keep him in darkness, but remove all clothing, restrain him, deny him the normal facilities of a bathroom and abuse the victim physically, probably by irregular sessions of violence. These could range from beating up people to giving them so-called shock or burn treatment.

Allied to these first premises, there was another, possibly the most important step. The hostage had to be removed from what psychiatrists called 'normal daylight patterns'. In simple language, they would be, literally, kept in the dark.

'Once you have unbalanced a person through abduction, restrained that person, made that person vulnerable, and disorientated that person by removing his time pattern, the rest is relatively simple and can be divided into three stages,' Franks continued in his cold, matter-of-fact tone which made Bond wonder how many times this man had practised these very techniques.

'You begin to control through random violence and random reward. A person is beaten up three times in, say, five hours, but between these acts of violence there is one reward – a glass of water or a hunk of bread, a cigarette or the use of a bathroom. But always in the dark, always isolated, always unsure of why this is happening.'

Further, Franks told them, there were other pressures – threats to the victim's family, threats of harsher treatment by some unseen and unknown person who is painted as a monster, sudden and irrelevant leniency. 'Four days of this kind of treatment can, in well-controlled circumstances, bring the victim to rely wholly on his captor. It is then that the captor makes himself known, makes promises and begins to show the victim that he is in charge. If the scenario has been properly played out, then the rest is child's play. Confused and lost, the victim will sign anything, give any information, just by being promised a return to normal life.'

Again, Franks maintained that so far, all five hostages had described their treatment in those very terms. They were held in dark cupboards, blindfolded and chained to the wall, naked and with no room to move. They were beaten up one minute, given food the next. They *all* appeared to have lost track of time. Each one claimed to have suffered horrific humiliation before Brokenclaw revealed himself as the man who pulled the strings. To clinch it all, they had identified the coffin-sized torture chambers where each of the men had been kept after their abduction.

'I defy anyone not to give up even stratospherically classified material under these circumstances,' Franks finished. 'I am certain, also, that all these men will suffer only a court of enquiry. None will be required to go through a court martial.'

During Franks' long explanation of how the kidnapped officers and men had been separated from the classified information, the CIA man, Grant, had taken two telephone calls and spent a short time whispering to M, who now told them that he could fill in the debit side of the balance sheet 'Indeed, I am in a better position to do that, for Mr Grant's colleagues have come up with certain pieces of new intelligence.'

Soberly, M said that the news was not good. 'First, it appears that both the Chinese General H'ang, and his associate, Brokenclaw Lee, have vanished into thin air.' The helicopter which had undoubtedly brought H'ang to what M referred to as Brokenclaw's lair, had been found abandoned only five miles north of San Francisco.

'H'ang came into this country posing as a Hong Kong businessman. That is now certain. We have details and records. The passport, visa and other papers were impeccable forgeries. Our CIA friends have yet to discover how he came to be provided with a helicopter, but doubtless the Lee fellow could tell us that, if we could find him. Naturally, all ports and airports are being watched. There is a police alert out for both men, but H'ang in particular.'

He went on to say everyone was convinced that Lee was essentially the leading Chinese Intelligence resident in the United States. 'As such, he is undoubtedly privy to the identity and whereabouts of every single Chinese agent at large in the United States. Therefore, it is essential that Lee is caught, sooner rather than later. I would go as far as to say that he is America's and Britain's most wanted man.'

Bond said nothing. Already he thought he knew where

Brokenclaw Lee could be found, but he was battered, bruised and very tired. He put the thoughts on hold. There would be time enough to follow up his theories which were more than mere hunches.

'Sadly,' M continued, 'we see no reason for keeping the *Curve* team operational, but we're going to wait until Monday in case anything else turns up. All of you are welcome to take the rest of the weekend off and reassemble here at 09.00 hours on Monday to make the final decision. I shall be staying aboard, but that need not apply to the rest of you.'

The words were hardly out of his mouth before Chi-Chi whispered in Bond's ear, 'Please, James, please, you stay with me, yes?'

He gave her a long look which needed no further explanation. 'Certainly. I'm honoured, Chi-Chi.'

'Hey, James.' Big Ed Rushia was behind him. 'You're welcome to come stay with me and my little child bride; she's the damnedest cook. Makes an incredible gazpacho, if you like cold soup. She also produces apple pies just like Ma used to make.'

'Unhappily, my ma never made apple pies.' Bond tilted an eyebrow. 'I'd love to stay, Ed, but I'm afraid I've had a previous invitation which not even the demon Brokenclaw could make me give up.'

'Ah!' Rushia said, looking at Bond and then at Chi-Chi. 'Ah!' again. 'Bless you, my children. May your days be long and your nights longer. I'll give you my number, though, just in case the novelty wears off.' He slipped his card into Bond's hand, and with a cheery wave, left the cabin.

Tanner approached them, saying they would have to delay any departure as Franks wanted to go through one or two points with both of them. It was well after five before they were taken back to the mainland.

Chi-Chi lived high in an apartment building on Union Street. 'It's not all fixed up yet,' she warned him, but, when they arrived, Bond was impressed by what he saw. It was not large –

a living room, bedroom and kitchen, but it had a huge picture window looking out towards the Golden Gate Bridge and the furnishings were new, modern and very comfortable. There were a couple of extremely good reproductions on the walls of the living room, together with an attractive, framed museum poster advertising a da Vinci exhibition and an excellent original oil by Eyvind Earle in the bedroom.

Within half-an-hour he felt comfortable and relaxed, as though he had lived in this apartment for some time. There was no clutter and the kitchen was what his old housekeeper, May, would have called 'prick neat'.

'Relax, James. I'll get us some dinner. Unless you want to go out and live it up.'

'I don't really think you're in any condition to go out and live it up, and I feel as though I've just gone four rounds with Mike Tyson. In fact, I really think you ought to go to bed while I get you something light on a tray.'

'That an invitation, James?'

'Could be. You Chinese are so inscrutable, though.'

'I'm an inscrutable American, Captain Bond.' She came to-wards him, her eyes again locking with his. She winced slightly as he put his arms around her and he quickly apologised for his clumsiness. Then his mouth was on hers and it was as though he had known her lips for years. He pressed harder and she pushed against him. In the bedroom he said, 'Your back, Chi-Chi. Be careful of your back.'

'James, my dear, I know many ways to please us both without lying on my back.'

Three hours later, he had to concede that she knew a whole encyclopedia of ideas that neither hurt her back nor his own bruised ribs. There were moments when Bond experienced that sense of wonder only granted to some men once in a lifetime, as her slim body seemed to float above his, light as a wisp of gauze yet giving and taking something more than just lustful pleasure.

They ate a simple meal of what Chi-Chi called *her* Caesar salad, but which Bond would have called a very good Salade Niçoise, followed by raspberries from her freezer with whipped cream. The coffee, he noticed, was Swedish, the Traditional Roast, freshly ground.

They sat over the coffee and brandy looking at the great undulating strings of lights marking the bridge, until Chi-Chi stifled a yawn.

'I'm sorry.' Bond reached over and held her hand. 'I haven't been talking much. A lot on my mind, Chi-Chi.'

'There is an old proverb.' She looked at him from under lowered lids. 'I think maybe it is Chinese, and it says, "Those who have love need no prattle."'

Bond gave her a smile with his eyes. 'I didn't know there was a Chinese word for prattle.'

'Maybe it's an old English proverb.'

'Maybe.' He was silent again for a moment. Then, 'You remember when we woke in Brokenclaw's lair? The morning when we thought we were in Virginia?'

'Could I forget?'

'I thought I had forgotten, but at one point during that day I remembered something. It was a sundial in Virginia. At the university of that state, there's an inscription on a sundial which says—

> Time is
> Too slow for those who wait,
> Too swift for those who fear,
> Too long for those who grieve,
> Too short for those who rejoice,
> But for those who love, time is
> Eternity.
> Hours fly,
> Flowers die,
> New days,

> New ways,
> Pass by.
> Love stays.

'I thought of that; remembered that, on the morning we saw the Blue Ridge from the bottom of a devil's pit, Chi-Chi, and I'll never think of you without remembering those words.'

She rose, took his hand and gently led him back into the bedroom.

They spent a lazy lovers' Sunday, rising late and eating brunch together on the small table by the picture window. It was two in the afternoon before they finished the meal – orange juice, eggs, bacon, waffles with real maple syrup and coffee. Then they showered and went back to bed, rising again around six.

'I wanted to make us a splendid dinner tonight. A kind of celebration.' Chi-Chi was in the kitchen. 'I have everything but wine, and you love wine, James.'

'I can live without it.' He kissed her. 'But why don't I try to find some? American cities always have shops open on a Sunday.'

She gave a little pout. 'There's quite a good liquor store two blocks up. But I don't want you to go. I'll put some clothes on and come with you.'

'And that'll take weeks. I'll try to get us some champagne. Does your liquor store sell champagne? And is that okay for the surprise you're preparing?'

'Couldn't be better.' She kissed him again. 'Please don't be long, darling. I can get my treat in the oven and we can have a whole free hour until it's ready.'

On his way out, Bond picked up the ASP which had never been far away from him since their arrival. 'The password's "Time",' he said, and she laughed.

'I mean it, Chi-Chi. Don't open up unless it's me. Our friend Lee's still around, and I don't think he's the kind of man who forgives and forgets. Eventually we're going to have to round him up or kill him. He *must* know that.'

'Time,' she said, frowning. 'Yes, I do know we'll have to get him and I can't wait. I can't wait to get him either.'

'Hussy!' Bond stuck the pistol in his waistband behind his right hip and left.

It took almost half-an-hour, and all he could get was Californian champagne, but by now, he was quite converted to American wines.

He knew something was wrong before the lift reached Chi-Chi's floor. Instinct, he wondered, then realised it had nothing to do with instinct; the lift held traces of Bal à Versailles, and that was what Chi-Chi had been wearing.

The door hung half off its hinges, and she had put up a struggle, for the place was a mess. One chair smashed, a table lamp thrown across the room, the glass over the poster fragmented and the drapes on one side of the picture window pulled so that they hung sideways from their fixings as though she had grabbed at them and fallen.

'Chi-Chi!' he called, knowing there would be no reply. Again, 'Chi-Chi!' as he ran to the bedroom.

She was not there either, but the beautiful Eyvind Earle oil painting was ripped and riven by an arrow from which hung a message.

> If you want to see her alive again, you will come to Muir Woods
> alone at one thirty precisely tonight.
> LEE

Bond went through to the living room, picked up an overturned table and found the telephone on the floor beside it. He was about to dial when he had second thoughts. Training? Experience? Or just the automatic reaction of one who always thinks in terms of listening devices and surveillance.

He rode the lift down to the street again, found a telephone booth and dialled a number.

When it was answered, he said, 'Ed, I need you. Now.' His voice was unsteady and the words, 'Flowers die, New days, New ways, Pass by. Love stays' screamed through his head.

18

THE CHELAN MOUNTAINS

He waited in the lobby of the apartment building until Rushia arrived fifteen minutes later.

'What the heck's the matter, James? You look like a ghost.'

Bond found himself unable to speak. He just nodded, indicating that Rushia should follow him.

'Well, that wasn't any lovers' tiff,' Rushia said, standing just inside the door of Chi-Chi's apartment.

'It's not funny, Ed. Look in the bedroom.'

'Oh, shit. No!' Rushia came out of the bedroom and motioned Bond into a chair. 'You called the cops.'

He shook his head. 'The last thing I want is cops.'

'Then you're going to Muir Woods? It's not exactly private there. They have forest rangers and all. It's a National Monument, for crying out loud.'

Bond had visited the woods on several occasions, and like thousands of others, had marvelled at the giant redwood trees which tower on the edge of Mount Tamalpais State Park. 'I'm going nowhere near Muir Woods,' he said, a dull edge to his voice.

'So what the hell happens to Chi-Chi? Lee says you have to be there if you ever want to see her alive again. James, old buddy, you're risking her life.'

'I don't think so.'

'Why, for heaven's sake?'

'Because I think the Muir Woods thing is a set-up. I think I know where that bastard Brokenclaw Lee is holed up.'

'You *think* you know? Hell, James, this isn't a time for hunches. You've *got to know*, not just have some kind of an instinct.'

'Okay, then – I *know* where he is. The Muir Woods meeting's almost certainly a blind. Sure, it's probably some sort of ambush as well, but I'm heading for the place I *know* he's at.'

'So what do *I* do? Sit on my thumbs and eat Gummi Bears?'

'We're all supposed to be in that conference tomorrow morning, Ed. Well, sure as hell, Chi-Chi isn't going to be there. Neither am I, and if you agree to help, neither will you.'

'Is that right? We going AWOL, James? If you say yes to that, I didn't hear you. What I heard was we're taking some of the leave due to both of us.'

'You'll come?'

'Only if you're really sure.'

'Near as dammit.'

'That's near enough for me. Hey,' Rushia's eyes were focused on something near the sagging drapes. 'What the heck's that doo-hickey down there?'

Bond saw it as Rushia pointed. Something small, glinting on the carpet. He reached down and came up with a stick pin, the kind of thing people wore in their lapels to show they belonged to the Rotarians or the Elks. This one had three tiny letters fixed to its head. The letters spelled out FBI.

'So now we know who snatched her.' Bond looked blankly at the pin. 'I'm not only going to get Brokenclaw, but I think I'll probably also have a go at those crooks Nolan and Wood.'

'Just say the word, James, and I'm with you.'

'It's more than just a word, Ed. I need inside help. Information. I need to know stuff that I think you can get for me.'

'Shoot.'

Bond talked carefully for a good half-an-hour. When he had finished, Rushia leaned back in his chair. 'There's an awful lot of it, James, but I can probably get it all within an hour or so –

make that two hours, so why don't you get this place squared away while I go and do the jobs? I'll call you as soon as I have anything. Better, I'll come and pick you up but I also think we've got to watch our backs; leave some billay doo, as they say in Paris, France, just to make certain the old folks at home know roughly where we're heading.'

'I leave that entirely to you, Ed, but the last thing I want is the cavalry coming to my rescue. If I'm going to do this, I'm going to do it alone. It's an end game. Me and Brokenclaw alone.'

'And what if he doesn't see it your way?'

'The man has a gigantic ego, Ed. I can't see him turning down a chance to beat me, one on one, as your people say.'

'A one on one with that guy could mean something pretty deadly, Jim.'

'Don't ever call me Jim.' There was no humour in his voice. 'I know a guy called Geoffrey in the business, back in London. He has a damned great notice in his office. It says 'The name is Geoffrey, *not* Geoff.' That's the way I feel. The name's James, not Jim.'

'Excuse me,' Rushia said with exaggerated politeness. 'Just didn't know you cared.'

When he had gone, Bond began to tidy up. He hauled the door back into place, took down the shattered poster and generally made the apartment look a little less messy.

The telephone rang around midnight. Rushia said he had everything they needed. He would pick him up within the hour.

'We'll have to charter,' Rushia said when Bond was seated next to him in a big green Chevy sedan. 'I don't see us getting on any regular flights. I left word, by the way. Said all three of us had gotten a sniff of Brokenclaw and couldn't raise anyone else.'

'Will that hold up?'

'Maybe not for ever, but it should give us twenty-four hours.' Then he started in on the information Bond required.

The area around the Chelan Mountains, high in the north of Washington State, was what Ed called 'Vacation Land'. 'There're

scenic routes to walk or drive. They ski there in the winter –
there's been no snow as yet this year, but it's going to be cold.
We'll need some heavy clothing, but most of the holiday stuff
goes on south of Lake Chelan. This reservation you talked
about . . .'

'Yes?'

'It's a semi-official thing. Washington State has a lot of regular
Indian Reservations. The one you're after isn't just confined to
Blackfoot people either.'

Bond waited. Since he had seen the arrow piercing the oil
painting in Chi-Chi's bedroom and read the message attached to
it, he had heard one thing over and over again in Brokenclaw's
voice—

'I doubt if I could live with myself if I did not spend time
among my other people. I need to recharge my batteries like the
next man. There are members of the old Blackfoot Confederacy
who live apart. High in the Chelan Mountains, in Washington
State, there is a peaceful camp where they live out their lives in
the old way. I go there often. I like to breathe the smoke from my
tepee, reflect on life, talk to my ancestors.'

It was not a mere hunch that had brought him to the conclusion that Brokenclaw had gone off to this 'peaceful camp' as
he had called it. This was logic. If Brokenclaw believed in his
own powers of escape, evasion and ability to remain outside the
law, the camp in the Chelan Mountains was the one place he
would go. Maybe to recharge his batteries, possibly to take stock,
to think out his next move. He would have funds outside the
United States, and in the peace of the mountains, he could, as he
put it, breathe the smoke from his tepee and make a decision.

If he wanted revenge on the two people who had been the
cause of his downfall, it was in those mountains he would wreak
that revenge. Chi-Chi would be there, and Brokenclaw's logic
must have told him that Bond would eventually follow.

'Not just Blackfoot people?' he queried.

Rushia took the car on to the airport road. 'Nope. Around

twelve years ago a number of Indians from various tribes settled in the Yakima, Colville, Warm Springs and Nez Perce Reservations, asked if they could live outside their allotted reservations in a camp of their own choice. There were Blackfoot Confederacy people, Cheyenne, Sioux, Crow and Mandans. They swore an oath that they would live together in peace, but they wanted to live in the old way. Up there they don't bother anyone. They're self-supporting, they use original tools, they hunt game and small animals and they keep to themselves.

'Somehow they've worked out a common understanding with one another. There have been rumours that they practise a lot of their old, somewhat barbarous ceremonies, but, as long as nobody bothers them, they don't cause any trouble. I have a map that'll take you right up to the camp.'

'Where do we go first?'

'We hire an air taxi, James. That'd be our fastest route, a jet if possible, to the field at Wenatchee. Then we hire a Range Rover or some such. There's a track that'll take us to within five miles of the place. It's uphill, through wooded country, but the paths are there if you look for them. Map's in the glove compartment here.'

'I'll look at it on the aircraft. If we can get an aircraft.'

They got a Learjet, and when they said where they wanted to go, they also got a strange look. 'Something going on up near Wenatchee?' the man from Weatherproof Air Services asked.

'Not that we know of. This is a mission we're on. Government business.'

'Why don't you get a government airplane, then?'

'You know what it's like.' Ed became very confidential, very trusting. 'So many damned forms. We want to get up there as quickly as possible, not wait for a week. We put the Learjet on Amex and shove it in for expenses when the time comes. You know how the old song goes?'

'Sure.'

'Why did you ask if something was going on up in Wenat-chee?' Bond asked.

'Because you're the second job we've had tonight. Same route. Had to use our one DC-3, the old workhorse herself. Slow, but still flying.'

'You couldn't give them a Learjet?'

The man shook his head. 'Another government job.' He dropped his voice. 'FBI. One agent and a male nurse. Taking a woman back home. She's been in some accident. Looked in a bad way. Unconscious. Had to get her on a stretcher.'

'How long ago?' Rushia asked.

'Why the interest?'

Rushia sighed. 'If you really want to know, it's connected to the case we're on.'

'Well, they left about three-quarters of an hour ago. If we get your flightplan filed and okayed quickly enough, you'll be landing within ten minutes or so of the DC-3.'

'Let's go then.' Bond was not smiling.

The DC-3 was parked near the terminal building at Wenatchee, under the big floodlights. They saw it as they came in to land, and, as the Learjet taxied in, both Rushia and Bond craned to see if there was any activity around the aircraft.

In the terminal, Rushia went in search of the crew while Bond headed for the car rental services. He tried Avis first and found they had only just let their last Range Rover go. 'Big call for them around these parts,' the girl said. 'I can let you have an almost new Isuzu Trooper. It'll do the same job for you.'

It was two thirty in the morning when, with Rushia at the wheel and Bond following the map, they left the airport, heading north.

'They're coming back,' Rushia announced as the Trooper pulled away and picked up speed.

'Who's coming back?' Bond's mind was ahead of them.

Already he was flexing his mental and physical muscles for the showdown with Brokenclaw.

'Who d'you think, dummy? Dorothy and Toto? Your friends Wolan and Nood . . .'

'Nolan and Wood. They're coming back this way?'

'Certain as the unexpected.'

'Speak to me, Ed.'

'Okay. Read my lips. Your two ex-FBI buddies are coming back. The DC-3 crew are waiting for them. They hired a Range Rover and they've got twenty minutes' start on us.'

'Then . . .'

'You haven't heard the best part.'

'Well?'

'They're coming back with another guy. One of them told the pilot. They want him to take them to Bracket Field, the other side of LA. You might like to know that the other guy's an Oriental gentleman. Old and infirm, they said. Some charter is picking him up from Bracket Field. Right? Happy now?'

In the darkness, Bond smiled.

They drove for ninety minutes, keeping to the Columbia River on their right and the dark mass that was forest and mountains to their left. They went through the town of Chelan and on, until they reached a narrow road to the left.

'This the one that peters out into a track about twenty miles up?' Rushia asked.

'About five miles from the camp, yes. Can you do it without lights?'

'Not yet I can't. Not if you want to get there.'

'Pull over at any sign of lights.' Bond already had his automatic pistol out.

The road was little more than a track, and both expressed their doubts about getting vehicles past each other. 'If they suddenly come hurtling down with their Oriental gent on board, we're in for H'ang Chow Mein,' Ed chuckled. 'Or Bondburger.'

The going was slow, and thirty minutes later it was light

enough to kill the headlights. Ten after that they saw the Range Rover.

It was pulled hard in to the right of the track and seemed empty and deserted.

'I guess I'm going to do the famous Rushia backup. Watch out for me, James.' Slowly the Trooper rolled in reverse, weaving a little until they had moved about thirty yards back, and just around a bend which would hide them from anyone approaching the Range Rover.

'I don't suppose you came ready for a shooting war?' Bond's finger was itching.

'You don't? Well, James, I came prepared for all eventualities.' Ed jerked at his waistband and drew out a massive Colt revolver with a six inch barrel. '.357 Magnum,' he grinned happily. 'This is my "Make my year" gun. I also have accessories, like handcuffs. I was going to use them on your good self if I came to the conclusion that you were going to do something really difficult . . .' He let the sentence trail off at the sight of Bond's eyes narrowing. 'No, well, perhaps not. Let's get ready for these palookas and the famous General H'ang.'

'When we take them, I want you to drive them down to civilisation and turn them in.'

'Can't I hang around and wait for you?'

'I'd rather you had them in some lock-up. I'm not certain, but I think if they were near me for any length of time, I might just kill all three.'

They moved quietly up the track. There was enough tree cover for Rushia to sink down, hidden by the Range Rover, and Bond to find a nice covert on the far side. From it, he had a view of the path snaking upwards through the trees which, he knew, led to the camp and Brokenclaw.

They waited for almost an hour before the sound of voices began to float down from the track. Neither Wood, Nolan nor the general seemed to have the slightest care in the world. As far as they were concerned, they were invisible. Bond had a sudden nudge of anxiety lest Brokenclaw had sent some of his people from the camp down with the ex-FBI men.

When they came into view, however, there were only three, moving slowly, two of them keeping time for the general's dot-and-carry-one limp. They let them actually start to get into the Range Rover.

'I really wouldn't try anything silly, like going for catapults or shouting rape!' It was Ed Rushia who broke the silence, and they all froze, for the long barrel of the Colt was placed neatly in General H'ang's ear. 'I could deafen him a mite,' he continued. 'Also my buddy just behind you, Wood – or Nolan – whichever you are, has a strong conviction that you are all expendable.'

H'ang dropped the briefcase he had been holding.

They came quietly enough, though they were all three carrying pistols. Both of the former FBI men still had handcuffs on them. 'Needn't have brought them after all, Ed,' Bond said cheerfully as they cuffed all three men together, helped them into the rear of the Range Rover and used the last set of cuffs to secure them to part of the metal framework.

'Commander Rushia's going to take you boys down to the nearest cops.' He fiddled with the briefcase, which opened easily enough, the combination lock having been used so often that the numbers almost fell into place by themselves.

Inside was another set of the Lords and Lords Day documents, and when he saw them, Bond realised his hands were trembling. 'Take this lot, Ed, and burn them the first chance you get.'

'Okay, buddy. Good luck. I'll be waiting for you.'

'I wouldn't bother,' one of the ex-FBI men growled. 'He's never coming out of there alive. I can promise you that.'

'You'd be surprised at the places Captain Bond's come out of alive.' As he said it, Rushia thought he would possibly inter-rogate the boys on the way down. He had picked up a wrinkle here and there. If James was going into a certain death situation, it was better for ole Ed Rushia to be warned so he could send in the cavalry.

Bond must have read his mind. 'Ed,' he said quietly, 'only in the last resort. Please promise me that. It has to be very bad. I must do this on my own.'

Rushia nodded, raised a hand and started the Range Rover's engine as Bond slowly began his hike up the path which rose to lead him to his destiny.

He knew the real danger was only just starting, and after a mile, had that uncanny feeling that there were several pairs of eyes on him.

Slowly, the path flattened out, and then, quite suddenly, he was at the end of the treeline. The woods grew to the edge of an oval depression, about a mile long and half-a-mile wide. Smoke rose from camp fires, teepees were sited neatly in two long rows. At the furthest point, standing apart from the teepees, there was a large circular structure built of hides stretched over wood. It had a high curved roof and a totem stood directly in front of it. The ceremonial Lodge, Bond thought, bringing his eyes back down the lines of teepees. At the end nearest to him was a tent taller and bigger than the rest. 'Buck House,' he muttered to himself, stepping from the trees, his arms high over his head, his pistol held by the barrel, to show that he came in peace.

Women, and a few men, had been moving through the camp, doing the usual morning chores of any society, lighting fires, starting to cook. As they saw the white man approach, they stopped and watched, faces expressionless, as he headed on down to the large teepee.

He could smell the woodsmoke mingled with burned meat and expected to be called to a halt at any minute. But the men and women did not move. He realised that, after the initial interest, their combined gaze had now fallen on the teepee which he was nearing from the rear.

He moved slightly to one side, so that he could approach diagonally, and then reach the entrance flap at the front. As he moved, a figure stepped from behind the teepee.

'Captain Bond, what a pleasure to welcome you to our camp; and what a pity you did not obey my orders two nights ago.'

'Where is she, Brokenclaw?' He stood stock still, holding eye contact with the huge man who was now dressed in buckskin and wore a long hunting knife at his belt.

'Where is she?' Brokenclaw's voice was friendly. 'She is safe, James Bond. She is here and she is safe. Why, do you wish to fight me for her?'

'That was my intention. One to one, head to head, Brokenclaw. And I'm quite willing to do it on your terms. You choose the weapons, so to speak.'

Brokenclaw put back his head and laughed. 'You think you're man enough to be a chief? All right, Captain Bond. There is one way we can find out if you have the strength to be a leader of men. Come, I will introduce you to a little ceremony invented first by the Mandan nation. It was designed for just such a purpose – to choose leaders. It is called the torture rite of the *o-kee-pa*.'

19

CHALLENGE BY TORTURE

'You see, when men and women from many different Indian nations sought permission to come and live here, adhering to the old ways, there were many things we had to decide as a community.' Brokenclaw still maintained that perfectly composed manner, his voice never once indicating emotion.

They sat on skins in his teepee, with a young Indian woman serving them with a kind of stew made from rabbit, wild onions and other root vegetables. They ate with spoons, from bowls, both fashioned from wood.

'It was necessary for us to have a mutual understanding regarding things like our religious beliefs, and the ways in which we chose our leaders. We had to agree on ritual and etiquette,' Brokenclaw continued. 'One of the terrible things the white man has done to those I regard as my people, is to introduce a different way of life – a way alien to our forefathers and a way which has brought great degradation on the proud Indian nations. You see it on the reservations, you see it in disease and the horrors of alcohol. This was one of the reasons I was a prime mover in bringing strong people from various tribes together.'

'I understand that.' Bond tried to remain calm in the presence of this man who sat patient, soft-spoken and reasonable. It was difficult, for he knew that here was evil personified, a monster who claimed two sets of ancestors, two traditions and could slip between them like someone inflicted with a multiple personality. He was a man who had held together the San Francisco underworld and ruled through brutality and fear. Listening to him talk, it was difficult to accept the truth about this appalling aberration locked within a human body.

'Among the most important of our rituals, we agreed, was the appeasement of the spirits, particularly the spirits of earth, fire and the water which once covered the entire earth. You can understand this, Captain Bond?'

He nodded. Inside, his stomach churned as he waited for Brokenclaw Lee to come out with the real object of this little lecture.

'Just as Christian peoples have their ceremonies which speak of death and rebirth – the rituals of Spring, the Easter rituals – so we had to look back to the old ways and resurrect *our* rites of appeasement, so that the spirits would not forsake us, so that we would live to see the crops ripen and be blessed with good hunting.

'One such ritual which emanates from the Mandan Indians, the Plains People, is that of *o-kee-pa*. This is a long ceremonial period, in which there are spirit dances and sacrifice. Part of the ancient *o-kee-pa* rites concern the choice of future leaders.' He paused as though waiting for Bond to show comprehension.

Brokenclaw maintained that the *o-kee-pa*, when first discovered by the white man, had offended. 'They considered parts of it so brutal and degrading that when an explorer from your own country, Captain Bond, took back evidence of the ceremonies, the Victorian British maintained that the poor wretched explorer's mind was filled with bizarre and morbid fantasies. That was rich coming from the Victorians who exploited their workers, and who brutalised the poor, don't you think?'

Bond merely nodded.

'We decided that part of the *o-kee-pa* was ideal for choosing future leaders from among our people here. The torture ritual had long been used to weed out the strong from the weak. So, some twelve years ago, we performed the ceremony again. Out of eight men, only two of us passed the test, and I have scars to prove it to you. See!'

He rose, stripping off his buckskin jerkin to display his back. Below the shoulder blades there were long, thick ugly scars. 'There are two more.' He rolled up the loose trousers to show that there were jagged, rough scars on both of his calves as though a bullet had passed through the flesh and exploded, leaving torn and ragged wounds.

'You tell me that you will fight me on my own terms, then these are my terms. I shall explain.'

Bond listened with mounting horror, knowing that this man had already been through this vile and obscene test and won.

'Those who would seek to be leaders were first taken to the Sacred Lodge and there smooth, strong pegs were driven through their flesh, one on each side of the back, below the shoulder blades and another two deeply through each calf. To these skewers, rawhide ropes were attached. At the end of the ropes leading from the calves, buffalo skulls were tied as weights, then they were suspended from the ropes tied to the skewers in their backs.

'There are intricate, special chants which are sung during this phase,' Brokenclaw continued. 'The pain is intense, but you must remain conscious. If a man loses consciousness, then he is cut down and must drag himself to the Medicine Man, who will chop off one or two of his fingers.' He played his own hands, one palm forward, the other twisted so only the back showed. 'As you see, I have all my fingers intact. There are six men in this village who are without fingers.' The smile was of intense pleasure melded with evil.

Those who sought leadership, he said, were required to hang through the length of the chant. 'In modern time that is about twenty minutes. Then we are lowered to the Lodge floor and the pegs are removed from our backs, but not from our legs, for the next phase is a race. The course is prescribed, around the village, and the buffalo skulls remain in place. This means that participants are hampered by the weight and sometimes have to be assisted around the course. Inevitably, the buffalo skulls drag the pegs from the calves which causes more pain but allows you to run faster. That, James Bond, is the torture rite of *o-kee-pa*. It is also my offer of a single test, one on one, though there must be a final decision in the unlikely event of us both completing the ceremony. So far, do you accept my terms?'

He had expected some form of hand-to-hand combat with a choice of primitive weapons, or at least a match against Brokenclaw with no weapons. The last thing Bond had expected was this savage test of torture. But he had no option. He had placed himself in this situation, so he had to abide by it, even if it meant mutilation.

'What is the final test?' he asked.

'The course we will construct,' Brokenclaw spoke very softly now, 'will bring us to two separate finishing points. We would each have to run the same distance, but we will end up some fifty yards apart. At the finishing mark there will be one bow and one arrow. If we both complete the course, then we must finish the matter. One shaft against one shaft. The first to reach his mark may shoot, and I should warn you that I am quite extraordinarily accurate with the bow.'

Bond took a deep breath. 'I will offer myself to this torture ritual on three conditions . . .'

'Ha, you require conditions . . .'

'They are perfectly reasonable . . .'

'Tell me.'

'First, I must have your word, spoken before the assembled braves and Medicine Man of this village that, should I win this test, I will be allowed to leave in peace with the girl.'

'Agreed, of course.'

'I must examine the bows and the arrows and have the word of your Medicine Man that neither will be tampered with before we end the test.'

'You have *my* word . . .'

'Your word is not enough, Brokenclaw. I require the word of your Medicine Man.'

Brokenclaw gave a curt nod. 'Your third condition?'

'This covers two parts. First that I am allowed to see the girl and know that she is safe and well . . .'

'Of course she's safe and well . . .'

'Good. I must see. I must also have a solemn oath that no harm will come to her during the test.

'She will be free to go, naturally. But I fear, Captain Bond, that, while you might just have the courage and stamina to reach the end of the course, you can never beat me with the bow.'

'We shall see.'

'Then you accept the challenge?'

Bond did not hesitate. 'I accept the challenge, for you deserve to die, Brokenclaw Lee, and I fear that, though the authorities will eventually catch up with you, they will only imprison you. Prison is too easy. Your way is good. It is a test of manhood, leadership and courage. You merit death.'

Chi-Chi was terrified. She did not have to tell Bond for it showed in her eyes and her whole demeanour. She looked more fragile than ever, he thought, as he told her that all would be fine.

'I just want to get out of here, James. I want things to be as they were when you went out for the wine.'

'The wine'll keep. It's a good year.'

'Yes, but . . .'

'I'm negotiating.' He was not going to tell her how or make her even more frightened. As he left the women's teepee, where she was being held, his one thought was that he *had* to survive; he *had* to win. Chi-Chi had become too precious for him even to think of losing.

With Brokenclaw, he met Bear's Head, the village Medicine Man and some of the senior braves. Using sign language, and watching his adversary closely, he felt confident that Brokenclaw was sticking to his side of the bargain. But there was still the nagging thought in the back of his mind that should he be close to losing the contest, Brokenclaw might have arranged some kind of backup. The one person Bond did not trust among the other senior braves was a short whippet of an Indian called Even Both Ways. To Bond, he looked to be the kind of Indian who had seen a lot of the world outside the reservations and this particular village. He also appeared particularly attached to Brokenclaw.

They were led around the running course. From the Sacred Lodge, Brokenclaw had to run to the left and Bond to the right. They would cover the entire length of the village, running behind the teepees until they were on the far side of Broken-claw's own tent where their final goals were marked by white stones set roughly fifty yards apart. Here, one of the Medicine Man's assistants set down the two bows and their accompanying arrows.

Both bows were strong and almost identical, fashioned from good ash backed by animal sinew. The taut strings were also, in Bond's judgment, made from the sinew of animals, and the arrows were firm, straight and iron-tipped, their flights made from large bird feathers.

As much as he would have liked to try his own bowmanship, Bond knew that this would only be taken as a sign of weakness and uncertainty. Half the battle, he had decided, was to show no fear and display only great confidence in the outcome. To this end he now asked if he might be left alone for half-an-hour. He consented to sit in full sight of everyone, but, he indicated to the Medicine Man, he wished to talk to his gods.

By this time he had taken to passing messages to Brokenclaw through the dignified, sinister man clad in garish skins and hung about with charms, face covered in a white mixture and his hair plastered to his scalp with some sticky red-coloured daub. Once he had accepted the challenge, Bond felt it was more impressive to ignore his opponent than appear friendly.

His request was granted, and he moved a little way up the

bowl of earth surrounding the village, finally finding a small ledge on which he squatted in the lotus position and closed his eyes. This was the only way he could face what was to come, to will himself into a mental and physical state which would guarantee his winning.

First he settled his mind on his enemy. Brokenclaw had gone through this ordeal before, but that was some twelve years ago. In the time that had passed, the man had almost certainly lost some of his stamina. Yes, he appeared fit but Bond judged him as being a little overweight, certainly heavier than he had been a dozen years ago. It was possible that the strain would now be too much for Brokenclaw Lee.

His own position was different. He was strong and fit. He knew it and drew consolation from it. The pain would, undoubtedly, be a shock to his system, but he now had to distance his mind from pain. It was a trick already learned. Pain *could* be borne. Pain did not kill, it merely blunted the other senses. Bond focused on keeping his other senses withdrawn from the physical pain, and this was the most important facet of being psychologically prepared for what was to come.

Finally, with his mind distanced from his physical being, Bond rose and walked down to the braves waiting around the Sacred Lodge, ready for the last challenge, the *o-kee-pa*.

20

O-KEE-PA

The Sacred Lodge seemed to be filled with a film of smoke from the pipes of the older men who sat in huddled clutches near the triangular, gallows-like structure erected from thick weathered trees.

First, Bond was stripped and a soft loincloth placed around his waist and between his legs. His feet were left bare, then he was led by two of the Medicine Man's assistants to his place below one of the crossbeams, and turned to face Brokenclaw. He gazed fixedly at his opponent's left ear. It was an old trick which could sometimes give the impression that he was staring out an enemy.

The drumming began, deep thuds, almost in waltz time, but slow and hypnotic. The chanting followed, eerie and as though from throats that had little to do with mankind. Bond fixed his mind on the rhythm, taking deep breaths, ready for the first shock of pain.

One of the assistants gathered a handful of flesh from directly under his right shoulder blade, and the agony leaped through him as the first sharp peg pierced his skin and slammed through the flesh, searing his whole back. He could feel the blood wet below the wound and struggled to force mind away from body.

Then the next peg went in on the left side and the hurt doubled – huge sharp needles seemed to have blasted through his back, and he began to feel dizzy at the effect. He took in deep breaths, concentrating more and more on the throbbing of the drums and the guttural wail of the chant.

He was hardly aware of the men making ready his right calf until the sharp peg slashed into his leg, sending pain drenching through him. At the insertion of the final peg, Bond thought he was going to lose consciousness there and then, but he managed to keep the still centre of his mind on the need to overcome the anguish.

They had told him that the buffalo skulls were very old, and had remained with some of the tribes for many years. Though old they were still heavy. He suspected they were also weighted with stones.

Brokenclaw had made no sound as they were piercing his body, and Bond knew that but for a quick intake of breath at the first penetration, he had also kept from crying out. He kept his eyes to the front, feeling the sweat run down from his forehead, bubbling over his eyes.

From far away he heard the Medicine Man give a long shout which seemed to rise and fall, then merge into the chanting. A second later his brain reacted to the knowledge that this was the signal for the slack to be taken up on the rawhide ropes. He thought the whole of his back was going to be ripped apart as his body took the strain once his feet were off the ground. Then his back became one blazing area of fire, and as he was lifted higher, he felt the unbearable weight on the pegs in his calves. Pain seemed to saturate his entire being then stab out in great eruptions from the points where the four pegs had been driven, so that, while the agony was complete and in unison from toe to head, even worse, sharper, knife-like stabs shot through him.

The drag on the calf pegs became stronger, and he realised that there was added agony because his body had started to oscillate slightly. It was as if the pegs in his legs were razor sharp and being slowly drawn down, as though they were knives being sliced through the butter of his flesh.

Again and again he had to force his mind away from what his body was telling him, that he was being rent and ravaged by the pegs. The sense of total suffering seemed to be without end.

He could see, or feel, no relief, no solace, just the raging fires consuming him. Twice he managed to bring himself back from the brink of unconsciousness, and once he tried to see how Brokenclaw was holding up, but the sweat ran in small waterfalls from his hairline down across his eyes.

Nausea gripped his stomach, then the cramps began, shouting above the harsh, slashing explosions of torment which came from the pegs.

Then, without warning, he heard, as though from far away, the drum beats taking on a new and faster rhythm and there was movement. The hanging was over, and they were slowly lowering him to the ground.

The weight came off his legs, and the strain from the ropes attached to the pegs in his back was released. At that moment, Bond had to struggle to remain standing. He was aware of the thongs at his back being cut and of the two assistants jostling him, pushing, shouting.

Through the white heat of what felt like a thousand wounds in his body, he realised it was time to begin the run. He fought the almost overpowering discomfort, focused his mind first on Chi-Chi, then on the necessity of beating his adversary. If you don't win, James, Brokenclaw Lee will go on to more evil, his mind shrieked at him. The agony shrieked back as he put one foot forward and pulled against the rope and the buffalo skull.

He managed two steps towards the doorway of the Sacred Lodge before he slipped and fell. As they pulled him up, he caught sight of Brokenclaw, his face contorted in his own private hell, also being helped forward.

There was one way, and one way only. He must rid himself of the weights. Clenching his teeth, he kicked back and then forward. He felt the flesh being torn, and a new highly tuned pain in the right leg.

He performed the same action with his left leg, and, this time, actually felt the flesh give way, a terrible cutting and wrenching as the peg was torn out and the wetness of the blood sliding down his leg.

But the peg remained attached to his right calf. With his mind still centred on Chi-Chi and the need to win, Bond reached down, grasped the leather rope and heaved the peg from its place. He felt the searing heat of the wounds, but was able to stagger forward, using both legs.

He brought his hand up to wipe the sweat from his eyes, gathered his strength and began to move. Not far, he thought. It is not far to go. But his legs burned as though the Medicine Man's assistants were lashing at his calves with red-hot pokers.

Get into a rhythm, he told himself. To hell with what you are feeling. Just get the rhythm. The drums seemed all around him; he was aware of Indians shouting, as though urging him on, and, slowly at first, he began to get one leg in front of the other.

As he reached the door, his shoulder jarred against something and he looked to his left to see Brokenclaw, staggering, dazed but forcing his body through the opening at the same time. They were neck and neck, Bond thought, and somehow this seemed to give him more heart. He began to jog, but the suffering which swept upwards through his body at each stride made him want to vomit. He bit his lip hard, in that old trick of inflicting a new pain on himself in order to try to overwhelm the old.

Another four steps. His mind began to tell him the old pain *was* old. It had been with him for an age, not simply half-an-hour or so. His mind began to welcome the eternal throbbing, the pulse of the fire that consumed him, and through the depths of despair, measured in the thousand sharp objects cutting into his body and drawing out his lifeblood, he saw the way ahead. Slowly now his mind had begun to triumph over the exquisite torture racking him.

His strides lengthened; somehow he was actually running, head down, forcing his riven body through treacly air, for it was as though what he breathed had solidified, surrounded him, and was trying to force him back.

There was no sense of time now, just the determination to ride it out, to get to the finish, to reach a point where the pain would cease.

He felt encased in blood and sweat, so that he was constantly using the back of his hand to clear his eyes. People still surrounded him and the drumming began to get louder and louder, filling his head, then his whole being.

Quite without warning, the drumming stopped. Silence followed, with only his heavy breathing and the quick thump of his heart in his ears to tell him he was still alive. Then, a few paces away, he saw the white rock and his bow and arrow lying ready.

With a mighty leap forward he seemed to gather strength from somewhere, launching himself at the weapons. One hand grasped the bow, the other caught hold of the arrow.

His vision blurred and he knew his knees were buckling under him, but his sight cleared enough to position the arrow against the bowstring, to pull back on the pressure of the string and lift himself to his full height, turning in the direction where instinct told him his target waited.

Brokenclaw, covered in blood, his huge body fighting to stay upright, was already drawing back the bowstring carrying his arrow until the bow was at arm's length and the missile wavered in Bond's direction.

Bond could not get his feet into place. He could not maintain the stance. He knew that Brokenclaw had won; he even thought the arrow was already launched, and at that moment, his legs gave way and he fell to his knees.

Brokenclaw's arrow hissed inches above his head, thudding into the earth behind him.

One more push, one more reach into whatever reserve of strength remained. He straightened, found his eyes clear of sweat, saw his target, swaying but upright, the bow, meant for him, falling to the earth.

Just before he shot, Bond imagined he could see Brokenclaw's eyes bearing in on his own, but this, he thought later, was probably his imagination, as was the feeling of a great arc of evil surging from the man's body.

Bond knew he was on target. He loosed the arrow and saw it strike firmly into Brokenclaw's throat. There was a noise which he recognised, he had read of it somewhere, the noise like the muffled murmur of a great torrent advancing through woodland, a howl of despair.

He clearly saw Brokenclaw clutch at the arrow, as though trying to tear it from his throat. Then the huge Chinese Indian gave a long, hoarse choke, his hands dropped from the attempt to withdraw the arrow, his arms flew outwards, flapping like some wounded bird cut down by a shot. They were still moving in a flying motion as his body hit the ground.

'James! Behind you! Behind you!' He knew the man's voice, and even as he turned, saw that the Indian, Even Both Ways, was poised on the rim of the oval bowl of ground surrounding the encampment, his bowstring drawn back, the shaft ready to fly. At the same moment, there was the sound of a shot which echoed around the camp as Even Both Ways threw back his hands and was tossed like a piece of garbage into the air.

Bond tottered forwards towards Brokenclaw's body, lying very still. Then his knees gave way and he sank into a grey mist.

'Hey, James? James, it's okay. You're going to be okay.'

The mist swam in front of his eyes and he was again submerged in a great undulating wave of pain, but he could just make out Ed Rushia's craggy face above him.

'Hell, Ed,' he croaked. 'I said only in the last resort. I had to do this on my own.'

'You did, James.' A different voice. 'Ed saved you when one of Brokenclaw's men tried to take you out. It was all over by then. Oh, James, darling. What you did was . . .'

He knew the voice belonged to Chi-Chi, but somehow it began to slink away into another land as the darkness came in.

They operated five times during the next six weeks. In spite of M wanting Bond to be moved back to the United Kingdom, the Americans insisted they should do everything. 'In any case, we need your boy for a good debriefing,' John Grant had told the chief of the British Service, so M gave in with grace.

Grant's people came to see him in the Naval hospital at regular intervals, and he learned a little more about the late Brokenclaw Lee's empire. For one thing, everybody was convinced that his melting pot of Indian tribes in the Chelan Mountains had been for some eventual purpose. 'They seemed peaceful enough,' Grant told him, 'but we figure he only took in the most basic types, those who would return to the old brutal ways. No reservation Indian would ever think of performing the *o-kee-pa* torture rite nowadays. We're pretty sure he had some reason for building a private Indian army that had nothing to do with peace.'

Eventually, Bond was able to walk again with hardly any pain. The damage inflicted on his legs had been worse than that on his back, but the doctors said that, eventually, he would only have the scars to prove that it happened at all.

Sue Chi-Ho visited Bond every day, and every day thanked him for what he had done. 'I have been reading the lives of those two whose names we took,' she told him one afternoon. 'Abelard and Héloïse. I came across a quote from one of her letters to him – after she went into a convent and he lost his manhood. It seems something good to live by. She wrote—

May it be sudden, whatever you plan for us; may man's mind
    Be blind to the future. Let him hope on in his fears.

I am glad we're blind to the future. If I'd known what lay in store for us in *Operation Curve*, I'd never have gone ahead. I don't care what happens now, I just don't want to know what tomorrow will bring.'

Finally they told Bond he could leave the hospital. Chi-Chi picked him up late one afternoon and drove him back to her apartment. He had telephoned M privately and had been given four weeks' sick leave, though they both knew there would be a year of physiotherapy before Bond's muscles could be completely restored.

The apartment was back to normal, and even the shattered glass on the museum poster had been repaired.

'This is where we came in,' Bond said.

'Yes, but tonight will be different, James. I really have planned a wonderful meal. Just sit down, relax and I'll get it started.' She went into the kitchen, and a few seconds later Bond heard her explode with anger. She came storming out – 'Guess what I've done? I've forgotten to get the wine. James, would you be a darling and . . . ?'

'No!' Then he saw her begin to laugh. 'Absolutely no! No way! Never! Negative and out!'